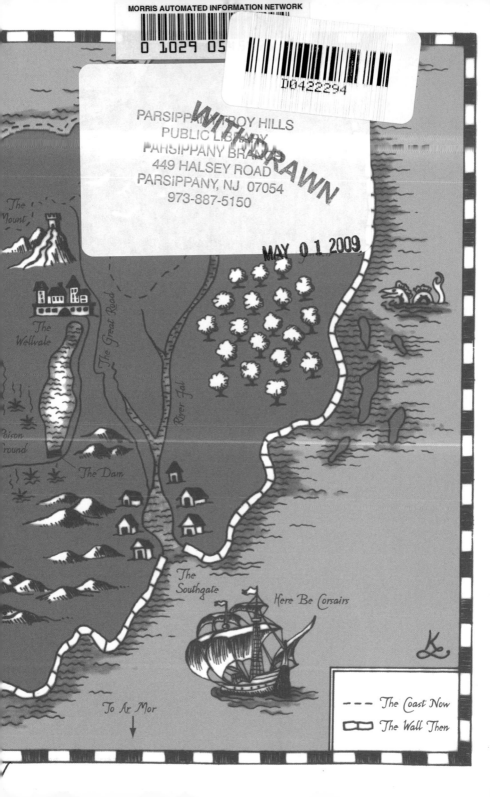

The Mount

The Wellvale

The Great Road

River Fal

Poison Ground

The Dam

The Southgate

Here Be Corsairs

To Ar Mor

The Coast Now
The Wall Then

LYONESSE

THE WELL BETWEEN THE WORLDS

LYONESSE

THE WELL BETWEEN THE WORLDS

SAM LLEWELLYN

ORCHARD BOOKS
NEW YORK

·

An Imprint of
SCHOLASTIC INC.

For Innis, my mother
and Teona and Alexandra,
my cousins

Published in the United Kingdom as The Monsters of Lyonesse: *The Well Between the Worlds.*

All rights reserved. Published by Orchard Books, an imprint of Scholastic Inc., *Publishers since 1920,* by arrangement with Scholastic Ltd. ORCHARD BOOKS and design are registered trademarks of Watts Publishing Group, Ltd., used under license. SCHOLASTIC and associated logos are trademarks and/or registered trademarks of Scholastic Inc.

Library of Congress Cataloging-in-Publication Data

Llewellyn, Sam, 1948–
The well between the worlds / by Sam Llewellyn. — 1st ed.
p. cm. — (Lyonesse; bk. I)
Summary: Eleven-year-old Idris Limpet, living with his family in the once noble but now evil and corrupt island country of Lyonesse, finds his life taking a dramatic turn when, after a near-drowning incident, he is accused of being allied to the feared sea monsters and is rescued from a death sentence by a mysterious and fearsome stranger.
ISBN 978-0-439-93469-5
[1. Fantasy.] I. Title.
PZ7.L7723We 2009
[Fic] — dc22
2008020075

ISBN-13: 978-0-439-93469-5
ISBN-10: 0-439-93469-9

10 9 8 7 6 5 4 3 2 1   09 10 11 12 13

First edition, February 2009
Book design by Christopher Stengel
Reinforced Binding for Library Use
Printed in the U.S.A.

·PART ONE·

The darkgardens were deepest green shading into black, fed with the finest blood. Darkness was the loveliest thing, of course — colored darkness, with little red flecks swimming in patterns, glowing, perfect, always the same in this world that always changed.

The woman's mind cruised the darkgardens, speaking with the giant Helpers. Her body lay in the tower high above the land, breathing only four times a day. . . .

Deep in the darkgardens, she rested and made her plans. The time was drawing near when the worlds would become one, and she and hers would rule them all, and darkness, beautiful, would cover the earth.

Brightness was weakness. Darkness was power.

She rose from the darkgardens to look at her kingdom.

Up raced her mind, through the dark water, up the rock shaft until rock became builded stone, up, up the chimney of the Well, through the secret tunnels into her chamber in the highest tower of the Mount. The body drew a breath. The fluids of life gurgled in their tubes. The woman rose, and went to her window, and opened her night-black eyes, and turned them down upon the bright world of Lyonesse.

It was dawn.

Below the Mount the land sank into a valley still untouched by the day. In its bottom lay the lake, with the walled city at its head. Night fog hung in the walls and buildings like beast guts on a slaughter-rail. The city was crowded with buildings — hovels and cottages by the lakeside, and farther back heavier blocks and ranges, blackened and lofty.

A chimney spat chemical smoke. Through the air came the thump of a machine. The black eyes crawled beyond the valley, over long leagues of hills to the oak forest of the Shipwright's Garden, where the River Fal ran through green meadows to the ship basins and wharves of the Southgate. They scorched over a barer land with standing stones and shadow-filled vales, far, far, to a thin black line that dammed the gray downs. The line was the Wall. Beyond the Wall the sea shifted, stretching away forever, bright, weak, hostile.

The eyes closed. A bronze shutter wheezed. Inside the tower, night fell again. The woman lay down on the black stone bed. The chest stilled. The tubes ceased to pulse. The mind plunged back through the twisted tunnels into the deep. The time of darkness would be very soon.

But far away under the Wall, in a town brilliant with morning light, something was beginning that would turn her wicked dreams to nightmares.

Listen.

ONE

The town is Westgate. And bursting out of the school into the warm afternoon sun, here comes Idris Limpet, eleven years old at this time, swinging a rope of books around his head, mad with joy at being released. They had been doing the Treaty in school. They were always doing the Treaty, and they were sick of it, Spignold and Erys and Mawga and Cayo and everyone. "Books on the roof!" cried Spignold.

Up on the thatch of the net shed the children slung their books, the ropes hanging down so they could pull them off later. That was the idea, anyway. But Spignold obviously threw his too hard, so the rope was out of reach, which he would eventually blame someone else for. And Mawga threw hers too softly, so they slid down again. Idris took the time to dust off Mawga's books the glittering powder of mica sand and fish scales that floored the narrow streets of Westgate, and tossed them neatly onto the roof. Mawga sniffed at him and ran on.

Idris paid no attention because he was leaping in the sun, saying good afternoon to his pet gull, Kek. He knew that

Master Omnium, the teacher, would be watching, him in his dusty black robe. And with Master Omnium that day was a man with a thick red tunic bearing the silver device of an eel devouring its tail, and a dark face, and a nose ring of heavy gold. Master Omnium and the man with the nose ring were staring at Idris. The nose ring man had a tablet in his hands, on which he was scribing in squidink. Master Omnium said something. The man raised surprised eyebrows and wrote again. Idris's joy quailed before an uneasy sense that they were talking about him.

"Oi!" cried Spignold.

And off they went, running, hands out for balance, up the cracked and sea-pink-tufted steps to the top of the Wall. And there was Westgate spread out behind and below them. There was the crumbling Wall, the high harbor, the Seagate with its chain to keep out wicked, murdering, sea-roving corsairs and Aegypt slavers, its turrets once proud and fierce now glassless and blind, battlegrounds for gulls and owls at the hinges of the day. And ahead, the surprise of the sea, huge, blue, and shifting, battering the Wall with the creamy edges of its waves.

The sea was higher than the land. Much, much higher, the height of nine tall men standing on one another's heads. It had always been thus, though if you listened to old people it was rising steadily. Spignold laughed at this; life was good, the old people were idiots. Idris was not so sure. He was a respectful boy, and he did listen, even if he did not in the end agree.

"To the Fort!" cried Spignold.

To the Fort they ran, along the Wall, up the steps, into a spiral stone staircase that smelled of rotten seaweed and up a tower at whose top was a chamber like a huge stone lantern, a round room with an all-around view and a partly fallen ceiling, built by a merchant to watch for his ships in the distant days of Westgate's prosperity.

On the inland side, the empty window sockets gave a view over the Westgate and the hills beyond. Once, the town had been a great port city. But the sea currents had blocked the channels with sand, and now it lay half-ruined. The Castle still stood on its hill, a grim drum of black stone over which flew the red-fist flag of the Town Captain. But the grand houses on the hill below it, once home to purple-cloaked merchants, now stood empty and rotten, their roofs sway-backed, their windows blinded by white crowds of gulls. The people, Idris's parents among them, now lived in the narrow, cozy streets that ran back from the harbor.

Behind the Castle the road ran up a long valley, shrinking with distance, and vanished among the rounded summits of the Downs. Apparently if you followed it for a week you would come to the Wellvale, far to the east, where the Captains lived in splendor. The road had once been full of traffic. Now there were weeds in the paving and few traveled it. . . .

Idris frowned. For as long as he could remember, the road had been part of what he saw every day. But now he found himself thinking: What would it be like to travel along it? He felt uneasy. The thought was an odd one, mixed up in some way with the nose ring man who had been talking to Master Omnium. And a stupid one. People did not leave Westgate.

"Idris," said Mawga's rather whiny voice. *"Idris!"*

Idris turned. It looked like they were playing Kingdom. It was a good game.

Spignold sat on a throne of stone lumps in the middle. Mawga sat at his side with a gull's feather in her hair. Spignold's pug nose was high, Mawga's eyes crossed and narrow. They were the king and queen, as usual. Kek the gull sat on the parapet, watching.

"Repel corsairs!" cried Spignold.

Everyone ran around, half mad with excitement, boiling imaginary oil and firing imaginary crossbows at invading slave ships. Spignold was shockingly wounded but cured by Mawga's keen nursing. Erys and everyone else were less badly wounded, except for little Cayo, who took a poisoned arrow in the shoulder and expired horribly, twice, because nobody had been watching the first time.

"Corsairs repelled!" cried Spignold.

"Oh," said Mawga, put out, because she liked being queen almost as much as pudgy, mean Spignold liked being king. "What now, then?"

"The plank."

"What's the plank?"

"New game," said Spignold.

Idris felt a return of his uneasiness. There was an odd look in Spignold's eye, half excited, half frightened. Idris noticed things like that. Nobody else seemed to. "Meaning?" said Idris.

Spignold walked over to a pile of rubble in the corner and hauled out a long board of reddish wood. "We stick one end out of the window," he said. "Someone sits on the inside end. Someone sits on the outside end. We rock. Like a seesaw. But better."

Idris looked out of the window. A long way below, a blue tongue of sea licked up the wall. Whoever was on the outside end of the seesaw would be in some danger. Plenty of danger, actually. You could bet it would not be Spignold.

"I'll go on the outside," said Cayo, always ready to make up for his lack of size with wild boldness.

BONG, said the great bell in the town. The air shivered. The children stopped looking at Cayo. They stood with their feet together, heads bowed. It was the Hour of Thanks. "The Well," said Spignold, taking over as usual.

"The Well," said the other children. Idris watched an ant walking over his bare brown toe. He tried to feel solemn, but the ant was more interesting. The Hour of Thanks was just a muddle of words about towers and Wells and a lot of other things that did not make much sense. He had said them ever since he could remember. They had long ago stopped meaning anything.

"Thanks to the Well and the waters therein," said Spignold. His father was the Town Captain, hander-down of justice in the name of the Mount. "For they bring forth monsters that we may live free. And thanks to our Captains who show the monsters the glory of day who else would know only night."

"Thanks to the Well," said the children. The noises of the day had stopped. The words rose in a murmur from all over the town.

Idris's mind moved from the ant to Spignold. He did not actually like Spignold very much. He did not like the way he automatically took control, or the way he deliberately set people against people, or the way he thought that just because his father was the Captain he was some sort of Captain, too.

BONG, said the great bell again. Far below on the street, voices started to gossip again, tin pots to bang on stoves, and cart wheels to grind the sandy cobbles.

"Right!" cried Spignold. "Cayo! The plank!"

Idris looked across at Cayo. The small boy had not been concentrating either. He had been using the quiet time to feel sorry he had ever volunteered. Now his eyes were too wide, and he was munching his lips from the inside, and his knees were shuddering faintly beneath his school kilt.

"Or maybe," said Spignold, with a mean, narrow look, "you are chicken."

All eyes were already on Cayo. All eyebrows were up and all lips pursed. It made Idris uncomfortable. Cayo turned pink. He opened his mouth to say that he was certainly not chicken, no way. But even as he did it his lips wobbled. Idris at this point was certain about two things. One, if Cayo went bouncing around on planks he would fall into the sea and drown, for it was one of the rules that nobody in Lyonesse was permitted to learn to swim, on pain of death. Any swimmer might be a Cross, a child of human and monster, and it was the law that no Cross could be allowed to live. And two, it was unfair, and everyone knew it was, but nobody would say anything, for fear of Spignold. Except Idris, who disliked bullying and could hardly ever stop himself from saying what was in his mind.

"Kek," said Kek the gull, standing on the parapet.

"Cayo," said Idris. "Would you mind if I had the first go?"

He saw Cayo's face turn bright red with relief, then assume a tough though tiny scowl. "Werl," said Cayo. "I dunno. If you really really want to —"

"Hey!" said Spignold, looking sulky.

"Plank out, then," said Idris before anyone could object. "Grab the other end, Mawga."

Normally Mawga would no more have gotten her hands dirty than walk across the sea to the Outer Banks. But Idris could feel a thing in him that he had felt before, a sort of energy that spread to other people and made them do what he wanted them to do. Spignold had it, too, in a way. Spignold managed it by being big and mean. Idris was not big and not mean. But sometimes he seemed to be able to tell exactly what other people were thinking. "Look," he said. "If you do this seesaw thing it's not going to work." He took possession of the plank, shoved its end out of the glassless window, and jammed its inside end under a great lump of stone, once part of the roof. Kek flapped into the air and hung on the breeze, watching. The plank now stuck out over the sea like a long, narrow diving board. "Watch!" said Idris.

He stepped onto the board and walked out of the window.

Now he was outside the tower, the sun shone hot on his head. Behind him was the kind of silence that comes from your classmates when their mouths are hanging open. A hundred feet below, the sea boomed hollow on the Wall of Lyonesse. He felt happy, because he could tell that Cayo was thinking that if it had been him he would have gotten the knee wobbles and drowned. Idris was light, and free, and he had done good.

He flexed his knees. The plank flexed, too. This was good, but frightening. He flexed again, with more power this time, and gave a little jump. The plank sprang under his feet. The fear faded. He did the next jump, a little bigger. Up he went into the warm breeze, arms straight out from his shoulders, weightless for a brilliant second, no fear at all now. Then down again, feeling the comfortable bend of the plank, the pressure in his knees as it shot him upward, the lightness in his stomach at the top of his leap.

"Woo," said the children in the Fort.

"You and me, Kek," Idris said to Kek. Then he was down again, bounce, up again. As he went down through the joyful air he thought he heard a clatter of wood and someone shout. He cast his eyes downward, looking for the plank under his feet.

The plank was not there.

There was a confused shouting from the Fort. He fell past it straight as an arrow, hands by his side. He glimpsed the white lines of surf on the Outer Banks, a drift of gulls, blue sky, sun high. He was astonished. His mouth was open. He knew he should have been frightened, but he was not. Instead he thought: I will never see Mum again, nor Dad, nor the Boys, nor the Precious Stones. And he felt very, very sad.

For about a second. Then the water bashed the soles of his feet, a huge, stinging blow, and he was in cold, salty sea, drowning.

Drowning was not at all what he had expected. He had assumed that when you fell into water you would sink, and the air in your chest would keep you going for a bit, but only until you got that panicky feeling you get when you hold your breath for too long in a breath-holding contest, after which you would take a gasp, which would not be of air but of water so you would sort of strangle. Then the horrible bit would start, with your life passing before your eyes and a very nasty struggle, the kind a caught fish makes in the basket.

There was the smash of the water. There was the panicky feeling. And a question: *Why don't we learn to swim, like the seals or the fish?*

And an answer: *Because what swims is beast, monster, or Cross.*

Then there was the struggle. Silent screams, blood thundering in ears, panic, real, horrible. But no past-life stuff. Just a stopping of panic. And a shrinking of the mind. And a feeling of floating in deep green darkness, with little red flecks around him, glowing, perfectly beautiful . . .

Something was battering at his chest. He gave a huge cough, very painful, because what he was coughing out was not air but water. Strong light jabbed his eyes. He rolled away from the battering and rolled into a ball.

"Stone me," said a voice. "It lives."

Idris opened his eyes. The light was still like knives, so he shut them. "Oi," said the voice. "Come back."

Idris recognized the voice. It belonged to Daft Alb, a fisherman when he felt like it, the rest of the time the laziest man in Westgate.

"Silly bleeder," said Alb. "Lucky for you I was passing by. In fact," said Alb, a note of puzzlement entering his voice, "lucky for you I was a-dreaming of a man with a nose ring, me telling him tide's wrong for fishing, him saying give it a whirl anyway, and me doing it. Then having come out of the Seagate I goes not straight ahead for the Banks but turns hard a-starboard along the Wall like I never do, just in time to see you come a-thundering out of the sky like a gannet. Down you did go," said Alb, "and I made sure you was mullet bait. But then up you did come, so I grabbed you. I wonder," said Alb, "if I am in for a reward."

Idris was not in a position to answer this question, as he was being sick over the side.

"Better out than in," said Alb. "Whyn't you give me a hand to row this thing home?"

Down the Wall they rowed, between the towers of the Seagate and into the great stone basin built for the trading ships that had made the Westgate's fortune before the sandbanks had blocked the channels. The quays were empty, except for a handful of fishing boats, a couple of gigs, and the *Pride of Westgate*, a big corsair-chaser tied up to the Guardian Dock. Idris began to feel better. His head cleared. He had the energy to wonder about Alb's dream. And as he wondered, something odd struck him.

He frowned. He said, "A man with a nose ring appeared to you?"

Alb puffed, rowing. "Yep."

"What did he look like?"

"Told you. Nose ring."

Nose rings were uncommon in the Westgate. A nose ring had been discussing him with Master Omnium. And now a nose ring had saved him.

Odd.

But plenty of things were odd, thought Idris, always practical. The main thing was that he had not drowned. The boat was sliding alongside the quay steps, green weed waving below.

A small figure was waiting on the cracked marble paving, looking miserable. Idris felt sorry for him. "Cayo," said Idris, taking the mooring line up the steps. "You all right?"

Cayo did not lift his eyes from his feet.

"What happened?"

Cayo avoided Idris's eye. "It was Spignold."

"It was Spignold what?"

"He was angry that everyone was looking at you. He sort of bumped into the plank. He can't have meant to. Then he said he would save everyone a lot of trouble."

"Trouble?" Idris felt a chill. "What trouble?"

"You know what bighead rubbish he talks. I expect he's very sorry."

"Yes." Idris was not a naturally wary person. Sudden death was common in Lyonesse, and Westgate was a hard place. Games were dangerous and played for keeps. It was good practice (some people said, particularly the Captains) for later life. But what was this about saving trouble?

Idris started along the quay, sore in throat and chest. Beside him, Cayo had cheered up and was singing:

Out of the sky he plummeted
but much to Spignold's pain
though blue sea closed over his head
he plummeted up again.

Idris laughed, which hurt his chest. As he turned his head to tell Cayo the song was rubbish, two men were watching: Master

Omnium in his long black robe and the man with the nose ring. As Idris caught Nose Ring's eye, Nose Ring inclined his head in a small, knowing bow. Idris remembered Alb's dream. The hair prickled on his neck.

Suddenly he wanted home and warmth. He trotted down the fifty steps from the top of the quay to Wet Street. Thank the Well, it was nearly time for zupper.

The Limpets' house was not very big, but what it lacked in size it made up for in tidiness. "I'm back," called Idris to his mum, who was battering tin pots at the clay stove.

"Dinner in a whale's dive," she said. "Wash."

He dumped his books in the bedroom he shared with the Boys, his large blond brothers, Ed and Cadmon. He washed in water from the rain tank, rinsed the salt out of his school kilt, and put on clean breeches. He was trying not to worry about the man with the nose ring. Nose rings were a thing you generally saw in men from the Wellvale. He wondered what happened to them when you had a cold. Snot everywhere, probably —

Someone was calling him. His mother. Harpoon Limpet was tall and blond, like her elder sons. The corners of her eyes and her arms bore the luck tattoos of the guild of Fishers. Idris ran downstairs and started to bang the shell bowls around the driftwood table, his worries vanishing with the prospect of zupper. "Here's your dad," said Harpoon.

Ector Limpet was a small, upright man, with the sea-blue eyes of those whose duty it was to patrol the Wall of Lyonesse. He was wearing the dark-blue uniform of a Gateguard Wallwatcher and a slight frown. The frown deepened when he saw Idris, but the eyes looked more worried than annoyed. Idris felt a sinking of the stomach and ran over in his mind the things he ought not to have done that day. "Where are they all?" said Ector.

"The Boys are out till the five bell," said Harpoon. "And the Stones are at their friend Wilda's." The Stones were the Precious Stones, Emerald and Ruby, Idris's little blond sisters, who seemed to spend months on end in their friends' houses, except when their friends were at the Limpets'.

"Good," said Ector. "Siddown, then."

Idris sat down. Harpoon sloshed a pinkish stew into three shell bowls. It smelled deliciously of crab and of garlics from the garden path at the back of the house. Ector ate for a while, silent except for slurping noises. Then he looked at Idris with those sea-blue eyes. "And you," he said. "How's it been?"

"Same old stuff," said Idris, uneasy under his father's gaze. He did not want to tell his parents about the fall into the sea, and the odd stares of Nose Ring and Omnium. What was done was done, and it would only worry them.

But Ector was not a gateguard for nothing. "There was something, though," he said. "In that Fort of yours."

"Let him eat," said Harpoon, to Idris's relief. "Took some catching, those crabs did, then some boiling, then some picking —"

"And very nice, too," said Ector, forging on. "But I bumped into Ringnet Prorbus on the way home, and she told me a tale about her Cayo." The eyes drilled into Idris's. "She said you'd done him a good turn. Very happy about that, she was."

"Ah," said Idris, not wanting to explain. "Yes."

"And?"

"Very good, this, Mum," said Idris, eating.

"All right," said Ector. "That there dratted Spignold was throwing his weight around, and you thought you'd stop him. Is that it?"

Idris put down his spoon. This might get complicated; Captains like Spignold's dad were far above gateguards like Ector. Perhaps his dad would get into trouble. But there was no getting out of it now. He held his father's eye. "What would you have done?" he said.

Ector ducked his head. "Very good," he said. "Just the thing." He was a kind man, simple and straightforward and strong-minded.

Idris felt a moment's relief. Then he saw his father catch Harpoon's eye and look away too quickly, as if there was something they were hiding from him, and he felt that chill again. "What is it?" he said.

"Eat," said Harpoon. "It'll get cold."

Idris laid down his spoon. He hated it when they hid things from him. "Please."

If the Boys or the Stones had done this, Ector would have ignored them. But Idris had a knack for making people feel the same way he felt.

"Tell him," said Harpoon.

Ector shrugged and prodded a bit of crab in his bowl. "That Spignold said something," he said. "Nonsense, of course . . ."

"Tell me," said Idris.

"You fell into the sea," said Ector. "You went under for a good bit. Then Alb fished you out, and Alb still doesn't properly know why he was in a good place to do it at a good moment to do it, except for some dream he said he had, silly fool. They reckon—that is Spignold says—you swam, and you made Alb rescue you by talking in his mind." He fell silent. The terrible words hung in the air between them. Monsters could swim. Monsters talked in people's minds.

Idris's heart had started hammering. "So according to Spignold," he said, "I am a Cross or some such abomination?"

"We know what's true," said Ector, his face grim, but embarrassed, too. "But you know Captain Ironhorse. Big fish in a small pool."

Idris watched his father and saw the awful danger in his face. In his mind the words of the Treaty marched with a steady, doleful tread. *Men may catch Monsters for the benefit they give to Men. And Men will keep open the Wells from which the Monsters rise, that the Monsters may enjoy the bright plunge of day into their world. The one is a fair exchange for the nation*

But Man is Man, and Monster Monster. The Treaty permits no abomination. The chief abomination is a Cross. For there are Monsters that present themselves in mortal guise, yea, even in the guise of young men and women, that mortal women and men may be deceived by them and bring forth Crosses, a Cross being a creature gotten by men of monsters, yea, even if it be of the thirtieth generation. And the way ye shall know your Cross is if your Cross can swim in the waters on the face of the earth; so any man that swims shall be called Cross and must surely perish.

The Treaty was something you learned at school. It was words, that was all. Monsters lived in Wells and were useful in some way that nobody told you. But if monsters got loose they were bad and frightening and wanted to breed with humans and conquer Lyonesse. But somewhere far away. Not in sunny little half-ruined Westgate. It was ridiculous.

"I *sank*," he said slowly, so they would understand and tell everyone what was true. "I went on that plank because Spignold was bullying Cayo and I wanted to help. And Spignold moved the plank and I missed it and fell and sank, and Alb pulled me out just before I went down for the third time —"

"I know," said Harpoon, smoothing his hair with a hand hardened by nets and lines. "That Ironhorse is a fat fool, and the boy's as bad. You mustn't worry. We'll sort it out. Now I can hear your throat is bad. Time you were in bed."

"Things will be all right," said Ector. "I'll see to it."

Idris noticed that his father's eyes met his mother's as if things were not all right, were indeed a long way from being all right. But he was very, very tired, too tired to be unhappy about things he did not understand. He dragged himself upstairs and into his bed. Dimly he heard the clatter of Ed and Cadmon coming in, and the squeak and titter of the Stones. Then he went to sleep.

TWO

I dris woke once in the night. He could hear his parents in
the kitchen, the rumble of his father's voice, the sharp note
of his mother's as she said, "No!" Then his father started
talking again and he was asleep again, falling through green
darkness among glowing red fishes. . . .

He awoke. It was morning, and from below there came
the bright smell of weedwater and smokefish. He was late for
breakfast. He rolled out of bed and scroffed his hair tidy and
hauled on his school kilt and tunic. Someone had brought back
his books and put them on the work desk in his room. Yesterday
was hazy, like a dream. This was a day like any other, except
that he was even later for school than usual, and he had a strange,
uneasy feeling in the back of his mind.

The weedwater was lukewarm, and the Boys had eaten the
fillets of the smokefish, leaving only a couple of backbones to
gnaw. Harpoon was out fishing, and Ector was on the Wall. A
squid-inked shell on the table read COME HOME FOR NUNCHEON.
Idris trotted through the sandy lanes to school. The sun banished his unease, and he dribbled a knob of dried donkey dung

cheerily for the last couple of hundred yards, Kek gliding overhead. He was last into the hall, but the morning readings had not yet started. Boys and girls looked at him as he took his place — a strange look, admiring but nervous, probably because of yesterday. The only person who did not look at him was Spignold, who was staring reverently at Master Omnium, lips pursed. The sight of Spignold brought back the uneasiness, and with it a small, anxious knot in the stomach.

The children listened to the Readings of the Day. They sang Wellsongs in the four-part harmonies that came naturally to the children of Lyonesse. Then they went to their classes. This morning, it was first the Manner, then the Nature of the Land. The Manner taught you how to treat other people so the person you met could tell your name and rank and place, and there would be no possibility for rudeness or offense. The Nature of the Land was boring, because Idris was beginning to realize that he knew as much about it as his teacher did.

"The nature of the land is to sink," said Mother Arthrax, who was incredibly old and incredibly dull. She mumbled away about the Wall, the pumps powered by monsters that kept the land dry. Inside Idris's head, the thoughts hummed busily by. It was silly to be worried. Nothing had happened after yesterday's fright. He would get on with his studies and forget about Spignold and Nose Ring and Omnium. He did not intend to spend the rest of his life patrolling the crumbling Wall against corsairs that nowadays cruised miles away, far to the south of the Westgate Banks. When he grew up he would make things happen. Not the way the Captains did, pompous and moneyish and self-important. He would know the stars, talk to birds, become expert in the placing of standing stones. He would make things happen without spoiling other things in the process.

A fly landed on his desk and sat washing its face with its front legs. Fly, fly, thought Idris.

The fly flew.

Idris watched it go. Come back, fly, he thought.

The fly came back.

Fly.

It flew.

Back.

Back it came.

Fly upside down, thought Idris, so surprised he could hardly breathe.

The fly turned upside down, got confused, and crashed to the ground. Mawga put her foot on it.

By the Well, thought Idris, his heart hammering. What was that?

"Idris!" cried Mother Arthrax. "Name me the marks of the Approach from the Sea!"

"Um," said Idris, his mind still full of biddable fly. "You got your North Sundeeps Bank, your Outer Banks, your Outer Inner Gobbard —"

"You got?" said Mother Arthrax. "Exactly whom do you think you are addressing?"

There was a general giggle in the class. Schools in Lyonesse were formal places. Mother Arthrax did not like the giggle and decided to blame Idris. "If you want a whipping you may have one!" she shrieked. "Come to the High Seat at day's end, and we shall see who talks disrespect and casualness!"

Idris bowed, gloomy again. It seemed just about impossible to keep out of trouble. Spignold was reciting the marks in a smarmy singsong, getting them all right, of course. Idris found another fly and tried to make it fly. But the doom waiting at day's end interfered with his concentration, and the fly paid no attention. Perhaps he had imagined the first one. Idris's gloom deepened. All he could do was wait and hope it was soon over.

After a couple of hundred years, the Nature of the Land lesson ended, and the pupils rose for Seal's Milk. The day being bright, there was a general stampede for the yard, on whose walls were marked the circles that were the goals in the game of War. War was a good, violent game, and it was a relief to run and barge and get Mother Arthrax out of his mind. He saw Rarpa pick up the ball and start to run. Idris launched himself into the air, got Rarpa around the neck, and pulled him down with a crash onto the sandy paving, shouting, "Mark!"

Suddenly Idris had the impression that the sun had gone behind a cloud. He looked up. There was no cloud, but a tall man in a brown cloak. A Town Guardian. What was he doing on the War field?

Idris found out.

Hard hands grabbed him by the upper arm. He was lifted from the ground. Idris thought, panicky, Is that what you get for not thinking about the way you talk to Mother Arthrax? Then he saw two things

He saw the face of Spignold, watching him, lips pursed, shaking his head.

And he saw, staring down at him from a little carved-stone window, the face of Master Omnium: a face that often watched him. Normally it was closed and confident. This morning it was white and worried.

"What have I done?" said Idris, helpless as his heels dragged across the sand of the yard.

"Shut, Cross," said the Guardian.

Cross? thought Idris, frozen with shock.

The school gates slammed. Big hands threw him into a closed mule waggon bearing the red fist of Captaincy. The wheels began to grind.

Cross.

Fear dried Idris's mouth and loosened his guts. He sat on the low bench and clamped his teeth together and told himself that this was a mistake. Soon they would realize he was only eleven and send him back to his parents. To distract himself, he kept count of the turnings. The cart rolled away from the school, turned right up Burnt Frog Hill, and right again up a road through the ruined town that was either the Lower Inner Rampart or (by the steepness of it) Castle Gates. Here the fear tried to come back. Very few people who entered the Castle in closed carts bearing the red fist of Captaincy —

A long squeal of gate hinges. A winding of gears, as of a portcullis being raised. The wheels turning hollow on a drawbridge.

— ever came out again. Not even if they were eleven-year-olds with mothers and fathers and sisters and brothers waiting for them.

The cart stopped. The back doors opened. "Out," said a voice.

Idris got out.

The cart was in a small cobbled yard. Blank walls rose on all sides. The sky was a small blue square far above. The horse stamped and snorted, as if it could smell something it did not like. Idris screwed up his courage. "Why am I here?" he said.

"Shut. March," said the Guardian and pushed him toward a door.

Idris marched, on wobbly knees. There was a passage, three more doors, a flight of stone steps. Another door, iron-strapped and nailed. The door swung open, apparently by magic. Inside was a table, a stuffed narwhal, small lamps of seal oil flickering before sooty mica reflectors. A man stood behind the table, not very old but completely without hair. Idris recognized him as Leech Derek the surgeon, and made himself say a polite "Good afternoon," forcing his jaw not to tremble. Leech Derek looked at him with his cold, poached-looking eyes. "Strip," he said.

Idris took off his school tunic and stepped out of his school kilt.

"On the table," said Leech Derek. The door slammed, the fifth door, cutting off Idris from the world.

"What —"

"Go, or be put," said the Guardian.

Idris put himself on the table. Leech Derek examined him, crown to soles, like a doctor looking for signs of disease. "No outward trace," he said to the Guardian.

"Of what?" said Idris. This must be a terrible dream. But it was real.

The Guardian ignored him. "Nasty, deceiving reptile," he said. "Dress."

Idris dressed, doing the buckles with shaking fingers. The Guardian pushed him down a corridor with another door at its end. "Go in," said the Guardian.

The door opened. A hand pushed Idris through a narrow tunnel. The tunnel ended in a round stone enclosure. The walls of the enclosure came up to his chin and were armed with rusty iron spikes. Beyond the spikes was an enormous room. At the far end of the room were three big chairs, the middle one higher than the other two. The middle chair was empty. In the chair to the left sat an old scribe with a dried inksquid and a great sheet of sealskin on which he was making notes with a seagull quill. I must be dreaming, thought Idris. But he knew he was not. For in the right-hand chair, wearing the triple crown of Captaincy, tin, copper, and gold, sat Captain Ironhorse.

Idris summoned up his courage. "Good afternoon," he said through the spikes, keeping his voice steady, but only just. He knew where he was now. He had been here on a school trip. This was the Hall of Justice.

And the spiked enclosure was the dock.

"Silence!" cried a voice from below. Idris stood on tiptoe. On the floor of the enormous room, a half-dozen people were sitting. He recognized a fish merchant, a shipowner, a couple of brown-tunicked Guardians, and a man who might be a clerk. The Captain's people, in fact. The kind Dad called fat bloodsuckers.

"The court is here," intoned Ironhorse. "The court will do its duty. However disagreeable." He smiled vastly. "What is the case?"

"Suspected Cross," said a voice Idris recognized as belonging to the Guardian who had brought him.

Idris's heart gave a great bang, then seemed to stop beating. Everyone knew Crosses existed and that they were taken away and destroyed. But there were no Crosses at Westgate School. He was a boy, not a Cross.

"Has he been examined?" said the Captain.

"Aye," said Leech Derek.

"Does he bear signs?"

"None evident," said Leech Derek, his brow greasy with its sweat. "A very perfect specimen of a man boy, indeed."

"Perhaps too perfect?" said the Captain knowingly.

Leech Derek gave an equally knowing wag of the head. "I have seen it so, with Crosses."

"There is other evidence," said Ironhorse pompously. "It comes from a man of the Wellvale skilled in recognizing Crosses." Into Idris's head came the dark face of the man with the nose ring, murmuring to Master Omnium. He looked at his feet, bowed down by an awful sense of powerlessness.

"See, he hangs his head," said Ironhorse. "My brave son Spignold has long had suspicions of his own." Dirty bully, thought Idris, with a sharp stab of anger. "And there is yet more evidence," said the Captain. "Yesterday, the creature Idris Limpet did fall by the ingenuity of my brave son from a tower and was seen to swim. There is a witness. Scribe?"

"I have here a paper from Alb Fishbee, known as Daft," said the scribe with the squid and the sealskin. "It goes like this. 'He come down like a gannet, splat into the water, very neat, and I made sure he was a gone goner. But after maybe ten breaths up he comes. And I grabs him. Is there a reward?'"

"Virtue is its own reward," said Captain Ironhorse, sniffing fatly. "I have also heard from this person's classmates —"

"Your fat, lying son!" said Idris, losing his temper.

"— that the accused was seen to swim. Scribe, read the law on swimming."

"It is written," said the scribe, "that what swims is a Cross, and shall not be suffered to live —"

"Wait!" cried Idris.

"— and shall not be heard," said the scribe. "For lo, the monster speaks sweetly and bends men's minds. Better a man die in mistake than a monster live."

"Very well," said Ironhorse. "Let it be done."

Idris's lips were numb with horror. "Let what be done?"

"One suspected Cross shall be drowned, and if he yet live and be verily monster, be crushed," said the Captain. "Let it be written."

"I want my parents!" said Idris, in the nightmare. "My dad's a gateguard! My brothers —"

"Put him away," said Ironhorse. "Next case."

"There is no next case," said the scribe. And he might have gone on, but Idris did not hear it. For the floor had dropped away under his feet and he was falling. A yell of horror tore his throat. For he knew to where he was falling.

Some Westgate mothers scared their children with tales of the Drowning Cell, connected with the dock of the Hall of Justice by Hell's Throat. Harpoon had not been one of those mothers. Harpoon had been sweet and kind and huge and gentle, and now he would never see her again. Because Hell's Throat had swallowed him.

So he fell. Then he was not falling but slithering, down a long chute of slimy stone. A smell of old mold and rot came up at him. It was dark. He put out his hand to slow himself, but the walls hurtled by, smooth as glass. Down he rushed, down and along, shooting under the roots of the town. Perhaps he was shouting, probably not, because the terror and regret were gone, and what remained was the knowledge that this was not fair. He was an ordinary boy. But this Nose Ring had singled him out as a monster. And Spignold had lied about him to please Ironhorse, who doted on his pudgy son. And Ironhorse had condemned him without question, the way you would swat a blackbeetle on the real phoare

Idris turned a somersault and came down with a bang on his shoulder, upside down, out of control, like the fly in the classroom —

The fly.

Something burst in Idris's head. It was as if an extra pair of eyes had opened, a pair he had never noticed before —

Bump, went something under him, a seam in the rock, perhaps. Over he tumbled and put out his hands to save himself. The heels of his palms crashed painfully against stone. Over he went again.

The new eyes in his head saw a town.

They saw the line of a sea wall, blue sea beyond, towers, spires, the blind sockets of windows. The town was Westgate, the wall the Wall. *He was seeing through Kek's eyes.*

For a moment his mind filled with wild thoughts of escape, taking wing away from all these horrors. Then over he tumbled again, and he knew he was not the gull, but only seeing with the gull's eyes. He slid flat on his belly. His knee hit an edge of stone, hurt. He was slowing down, the slope growing less, the floor wetter now, flattening out. And finally he coasted to a halt in pitch darkness, sitting in cold water.

Behind him, something went *click*.

He tried to stand up. When he was half up his head hit stone. He started to crawl backward, the way he had come. The stones were horribly slippery. The floor started to slope upward. His hands and knees found no grip, so he crept on his belly, the cloth of kilt and tunic providing just enough friction for him to make his way, his hands out in front of him, until he was out of the water.

His hands hit stone.

He felt up and around. Then he laid his forehead on his arms and closed his eyes.

He was in a stone pipe, perhaps a clothyard in diameter. The click he had heard was a balanced stone that had risen behind him to block him in. In front of him would be another wall, only this one would have vents at its base to admit the sea and drown him.

Idris knew that he was dead. The problem was that he could not make himself believe it.

His mind went inward. It went to the first things he could remember, when he had been tiny. Family things: Harpoon, his mother, the smell of her, warm and kind and tinged with fish-smoke. The hands of Ector, his father, carving him a little corsair boat out of a bit of driftwood, the fingers sunburned and clever, the eyes watching him as if in a sort of wonder at what he saw. The ragtag of the Boys and him, playing like puppies under the table. The Precious Stones, tiny, smiling at him with the perfect happiness and trust of babies who had not yet learned that the world was not a happy place and could certainly not be trusted. And now all that warmth and kindness had gone because of lies that Spignold and Nose Ring had told. Gone forever. Because his family would be alive, and he would be dead.

No, thought Idris. This cannot happen.

He jumped. Cold water had sloshed against his foot.

The tide was coming in.

It was happening.

His heart was hammering. He made himself breathe slowly.

The new eyes opened.

The town from above again, the Wall, the Castle. A street, Eel Alley, winding through houses. And down the street two men running. Even from above, Idris recognized his father. A lump came into his throat, and tears stung his eyes but did not dim them, because he was looking through Kek, and gulls do not cry. The other man was dressed in a dark-red cloak. He looked up, straight at the gull. Idris felt a chill of horror. It was the man with the nose ring, the Crosshunter. What did he want now? Ector bent and seemed to pull at something on the ground: a stone with a ring in the middle.

Somewhere in the solid ground far above Idris's head, stone grated on stone.

Suddenly he was seeing through his own eyes, and the world was pitch dark, and his heart was hammering again, and he was terrified enough to whimper. Whimpering was no good. Think. He stood up, got into a sort of crouch, and banged his head on the roof. The water was at his knees, rising fast. Thinking was no good either. The panic rose again. He shouted, "Dad!"

Nothing. Only the slosh of water. Water rising to his thighs now, as he crouched, nose uppermost, jammed into the arch of the tunnel top. Above the gurgle and slosh he thought he heard more grinding, a hammering, perhaps. But the water was at his collarbones now, and a ring of cold was rising up his neck.

"Dad!"

That was the last shout. The water covered his mouth. He took a last quick breath through his nose, and the water covered it, and he vowed not to give Ironhorse and Spignold and Nose Ring even in his death the satisfaction of terror. *Honor is a thing that is inside you,* he heard Ector say.

All that remained was an honorable death.

No air. Green darkness, shot with little red gleams . . .

The death struggle.

There was light. A yellow blur in the water. Arms and legs flailing, he thrashed toward it. Something grabbed him by the collar of his tunic and pulled him upward. He had to breathe. Breathed. Air, not water.

He was in a little stone room, leaning against a wet wall that flickered orange in torchlight. His father was bending over the trapdoor in the floor through which he had pulled Idris. Embossed on the door was the fist of Captaincy. His father was battering bronze wedges into hasps, securing the trapdoor. Water was welling up from its sides.

"It would seem," said another voice, "that you were not born to be drowned." It was a cold voice, on the edge of sarcasm. It belonged to the man with the nose ring.

Idris stared at him for a moment in horror. Then he pulled the short bronze sword from Ector's scabbard and hurled himself at the man, wanting to kill, stab, destroy. He heard Ector shout, "Idris!" But Ector did not understand what this Nose Ring had done.

A cloak muffled his face. A hard hand gripped his sword-wrist. Another lifted him from the ground by his collar. Nose Ring's voice said, "I am here to save you, idiot child."

"But you had me taken up and put down Hell's Throat and nearly drowned —"

"Hush now," said Ector. "I know this man. Now be quiet and greet him in the Manner and do what he says."

Idris's fingers opened. The sword clattered to the stones. He felt himself lowered to the floor.

"Offer him thanks," said Ector.

"Never," said Idris, between clenched teeth.

Nose Ring laughed, infuriatingly superior. "One day you will change your mind."

"The Manner," hissed Ector.

Idris did not see why his good father should abase himself before this Nose Ring. But a father was a father; that was in the Manner, too. So he took a deep breath and managed to bow respectfully, as was expected on meeting a stranger. He said, through clenched teeth, "Revered father and honored sir, I thank you for your coming."

"Up we go, then," said Nose Ring, sounding bored. "You first."

Above the little room was a shaft, with bronze rungs up its side. Ector looked at Idris. He winked, patted him on the shoulder, and started to climb.

"Very touching," said Nose Ring. "Go on, then." He boosted Idris up so he could catch the first rung. Idris began to climb. Nose Ring came behind him, talking. "This is the shaft they haul the bodies up," he said. "They've got a windlass at the top. Nasty place, nasty people." Pause, with climbing. "Still, you won't be seeing them again."

The muddled thoughts stopped. Suddenly Idris's head was clear and cold. He said, "What do you mean?"

"Get a move on," said Nose Ring. "I hope you said goodbye to everyone this morning."

"What are you talking about?" said Idris, guessing what he meant but not wanting it to be true.

"Your mother and all the rest of that lot," said Nose Ring. "You won't be seeing them for a while. If ever. Use your brains. Obviously you can't stay here. So I'm taking you away. Before someone finds you and drowns you. Properly, next time. And your family with you."

Idris had an awful vision of the Boys and the Stones and Ector and Harpoon behind the iron spikes. He saw the floor give way, heard the screams. "Oh," he said, in a small, small voice.

"Climb."

Light was pouring down the shaft now, the bright, golden light of a Westgate evening. Idris scrambled out of a hole in the pavement. They were among the ruined and uninhabited houses of Gone West Street. Four horses were standing in the street, two with packs, two with saddlecloths. Kek was standing on the ridge of a stone-tiled porch, and the western sky was a blaze of purple and orange.

Nose Ring looked up and down the street. "All right," he said. "Off we go."

"Go on, boy," said Ector. Idris was horrified to see a tear slide down on either side of his father's nose. He could feel tears of his own. "We'll see you one day, never you mind."

Metal boots sounded higher in the street. Nose Ring swung himself onto the saddlecloth. "Up," he said.

Idris was staring stupidly at his horse. It was sleek and glossy, the saddlecloth embroidered with the device of an eel devouring its tail.

The boots were coming down the hill. "Ahem," said Nose Ring. "Here come the Guardians."

Ector hugged Idris. "It'll come right," he said. "Be brave." He made a stirrup of his hands and heaved Idris onto the saddlecloth.

Tears blinded Idris. He could not speak. He was vaguely aware that someone had put something over his shoulders: a cloak with a deep hood. Someone seemed to yank his horse's head and lead him away into the lanes to the eastward, passing through the squad of Guardians. Out of the town they rode. He could not see where they went, except that it was away from the sunset. Then the hooves rang on granite paving, and he knew they were on the Old Road, heading into the darkness that pressed on the empty Stone Downs.

THREE

L ater, Idris remembered little of the first night's journey
to the east. His horse moved at the smooth, steady trot
of a passagemaker, and he twined his hands in its mane
and hung on as best he could. After a while he pushed back his
hood. He had had enough of crying. He even felt a tug of adven-
ture. The humpbacked Downs rolled by. Once he saw the shapes
of standing stones against the sky, glowing dull green as they
came into alignment with their mother star. A dog barked as the
little party skirted a village, and lights glowed yellow in a farm-
house's windows as they passed through its yard. The excitement
passed. He began to be tired. But on they went and on, the voice
of Nose Ring goading him awake when he started to nod.

"What is this road?" said the voice.

"The Old Road," mumbled Idris through clogging waves
of sleep. "Leave me alone."

"No," said the voice. "What do you know of the points of
Lyonesse?"

"Nothing." This was a lie, but Idris was too sleepy to
be bothered.

"Not so. Tell me."

Idris opened his eyes. The pony's ears jogged before him in the dark. "Around the land, the Wall," he said. "Inland of the Westgate, the Stone Downs. At the northwest of the Stone Downs, the moors. West of the moors the Sundeeps, which are mountains. To the south I have heard the Wall is broken and there are marshes, and beyond the marshes big hills, and beyond the hills the River Fal that flows through the Shipwright's Garden, which is so called because of its great oak trees. Also there is the Wellvale that I do not know about, and the Hoar Rock that is called the Mount where the Regent Fisheagle lives with her son the Kyd Murther on whom be praise and blessing. Beyond the Mount are the mountains of High Kernow, where barbarians live in huts made of bones and we do not go." His lids started to come down again.

"Is that all?"

"It is all I can be bothered to tell you, and anyway you know all this perfectly well," said Idris, cross with sleep. "Leave me alone."

"If I had left you alone, you would now be drowned or crushed," said Nose Ring. "Now. We are going to the Valley of Apples."

"Apples?" said Idris.

"It is what they call the Wellvale," said Nose Ring. "Though there are no apples there nowadays. The water from the Wells has made it stink. So we will go up the Old Road through the Stone Downs, then southeast across the Hundreds. Across the what?"

"Hundreds," said Idris, jerking awake.

"Indeed. Beyond the Hundreds are the woods, where we will rest."

"How far?"

"Ten leagues. As far as you might walk in two days. We will arrive at dawn. Then onward over the Poison Ground to the Valley of Apples."

"Oh." What would they be doing at home on Wet Street now?

Sleeping. Grieving.

Nose Ring spurred on ahead. Idris kicked his pony after him. On they rode.

Between misery and half sleep, the night seemed to last forever. Finally, the eastern horizon grew a narrow band of shell-pink and the crust of stars faded in the paling vault. As the sun stuck a fiery limb above the land, they entered an oak wood in which the road wound steeply uphill. "We are come to the Wolf Rock," said Nose Ring. "It is the home of Uther and Nena and their people. They are gentle in peace but fierce in war, like most Knights; old-fashioned, but loyal and good, and mindful of their honor and the duty of hospitality. Here we rest."

Idris raised a weary head. High above the green leaves rose a tower of yellow stone, up and up. And there, higher still, riding the wind, was Kek. Idris's horse whinnied. From the woods above, another horse whinnied back.

The road sloped steeply upward. A curtain wall. A gate. A challenge and response. Hooves in a courtyard, the clank of weapons. Voices, friendly voices. "Safe here," said the voice of Nose Ring. Idris opened his mouth to say that this time yesterday he had been safe in Westgate, which was his home. Instead he sat down on a mounting block and went to sleep.

He woke some time later. He was in a bed with soft blankets pulled up to his chin. Sun was pouring in through a narrow window, steeply, so he guessed it must be the middle of the day. He was very hungry. He sat up.

Someone had left a beaten-tin tray by the side of his bed. On the tray was a brownish-gold block of something. It looked edible and smelled excellent. It seemed to have a crust on the outside and delicious meat on the inside. Idris wondered if he should ask if it was for him. But there was nobody around, and by the time he had finished wondering he found he had eaten it anyway, and it was indeed delicious, far, far more delicious than the crab and eel and seal cheese you got in Westgate.

Where about now the Limpet family would be sitting around the driftwood table. Seven chairs. One empty.

They would be thinking Idris was dead, for Ector would never have told them the truth for fear of more trouble. They must be so sad.

Idris had never felt so lonely. Misery pressed him back upon the cloudy feather pillow.

He fell instantly asleep again.

Next time he woke, the window was gray, the room half-dark. He could feel that there was someone in there with him. "Who?" he said in a panic, groping beside him for something that might do as a weapon.

"You're awake," said a girl's voice, sounding not very interested in the fact or in him.

He blinked and sat up. Flint sparked. Tinder flared. A flame grew, moved to a lamp, and became a tall yellow leaf. It lit a girl's face. She had long red-gold hair and a small, slightly hooked nose, like the beak of a peculiarly elegant bird. "I thought I'd better bring you some zupper," she said. "Because we will be leaving at Crakerise. Crake is a star, you know."

"I know," said Idris, not enjoying being patronized.

"And you don't want to be sleepy on the road. Wits about you. I had a good nap this afternoon. We'll be riding all night. Go on, eat something."

Idris had seldom listened to anyone as bossy as this girl, but he did not answer, for he was already chewing another of the delicious meat pies. Then his mind caught up with his ears. "We?"

"To the Wellvale," said the girl, watching with a sort of horror as he wolfed down the pie. "Well, that didn't last long. I suppose you want another."

"No," said Idris, more to prove her wrong than because he didn't. "Thank you."

"I'm astonished," said the girl, seeing through him. "I mean, it must be much nicer than what you're used to."

45

Idris considered telling her to watch her manners, then decided that a remark as rude as this did not need an answer. He sat up in bed. "Clothes," he said.

"On the chair," said the girl. "They're new. The old ones were absolutely disgusting so I had them thrown away. See you in the courtyard. You'd better hurry." The door slammed.

The new clothes were a tunic and a coat of dark-red wool, and black three-quarter-length trousers. On the back of the coat and the left breast of the tunic was the device of the eel devouring its tail. Idris dressed, then went to look out of the window. Far to the west a half-moon hung low in the sky, and below it a glimmer that might be the sea.

The glimmer blurred with tears. Over there lay the Westgate, and Idris's life.

He took a deep breath. There was no going back there now. Nose Ring said his future lay in the Valley of Apples, or the Wellvale, or whatever it was called. Who was this Nose Ring? It seemed that he had singled out Idris as a Cross. Yet it was Nose Ring who had saved him from the Drowning Cell. I will become stronger, Idris told himself. Then I will discover the truth.

Firmly he turned his back on the window and strode down the stairs. Nose Ring was already on his horse, and a tall man was saying good-bye to the girl in a haw-haw voice, sounding sad, but something else, too — proud, perhaps. They mounted and rode through the gate and down the steep road into the green smell of the oakwoods, and the road winding white under the moon to his new life.

Whatever that might be.

They rode hard till moonset. Then Nose Ring said, "We rest here a glass."

Idris slid to the ground and went to help the girl down. "I'm fine," she said, sliding elegantly from her saddlecloth. They watered the horses. Then she said, "I've brought some food."

"Well, blow me down, she thinks of everything," said Nose Ring in his sarcastic voice. Except (Idris saw, as the dark face turned toward him under the moon) he was Nose Ring no longer. The ring was gone. The face was a forbidding landscape of planes and shadows, entirely concealing whatever lay buried behind it. Idris felt a stubborn refusal to be daunted by this. He was a boy of Lyonesse, among his countryfolk, and would not be cast down. He must introduce himself in the Manner, to show these people where he fitted into the land. He rose and bowed, as tradition demanded. He said, "I have been unmannerly. Permit me to name myself. I am Idris Limpet of the Limpets, Gateguards and Fishers of the Westgate."

As the Manner demanded, the girl now rose. "Permit me in my turn," she said. "I am Morgan ni Uther of the Wolf Rock."

Both of them now looked at Nose Ring. "Very mannerly, I must say," said that mysterious entity, with his mouth full. "This is really not a bad pie at all."

This was a horrible breach of the Manner — so bad, indeed, that Idris found himself wondering if it might not be deliberate, to test him. Anyway, it must be pardoned in one who had after all saved his life. "But what," he said, "are we to call you?"

Nose Ring took another bite of pie and chewed it with his mouth open. "I am called many things," he said. "On the whole, though, I think it would be best for the moment if you were to call me 'Sir.' Really excellent, this pie."

Idris thought he saw Morgan hide a giggle, though it was hard to tell in the moonlight. When they remounted, she rode ahead or behind, obviously not wanting to talk to him. This was wounding. But the shock of his trial and rescue was fading, and he was beginning to think about the future. So he allowed the horse to carry him along, and allowed his thoughts to take him away.

In an ordinary person, these would have been deeply gloomy. He was leaving his parents, his home, everything and everyone he knew and loved. But Idris had never felt quite ordinary. In his mind was an odd sort of satisfaction. Already he had traveled halfway across Lyonesse, and met with Knights. Now he was to work in the center of things. The future was dark and mysterious. But darkness and mystery were exciting.

He kicked the pony forward until he was riding knee to knee with Nose Ring. Bracing himself for more rudeness, he said, "When we reach the . . . Valley of Apples, what will we do?"

Nose Ring's face turned upon him. "You will be attached to the house of Great Ambrose the Mage, whose device is the self-devouring eel you wear on your tunic. There you will become a monstergroom."

The voice was not encouraging, but neither was it rude. It was merely matter of fact. Idris got the impression that this was a man who could be believed, and if that meant a lack of Manner, too bad. Idris did not care, though, for the words had woken memories of things half heard, things not to be spoken of by ordinary people. Very exciting things. He said, "And what are the duties of a monstergroom?"

Morgan made a tutting noise, as if this was a very stupid question. "To catch monsters in the Wells," said Nose Ring, ignoring her. "To tend and nurture them in the monsterstables until it is time for them to be put in the machines to burn. To ignore their wiles, and to learn the wiles of the Captains who own the Wells."

"Is the Great Ambrose a Captain?" said Idris, a picture of pompous Ironhorse coming into his mind.

Another scornful noise from Morgan. Nose Ring laughed. "Certainly not," he said. "He is a mage. A master of all sciences. You are fortunate he singled you out. Let us hope he will be as fortunate to be your master." He spurred on his horse.

Monstergroom, thought Idris. The word gave him butter-flies in his stomach. I am to care for . . . monsters. And learn the wiles of Captains greater, far greater, than Ironhorse, and with luck, destroy him. And what does he mean, I have been singled out?

He was excited now. But his eyes were still pricking with the thought of what he had lost.

Then his nostrils pricked, too. There was more than sadness in the air.

"Scarf 'round your face," said Nose Ring.

Idris wrapped his scarf around his face. The road had leveled out and now ran flat and straight into the distance. A tree held its branches out against the moon. It was leafless, although it was summer. The land beside the road looked sere and black. They passed a sheet of water that bubbled. The bubbles stank as they burst, somewhere between dead fish and bird muck. Idris heard Morgan cough.

"Welcome to the Poison Ground, my children," said Nose Ring. "The overflow of the sweet waters of the Valley of Apples." He laughed, harsh and ironic.

The marsh stretched on and on. At first, Morgan chatted with Nose Ring. Then she fell silent. Every now and then they crossed a river, running between stone embankments high above the level of the swamp. Mother Arthrax had talked about this. As the land had sunk, men had built up the banks of the rivers lest they flood all. At last they came to a low, barren mound, with a cluster of half-ruined buildings on its top.

As they rode up the slope toward the half-ruined barbican, little blackened men and women scuttled out of the buildings. They welcomed the travelers in hoarse, friendly voices, coughing as they took the horses and directed their guests to ill-smelling cells.

Here they slept for a while and woke in daylight; there seemed to be no longer any need for concealment. Idris was exhausted and his throat was sore. The same went (Idris guessed, though she kept her nose high) for Morgan. Idris's mind floated up to Kek. Once again he found he could use the gull's eyes. Kek was very high. He saw the road they had traveled, running through the woods, over farmland, until it vanished into the Stone Downs. And ahead . . .

Ahead, the thread of the road ran straight as a ruler across the black marshes until it met a short, thick line that must have been a wall or a dam. The blackened marshes fanned out from the line: *the overflow from the sweet waters of the Valley of Apples.* Behind the line was a lake, black from this height. Little things crawled on the the lake: barges, perhaps. At its far end was a smear of . . . what? Smoke, fumes. And buildings. Many buildings, confined in a wall. Behind the wall, down in the distance, rose a steep crag. On top of the crag was what might have been towers. Idris realized that Kek was looking at the Hoar Rock, and the mountains of High Kernow beyond it.

This was the land of Lyonesse, in which Idris had grown up. His mouth was dry. But not with fear, though it was huge and frightening — with excitement. The Westgate had been small, and he had known every cobblestone of it. In these great unknown spaces lay his future.

Idris returned to the jog and stink of the unending road, the hunched, cloaked figures in front of him. He said, "And soon we will see the Valley of Apples."

Nose Ring's head rose. He looked at the place where the road disappeared into the brownish haze. "Where?" he said, in the voice of one who already knows the answer.

"Beyond the dam."

Nose Ring turned to look at him. His face was shadowed by the hood, except for the eyes, which now had a piercing red light. "Have you been here before?" he said.

"Never."

"Then how do you know about the dam?"

Idris decided that it was time he had some secrets of his own. "I just know," he said.

The eyes rested on him for a worryingly long time. Then Nose Ring laughed, approvingly, as it seemed to Idris, and spurred his horse on without waiting for an answer. Morgan looked across at Idris, puzzled. But not scornful anymore, he was pleased to note.

Soon the ground began to rise, and the road led up the side of a valley. Ahead was the dam: an enormous wall stretched across the valley, streaked with black filth and shining with seeps of water, with long, low work sheds at its side. On top of the dam, people and fuming machines were toiling, adding extra courses of masonry. "What are they doing?" said Idris.

"The lake gets deeper all the time," said Nose Ring. "The water is from the Wells. It is poisonous, so it must be kept back.

They are making the dam higher. They are always making it higher. It is always leaking and overtopping. Come and see. You will not like it."

They rode up to a place where the dam met the hillside, hitched the horses to a rail, and walked out onto the dam top. A little crowd of men was gathered around a thing like a box on wheels. Next to the box stood a cart with an iron tank on its top. When the men saw Nose Ring, they bowed. "There is a monster in the tank," said Nose Ring to Idris and Morgan. "It has been brought from the Wells in a barge. Now it will be loaded into the machine. Watch."

A man pulled a lever on the cart. The tank tipped sideways. Water poured from the tank through a grid of bars. Something lay on the grid: something gray and shiny and shapeless, with holes in it, as if parts of it had been cut away. . . .

I'm drying! screamed something in Idris's head, an awful scream of horror and despair.

"Oh!" cried Morgan, hands over her ears, face as white as sea foam.

"Yes," said Nose Ring. "An unpleasant noise. The monster falls to the grid. The water drains through. The grid tilts. The monster is tipped into the burning chamber of the machine, so." The grid clanged shut. The shriek in Idris's mind was cut off. "The chamber is made of iron and clay. Clay against the heat. And iron, because thoughts do not travel through iron. The monster will now dry out. And when a monster becomes dry, what happens?"

Idris shook his head, still stunned by the scream. Morgan had stepped behind him, for shelter, he realized.

"You will see," said Nose Ring.

The men were moving the machine so that a nozzle at its front pointed at two huge stones lying next to each other. "Stand back," he said.

Smoke wisped from the nozzle. After the smoke came a flame, orange at first, then blue. Then it turned white-hot, and Idris saw the edges of the two rocks glow and bubble and fuse.

"It burns," said Nose Ring. "Monsters run pumps, and melt metals, and do all manner of things that people cannot do without." He yawned. "Shall we go?"

They went back to the road in a dazed silence. The scream was still ringing in Idris's mind. He had heard of monsters — everyone had. But he had not realized that they were . . . alive.

Nose Ring eyed him cynically, as if he could read his thoughts. "You'll get used to it," he said. "On we go."

On the hillsides running down to the lake, serfs were breaking stones. As the three riders passed, the serfs swept their hats from their heads and bowed. It seemed to Idris — perhaps he had read it somewhere, or heard it in one of the old songs — that the peasants were bowing to their uniforms. It was interesting enough to put the scream out of his mind. He said to Morgan, who was riding beside him, "Do the people take their hats off to your father's livery?"

"Only to my father."

"So if they bow to this Ambrose's mere sign, he must be a mighty man."

"Very mighty," said Morgan, hiding a smile.

Some time later they rounded a spur of the land. Ahead of them was a narrow theater of dun-colored hills, topped with bare rocks. Sprawled over the slope between hills and lakeshore, surrounded by a high wall, lay a city, bigger than any Idris had ever dreamed of. Behind the city, the ground sloped up. At the summit of the slope, a naked crag rose from a wood. The summit of the crag was crowned with walls. Inside the walls, towers of black stone frowned down on the valley below.

"Behold the Wellvale, otherwise the Valley of Apples," said Nose Ring and yawned. "Behind it, the Mount. That high building is the Kyd Tower. The grim one, I mean, with the pointed top."

Idris sat on his saddlecloth and gaped.

Every day of his life at the Hour of Thanks, he had imagined the Well. It had looked nothing like this. This was bigger. And . . . *dirtier.* But impressive. Vastly, horribly impressive. Even Morgan's highly sophisticated face wore a reverent expression.

"I will explain," said Nose Ring. "Look at the city. You will see many towers."

Many there were, tall, thick towers of stone, with pointed windows. Among the towers were chimneys and blocky buildings, windowless and stained with soot.

"The towers are the Wells," said Nose Ring. "The chimneys are the manufactories. The buildings are the homes of serfs. I expect old Mother Arthrax told you that the monsters live in the Wells. This is not true. The Wells are simply gateways between worlds. The world of the monsters is filled with water. We catch them by angling in the Wells. How do you catch a fish?"

"Tell a serf to get one," said Morgan, sniffing.

"With a net, or a bait, or a spear," said Idris.

"Good. And when do you use a bait?"

"When the tide is rising."

"Quite," said Nose Ring. "It is the same with monsters. There are tides in this other world of theirs. Once, the Wells were mere holes in the ground, kept blocked except at monster-tides. But the level of our land is sinking. As the land sank, men had to build towers around them, lest the poison water flood all. They are still building. What do you think?"

"Most impressive," said Morgan, drawling to hide her astonishment. Idris could only shake his head. Even the Westgate at the height of its prosperity had been a mere fishing village compared to this. The walls were tall and smooth, blackened as if by soot. They surrounded the city on three sides, the fourth being protected by the barge-filled wharves of the lakeshore. Inside the walls, the buildings were jammed like the spines of a sea urchin. As they drew closer, Idris saw houses and factories and towers and buildings that could have been temples or slaughterhouses. But most of all there were towers: towers plain and decorated, fretted and spiraled. "And that's the Old Well," said Morgan, evidently pleased to find something she could be an expert on. "The squat one. It was dug by the Old King, you know."

"Oh," said Idris, who had only the vaguest notion of this legendary figure

"It was him who found the seep between the worlds," said Morgan, as if the Old King had been a personal friend. "Oh!" For the ground was shuddering underfoot, and her horse had reared, and she was sliding over its tail.

"The tide is rising," said Nose Ring. "Onward."

They rode on, without further information from Morgan. The shuddering of the ground increased until it was difficult to stay on the saddlecloths. The towers came closer. The chimneys were leaking ugly smokes, slime green, muck brown, bile yellow.

They were right under the walls now. A great stone channel led from the city to the lake, wide enough for fifty horsemen abreast. Suddenly one of the fatter towers grew a dome of water that bulged, spread, thundered down its sides. A ten-foot wave roared down the channel and into the lake. Another tower fired, then another. The air filled with a sour, choking smell. "Catching more monsters," said Nose Ring, running a somber eye over the turmoil in the lake. "And for what?"

"To burn," said Morgan. "Obviously."

"But the water will overtop the dam," said Idris.

"Oh, dear me, no." There was something weary in Nose Ring's voice. "It is carefully controlled. You can't catch monsters without letting in water from the other world. So monsters must not be caught without licences from the Council of Captains. The Council measures the amount of water that comes into the land and the sinking of the ground. The Wellwater is poisonous. It must be kept in the lake here. Levels rise, of course. So the Council builds the dam higher. You saw the machine today."

Idris frowned. "So every time they catch a monster, water comes in, and they have to catch more monsters to control the water, and more water comes in," said Idris. "What happens when the lake's full?"

Nose Ring gave him a dark smile. "Do you know," he said, "I can see why that fat fool in Westgate felt he had to drown you. All you need to know is that it is the Captains and the Council who are the saviors of Lyonesse. And if you want to stay alive you must seem to believe it, even if you don't."

This did not seem at all fair to Idris. But now they had arrived at a gate in the city wall, and Nose Ring showed passes, and they entered and were threading a press of people and waggons and horses and piles of cloth and metal, each pile worth the whole of the Westgate, and the flood of faces and sensations drove everything from Idris's mind. The crush was ferocious, but people seemed to get out of Nose Ring's way. A Captain came past on a portable chair, wearing purple robes and a triple crown of tin, copper, and gold. Nose Ring waved a casual hand at him. The Captain looked sullen and turned his beefy face away. At last they came to what seemed to be the main door of a huge, straggling building at the base of a Well. Above the door was much carving, and the device of the eel in silvery mosaic tiles. Stable hands took the horses' heads. Nose Ring cast himself from the saddle. A magnificent woman in a grand dress of rarest crimson, her hair bound with gold wire, came to the door. She fell to her knees. "Master!" she cried.

Idris had never seen so obviously noble a woman in his life. He stood with his mouth open, but with an intuition beating at the side of his mind. He said, "Sir, if we are come to your house, it must now be mannerly to tell us who you are."

Nose Ring said, "Come up, Yseult, really," and helped the lady to her feet. He turned to Idris and bowed, as the Manner demanded. "Permit me to name myself," he said. "As Morgan already knows but has taken pleasure in not telling you, I am Ambrose, that men call Great, son of none, Mage of the Wellvale, Scourge of the Captaincy, Friend of the Old King, Monstermaster. And a lot of other things, Idris Limpet, that will become plain to you in due time." He paused, and a shadow crossed his face. "If," he said, "you live long enough. Now come in, both of you, find your cells, and eat, and rest. For tomorrow you begin your training."

FOUR

A dwarf wearing the red livery of the eel led them through rooms more splendid than any that Idris had ever seen. On the walls were great hangings dyed shellfish-purple, on which people and creatures waved in the drafts as if alive. He saw the glint of jewels, the gleam of heavy vessels made of gold, pottery of amazing intricacy. But all this he saw quickly, as the dwarf hustled him and Morgan deep into the stone maze of the building, up twisted stairs lit by little barred windows, and finally onto a high, dirty landing of naked granite. "Here," said the servitor. He pointed to two doors of nailed wood. "Choose one. Food coming."

"What —" said Idris.

But the dwarf had stumped away.

Morgan pushed a door open with a confidence Idris was pretty sure she did not feel. Beyond it was a cell, with a stone bed, a bright blanket, table, chair, and cupboard. The outside wall was curved, as if the cell was built in a circular tower. Idris pushed the other door and saw the same. "Which would you like?" he said.

Morgan said, "They're both absolutely revolting." She sniffed. "But probably better than where you live." Then she turned her face away quickly.

Idris's mind went back down the dark, weary road to the sounds of Harpoon banging the food shells on the kitchen table. "Not actually," he said, in a voice strangled by the sudden thickness in his throat.

Morgan made a tutting sound, marched into her cell, and slammed the door. Idris was ashamed of his weakness. She was just as homesick as he was, but better at hiding it. He went into his own cell and tried out the bed. "Hard mattresses," he shouted, though actually it was no harder than his mattress in the Westgate.

"These awful clothes," said Morgan in a new, low voice.

Idris walked into her cell and looked over her shoulder. Strange garments hung on pegs inside. There were a tunic of gray cloth, a suit made out of boiled leather with a helmet, and a limp gray jersey and trousers, all very secondhand.

The door opened. A servitor brought trays that smelled of food and planted one on each cell table. Idris waited for the man to leave. Then he said, "Shall I bring mine in?"

She looked up. The whites of her eyes looked thick and shiny, as if she was going to cry. "All right," she said, in a smaller voice than usual.

They ate in silence. There was good bread, meat, cabbage, a boiled root. "Not bad," said Idris.

"Stodgy," said Morgan. But he noticed that she ate it all.

"Good night," he said.

"Good night."

He went to bed, too tired to dream.

In the morning, a servitor woke him with breakfast. He struggled into the jersey and the trousers and the heavy boots on the cupboard floor, then went and banged on Morgan's door.

"What?" she said. Her voice was high and anxious.

"Can I come in?"

"Yes." She was sitting on her bed, looking down at herself in her work clothes. Her jersey was heavily patched over the heart. The edges of the patch had a scorched look. "What is it?" she said.

Something had appeared in Idris's head. It felt like telling the fly what to do, or seeing through Kek's eyes, yet not exactly like either of those things. "We should go," he said.

"Go? Where?" Her voice was cross and nervous.

"Down the stairs. Third on the left after the landing."

She was frowning at him. "How do you know?"

It was odd, now she came to mention it. "I just do."

"Uh," said Morgan. She tapped her forehead pityingly, to keep her spirits up, Idris guessed. But she followed him anyway.

Their heavy boots clattered and boomed on the stone stairs. Idris turned into the third entrance and found himself in front of a door. He turned the handle and pushed.

It looked like a classroom. Not a bright room like the one in Westgate, though. This one had walls the color of rusty iron, benches bound in ancient leather, desks pitted with carving. Faces looked around from the desks, the pale faces of about a dozen children dressed in work clothes like the ones Idris and Morgan were wearing.

At the front of the class was a huge iron chair with a back modeled on the wings of a giant gull. In the chair sat a figure in a black robe, the hood pulled down to hide the face. From the depths of the hood two eyes glowed, red as embers. "The last two," said a voice from inside the hood. It was deep and raw, as if it had breathed smoke all its life. "You heard."

"Heard what?" said Morgan.

THIS, boomed something in Idris's head. It nearly knocked him over. A slight frown crumpled Morgan's elegant eyebrows. "Did someone say something?" she said.

YOU COULD SAY SO, roared the silent voice. *IDRIS LIMPET, YOU HAVE THE GIFT. MORGAN WOLF ROCK, LESS SO. SIT DOWN.* By the time it had finished, Idris had found a way to pull up muffling folds of thought. Still, he felt weak and battered.

"I *did* hear something!" said Morgan. "Like a tiny little whisper right inside my head!"

"Silence," said the voice from the iron chair, aloud this time. "Be seated. Welcome to the School of the Captains. The others started a week ago, but better late than never. You are from all Wells — Brassfins, Initials, Ambroses, and the rest.

Your Wells may be different. But here you will learn together the Accomplishments of the Monstergroom. Monstergrooms supervise the catching and care of monsters. They can feel the thoughts of others, or muffle to keep them out. It is the power of monsters to put thoughts in human minds. Not everyone can hear human thoughts, or reply to monster thoughts, or stop them from coming into your mind. You have been chosen because you have that talent in a greater or a lesser degree. But do not think you can control the world with this gift. If you are in a mind, human or monster, the mind will feel you there."

I can make flies fly, thought Idris. I can see through Kek's eyes and hear thoughts. All this I can do. But how did Ambrose know this?

CONCENTRATE, CHILD, said the voice in his mind, catching him unmuffled, so he thought his head might explode.

"Huh?" said Morgan.

BONG, went a vast bell somewhere outside. Idris rose automatically to his feet and saw Morgan beside him, standing, too. The rest of the class was up. "The Well," said Iron Chair. The words were spoken. They stood in silence. But instead of the deep, pure silence of the Hour of Thanks in Westgate, there rose from the town a steady rumble.

Sacrilege, they would have called it in Westgate.

At last the voice in the iron chair said, "Thanks to the Well and may none of us die, or anyway not too many. Kay, you will please introduce the class to our latecomers, and though you are a Brassfin not an Ambrose show them the Well in action."

"Yes, Chair," said a boy with a long, serious face, light hair, and pinkish eyes. He looked weary.

"I'm Morgan," said Morgan brightly.

I know," said Kay.

"Oh. Did they tell you about us?" said Morgan.

"No," said Kay.

"How, then?"

Kay shrugged. Idris could hear a sort of murmur in his mind. The voice sounded like Kay's. He made a thought of his own. Is this the way? he thought.

Kay's pink eyes clicked on to him. "Ow," he said. "Too loud."

"Excuse me," said Morgan. "Are you both mad?"

Kay made a courtly bow. He said, "Morgan, I see that you are only beginning in the art. Now. Allow me to name the others. Here is Dawkins House Cutter of the Shipwright's Garden."

"Otherwise Dawkins the Great," said a small boy with a cheeky grin that reminded Idris of a more nervous version of Cayo.

Then there was Splee, who merely nodded, and Perce, tall, blond, and stolid, and Benrid, pug-faced, who looked down his short nose at Idris. There was Thorpe of the Captains, beautifully dressed in the richest cloths, who already had some of the unction of his Captain father. There was Bwrpau House Bwlch of the Stone Downs, thin and dark with eyes that added things up. And finally there was Gavin House Primrose of the Bees

Rock, tall, elegant, and dramatic, who took Morgan's hand and bowed over her fingers with a gallantry Idris knew he could never hope to copy.

"Now I must do our excellent teacher's bidding," said Kay. His face was smooth and pale, but Idris sensed that this was a person who would do one thing and say another. "Please follow me." He led the way through ill-lit corridors of stone. They clumped up stairs and more stairs, mounting higher and higher. The air was full of a bitter smell that caught in Idris's throat and made his eyes prick, as they had in the Poison Ground.

Kay stopped in front of an iron-bound door of massive oak. "Muffle," he said.

"Muffle?" said Morgan.

"Your mind. Muffle it."

"What?"

Idris caught her eye and gave her an encouraging smile. He could feel something terrible waiting behind that door.

The door slid back. "Behold the Welltop," said Kay.

It was a circular platform. Beyond the railing that surrounded its outside edge, the Wells of the Valley of Apples stood high and flat-topped, indistinct among the drifts of fume that hung in the air among their shafts. On other platforms on other towers, other little figures were moving. Beyond the towers, barges crawled on the dirty water of the lake.

It was horribly high. But it was not the height that was frightening.

Idris could feel the fear trying to make his feet take him back through the door and onto the nice safe stairs. He told it to go away. Turn around. Look.

Morgan glanced across at him. She turned around, too. Both of them looked at the middle of the platform.

The platform had no middle. Instead, there was a circular hole a stone's toss across. A perfectly ordinary hole, Idris told himself.

But it was not an ordinary hole.

"Behold," said Kay, in the voice of one demonstrating the fangs of a devouring animal. "The Well."

They stood silent in the fumes, looking at the black hole. Idris felt a pull, a sort of suction. He found his feet taking him toward the hole. "Keep the muffle," said Kay.

Idris nodded and closed his eyes. His mouth was dry, his heart thudding. The defenses in his mind had slipped. He pulled them up again. He took a deep breath. He walked to the inner edge of the platform and craned his head over.

The shaft of the Well plunged deep into darkness. There was a grinding of machinery far below. "Sluices opening," said Kay. "Normally they're shut, to keep the Welltides out. They get opened when we're monstercatching."

The grinding ceased. "Full open," called a voice somewhere.

Idris's ordinary eye saw only blackness in the Well. His ears heard a slosh and boom of water, huge and distant. His mind felt something else. A world. An entire world of black water. A world of darkness. Not darkness as absence of light. Darkness as an actual force —

Something roared at him. The noise was horrible, unearthly. It blasted him away from the shaft's lip. He fell to his hands and knees. His head was full of terrible pictures.

"Ears open, mind closed," said Kay, sounding bored. "Now look and listen and learn. Done any fishing with your daddy's riverkeepers?"

"My mother is a Fisher of the Westgate," said Idris, prickly with this languid Knight.

"How extraordinary," said Kay. "Well, monstercatching is just fishing, really. Look, they're baiting up."

A group of men in brown boiled-leather suits was working by a wooden derrick that projected over the shaft in the Well's center. A chain ran from a cabin perched on the rim of the shaft and over a pulley in the end of the derrick. The men were tying bladders to the end of the chain, bladders that dripped sticky red. "Blood?" said Morgan, in a voice too high.

"Of course," said Kay. "Now watch."

The men finished the bundle. Among the red globes the sun winked off something in it that looked like a polished needle as high as a man. "And that's a *hook!*" said Morgan. Idris was feeling better. This was fishing. Fishing was always exciting enough to make you forget about everything else, if you were a child of the Westgate.

"Letting go," said Kay.

The bait swung out over the shaft. Gouts of blood sailed down into the dark. A mind-scream of greedy delight howled out of the pit. Idris's flesh crawled. "They're feeding," said Kay, his eyes glittering.

"Oh," said Morgan, chewing at her lower lip.

"Now they get some encouragement," said Kay.

The men in leather suits started flinging bucketfuls of blood into the Well. The smell was revolting.

"Groundbait," said Kay. A man in the cabin moved his shoulders, as if releasing levers. The bunch of bladders descended dripping into the darkness.

Idris had done plenty of fishing off the ramparts of the Westgate. This did not sound right. "They catch something down there and pull it up?" he said. It was too far. If you pulled a fish up the ramparts, you could bet it would kick itself off the line by the time it was halfway up.

"Not quite," said Kay. "Watch the meter on the cabin side."

Idris looked at the meter. It looked like a clock with one red hand. The hand, which had been firmly on the bottom pin, had started to tremble. He held his breath.

"Here it comes," said Kay.

The hand was beginning to rise. The tower was trembling underfoot. Beyond the railings, Idris saw the other towers of the Wellvale shudder and sway. A breeze of foul air was roaring up the Wellshaft. He heard the shriek of machinery. He gripped the rail. This was not fishing. This was horror.

A disc of water was rising smoothly up the shaft. It was colored red with the blood that was leaking from the bladders floating in it. Under the bladders was something so dreadful he could not properly look at it, a huge pair of jaws wide open, full of enormous teeth. Kay had put himself against the railings around the chimney's lip. The whine of the engine in the crane cabin was a roar. The mouth came up and over and all around the bladders, and the water was level with the top of the chimney, then bulging over it, stinking, and Morgan shouted beside Idris, and he put out his hand and she grabbed it and the water from the Well bulged out of the hole and smashed into them.

Morgan's hand was torn from his. There was a filthy taste in his mouth and a stinging in his eyes, then a heavy blow in his ribs, and the water was gone, and his body was jammed against the railings around the outside of the ledge and he was looking at a waterfall pouring down, down, hundreds of feet down the stone flank of the tower, exploding into the gulley around its base. And through the stinging fog in his eyes he could see other towers firing, too, the poison lake lashed to dirty foam as thousands of tons of water poured out of the relief channel, and he felt the tremor of the ground as the towers rocked dizzily on their foundations.

And Idris saw, clinging to a railing by one hand, hanging over space, a limp, bedraggled figure. Morgan.

He ran forward and lay down and reached out and grasped her free hand. "Help," she said. The other hand came off the railing. The palm in Idris's was cold and wet. It slipped an inch.

He squeezed harder. It slipped again. Please, thought Idris. No. *"Help!"* said Morgan. Far, far below, the last of the water was draining from the channel, and blackbeetle carts crawled along a street that ran alongside it.

Idris said, dry-mouthed, "Kay. Help. Quick."

The pale-haired youth was looking at something on the ground. "Oh," he said, as if this happened every day. He trotted over and lay down and gripped Morgan's wrist. "The wrist, not the palm," he said coolly. "You get a better grip. Hookmen!"

A couple of the men in boiled-leather suits trotted across the Welltop. They carried long-handled iron hooks. They leaned over the rails, stabbed their hooks into Morgan's jersey, hauled her over the railing like a bag of seaweed, and trotted away. Morgan pulled the jersey down over her pale belly, sat up, and pushed her hair out of her eyes, not looking at Idris.

"Lucky you weren't killed," said Kay. "Plenty are." She smiled at him and allowed him to pull her to her feet. She still did not look at Idris. Well, thought Idris, they are Knights and I am the son of a gateguard, so I had better get used to it. He climbed to his own feet and spat the taste of bloody water from his mouth. The monster lay gray and formless, the size of a dead cow. . . .

He heard it.

Heard a growth of thought like a spark hitting tinder, making flame, exploding into a roaring inferno. *No,* howled the thought. *What? Where? No* —

Idris muffled. The men with leather suits and hooks ran across the Welltop and set their gaffs in the monster's flesh. Even through the muffling, Idris could hear its mind. *NO,* it bellowed. *IRON. PLEASE. NOOOOO.*

"Heave," said the hookmen and put their backs into their hook handles.

The monster slid across the pavement. A trapdoor opened. The front end of the monster slithered in, bellowing. The men twitched their hooks out. The monster kept sliding, faster and faster. The tail flicked and vanished. The trap slammed. The bellowing stopped, cut off short.

"The doors are made of iron," said Kay. "They hate it. The hooks are made of it, too. And the bars on the cages in the stables."

Idris nodded. He was trying hard not to shake.

A gentle hand took his arm. Morgan's voice by his ear said, "Thank you. It's good to have someone kind in this place. Cheer up."

Somewhere far below, gates of iron boomed. "How did you know?" he said.

"Minds are like books," she said. "Different people read different things." She turned a dazzling (and, Idris now saw, purely social) smile on Kay. "What have we just seen?" she said.

Kay seemed flattered. "The baiting of the monster," he said. "If you give him time to think, he'll see it's a trick. So you wait till just before the tide drives up the tower, and you put the blood down; they're mad for blood. And you drop the baited hook just as the tide comes in. The monster sees the bait rise, chases after it mad as an angry bull, nine out of ten times he doesn't even bite, just strands on the Welltop, the hook's only there for insurance. And before he can dry and burn down he goes into the monsterstables, where the groom and hookmen will be waiting to put him in a cage till he's needed for cutting and work."

"Wonderful," said Morgan, overdoing it, thought Idris.

"But how do you stop being washed away?" said Idris.

"We put ourselves across the railings, and let the water pour by. As will you next time," said Kay, bowing gallantly to Morgan.

"I will," said Morgan and laughed cheerily at him. He turned to lead them away. Morgan touched Idris's hand and winked. And Idris had the warm certainty that she had been nice to Kay because she wanted something. But she was nice to him because she was his friend.

Kay took them on a tour of the rest of the Ambrose Well, known as the Great Ambrose. The double walls were full of classrooms and sleeping cells and workshops. The ground floor was the gateway to Ambrose's quarters. In the basement were the cutting rooms, where men in leather face masks were doing sickening things to bits of monster that whined and twitched and glowed in tanks of slime. "They come here from the monsterstables," said Kay, coughing in the stench. "When they're cut, they go into tanks and then into barges that take them down the lake. From there they go into the dam machines, or into tank carts that take them to the pumps and the engines. They burn, you know. Hotter than wood or charcoal or anything. I'll show you the stables later. Have a shower, and back to class."

Ten minutes later they were in the classroom, waiting for Iron Chair. "Well?" said Benrid, who had a face like a nasty little dog. "What did you think?"

The showers had been warm water from a pipe. It had taken the stink of Wellwater from Idris's skin, but he had the feeling that nothing would ever get it out of his nose. "It smells horrible," he said.

"Oh?" said Benrid, with a sneer. "And what smells does your Majesty prefer?"

Idris found his heart beating slightly too hard. "Crab stew with wild garlics," he said. "The smoke of the driftwood that comes after a southerly gale."

"Really?" said Benrid. "Sounds as if you'd better go back to your mud puddle and get sniffing, then."

Idris thought about punching him in the nose. He made himself smile instead. "So you enjoy the smell of Wellwater?"

Benrid leaned back, as if he was copying someone older than him. "It smells of money," he said. "And power. I am going to learn to catch and care for and use monsters, because I want to be rich and powerful and take over from my father, who is a Captain, and throw him down a Well if I have to so

74

I can have his manufactories and get what I want. Yes, I enjoy the smell of Wellwater. Anyone who doesn't is a moron."

"Ah," said Idris. It struck him that it was Benrid who was the moron.

"And you'd better learn to love it, too," said Benrid. "Because if you don't, you will die. Have they told you about the Test?"

"No."

"We are instructed in Earth, Air, Fire, and Water, then we catch our monsters. Three out of five die. I will be amazed if you're not one of them. Sea filth and driftwood," said Benrid scornfully. "I would pity you if you weren't so stupid and vulgar."

Idris said, "Thank you."

"For what?"

"For your pity. And your great kindness to one as humble as me. I wish you success in the Test. And I do hope you manage to murder your father before he murders you."

Benrid looked baffled for a moment. Then he put the sneer back on. "You will see the power of monsters and those who manage them," he said. "And you will be ashamed that you were so cheeky, but it will be too late."

"Thank you *so much*, Benrid," said Idris, straight-faced.

Morgan kicked him under the desk and put her hands to her face to hide a giggle. Idris felt pretty good. He was a trainee monstergroom, which was apparently what everyone wanted to be. He lived in the Valley of Apples, capital of Lyonesse, bound

75

to a noble mage, not a fat old Captain. And he had a great friend whose life he had saved that morning.

Iron Chair limped in. The class arranged itself. Iron Chair started to drone about the cutting of monsters. Idris's mind drifted away.

He was brought back by a new noise: a great trampling in the corridor outside, as of soldiers marching. Idris felt his insides freeze. Had they come for him?

The door burst open. A man in a tasseled hat and tabard marched in. "He comes!" cried the man. "Be joyful! Be upstanding! By order of Her Sublimity Sea Eagle, Regent of Lyonesse, you are visited by His Wellblessed Immensity Kyd Murther, Dolphin of the Realm!"

FIVE

I ron Chair gave off a feeling of fluster. "Rise and bow, all," he said.

The pupils rose. The pupils bowed, and stayed bent double, eyes down, as prescribed by the Manner when in the presence of royalty. Idris had not been impressed by Benrid. But he was impressed now. Everyone knew that Sea Eagle was the Regent of Lyonesse. She lived in the black tower on the Mount and ruled the land. But the most important person in Lyonesse was not her, but her son, Kyd Murther. Kyd Murther was Dolphin of Lyonesse, which meant that on his fourteenth birthday he would become King. When speaking of the Dolphin in the Nature of the Land classes, Mother Arthrax's voice became an awestruck whisper.

And here he was, in the flesh.

Idris remained bowed. He had never met anyone royal before. But he had supposed that, according to the Manner, the royal person would demonstrate kindness by telling the bowers to rise.

The royal person remained silent. The class remained bent double.

Heavy feet trudged down the aisle between the desks. They sounded slow and somehow clumsy. Idris gazed at the squid-ink-stained wood under his eyes and tried to feel reverent. But his back was hurting. He was not feeling reverent. He was feeling cross.

The footsteps ceased. Moving his head back a thumb's breadth, Idris looked forward.

A boy was standing in front of Iron Chair's desk. A large boy, with a big pale face and a narrow golden circlet on his head.

Idris had never seen a legend before. Squinting through his eyebrows, he studied the face intently.

And found himself very surprised.

This was the face of the noblest in the kingdom of Lyonesse. But it was not a noble face. The lower lip jutted. The eyes were close together and narrow, as if the Dolphin could not be bothered to lift the lids properly. It was an overfed face, full of scorn and discontent, mingled with a faint malicious glee as it contemplated the bent and silent pupils. It reminded Idris of someone.

It reminded him, in fact, of Spignold.

To his absolute astonishment, Idris found that he did not like the look of the Dolphin of Lyonesse one little bit.

"You look like a lot of prawns," said the Dolphin. "All bent up like that, ha-ha. Stand up and let's have a look at you." He raked them with his hot little eyes, breathing through his wet

78

mouth. One of his retinue groveled forward and whispered in his ear. "I am told I must greet you," he said. "You are all of Captainly or Knightly birth, thank goodness, so you probably don't smell too bad. Ha-ha."

"Ha-ha," went Benrid and Thorpe and Bwrpau. The rest of the class forced a smile.

Except Idris. Idris stood, his heart hammering with anger. Then he put up his hand.

"What?" said the Dolphin, apparently shocked.

"Sire," said Idris. "I am not of Knightly birth, and my family has no tower. My father is a gateguard and my mother a Fisher of the Fishers. They are good people, and kind, and loyal. And we smell no worse than Knights or Captains."

"Oh?" said Murther, with a dangerous narrowing of the eyes.

Idris knew that he had committed a folly by opening his mouth and would commit another by explaining himself. But his family was as good as anyone's. He began to tell the Dolphin that what he had said was an affront to the Manner. But something odd happened in his mind. His tongue was saying something, but he could not hear what it was. Then he was standing there with the blood hot in his face, and the class was laughing at him, and Kyd Murther was laughing, too.

"I am sure your mother is very beautiful," said Iron Chair. "And I am sure that your father was very proud that she went off with a handsome Captain for a year, and that she came back with you in her belly. Which makes you half Captain, in a way."

An atmosphere of menace rolled from under the cowl. "But sometimes it is best to keep these things to oneself."

Idris turned cold with shame. He opened his mouth to say that this was not what he had said. No words came.

The Dolphin gave him a pitying sneer. "You have a chance, peasant, so make sure you use it well. And mind your manners in future."

The class demonstrated monstercutting for the royal benefit, but Idris was too mortified to pay it any attention. What he had said to the Kyd must have been a betrayal of his family. That was bad. What was worse was that a mind had taken his, and done with it what he had done to the fly in the Westgate classroom.

Idris put his mind away from the classroom and up to Kek. Below the gull the streets hummed and thronged. On a grassy terrace of the Ambrose a man had stood up from a table that bore a half-eaten nuncheon on golden plates and ewers. The man was staring at a barred window in the tower that rose before him. And Idris put out his own mind and touched that mind, and knew for a great certainty that the man was Ambrose, and the window was the window of the classroom, that the occupier of his mind and the thief of his thoughts had been none other than Ambrose himself.

"Well, I must go," said the Dolphin, yawning.

"All bow!" cried the herald.

Everyone bowed.

The Kyd lumbered out of the classroom.

"Dismiss," said Iron Chair to the class. "Except Idris."

Idris walked sullenly up to the master's chair. Iron Chair's smell was sour and musty, his eyes a dull glow deep in the hood. The gloved hand went to the hood and pushed it back an inch. Idris's heart jolted, and he took a step back.

Below the cowl was a red, cratered horror with inlays of metal in which gleamed eyes of raw red. "I sought to tell the truth to Fisheagle the Regent," said Iron Chair. "I should have been content with small lies. Now pay heed to your masters and be invisible to your enemies. I wish you life unburned. Go."

Idris bowed, as the Manner required. But he was not bowing in his mind. In his mind, he said: *I cannot be silent. I cannot tell small lies. And I shall tell this to the Great Ambrose himself.*

So that evening, Idris walked from the stone corridors of the Well onto the soft-carpeted marble floors of Ambrose's apartments, through arches and onto a terrace where a table stood among full-sized oaks.

Ambrose was sitting at the table alone. Idris had meant to start softly. But Ambrose's face was cool, his eyebrows raised. Idris found his nervousness replaced by generous anger.

"Sir," he said, "you have dishonored my mother."

Ambrose's right eyebrow rose a little farther. "How so?"

"You sent thoughts to my mind. I spoke them before Kyd Murther."

"Just as well," said Ambrose. "If you had spoken what was in your mind, you would be strapped to a burner in the Kyd Tower for your impertinence."

"Dishonor is dishonor," said Idris.

"And alive is alive," said Ambrose. "Apparently it is my job to keep you so. So I will apologize to you for those words if you will apologize to me for excess of honesty."

"I will not apologize for honesty."

Ambrose smiled. "Quite right," he said and rose. "I much regret the distress I have caused," he said, and bowed, as the Manner demanded.

"Oh," said Idris, deprived of an argument.

"Now," said Ambrose, "we will not sit here." He led Idris back into his chambers and into a room with walls of shiny metal. "Iron," he said. "Thoughts will not travel through it. Now sit down, and have some sunapple juice, and ask me some honest questions."

Idris looked at him narrowly, afraid he was being made fun of. But there was something new in Ambrose. The mocking edge was gone, and in his place was someone friendly, almost . . . *respectful.* "Very well," he said. "Why did you come to the Westgate and report me to the Captain?"

"Report you?"

"I saw you talking to Master Omnium. Looking at me."

Ambrose nodded. "Of course you did. We had been watching you."

"Why?"

"Oh, we had our reasons. Then I heard you giving orders to a fly in the classroom, and I knew that something must be done."

"You heard?" said Idris, astonished.

"It is not difficult. Your powers are . . . special. We have brought you here to keep you safe. You must be careful to do nothing to make them notice you, at least for the moment. Muffle your thoughts, stay out of the minds of others. Be an ordinary monstergroom and nothing else."

Idris had forgotten his anger. "Sir, I do not understand the first word of this."

"That is why I brought you to the Valley of Apples," said Ambrose. "So that you may come to understand, and perhaps even survive to be useful. When your gifts were becoming apparent, Master Omnium told me." Idris remembered Omnium's face at Westgate, watching through the little carved window. So *that* had been why. "We found an opportunity to have you arrested and condemned, and now you have vanished, and the Westgate guardians and their crushing hammers will be convinced you shapechanged and swam out to sea, and they have been told that as a baby you were taken in adoption at my orders, so the good Limpets will not suffer. All will be well for you and the Limpets as long as you do not go back to the Westgate."

Idris had turned cold. "Never?"

Ambrose shook his head.

"But my parents. The Stones. The Boys."

"You will see them," said Ambrose, his eyes far away. "After a while. Perhaps. Listen, though. There are things you have not been taught."

Idris was still thinking about his parents. Never? He said, "I know everything I need."

"Tell me."

"The Old King built the walls," said Idris, gabbling. "To protect the kingdom after the sinking and the floods. We benefit from these walls, and from the Well, and what it brings forth."

"Do we?" said Ambrose.

"The Captains prosper, so the Mount prospers, so the people prosper. Could I not go to Westgate in disguise?"

"Dismiss the idea from your mind," said Ambrose. "It is encouraging to hear that you have learned your lessons like a jackdaw. Has it occurred to you that they might be nonsense?"

Idris said, "Nonsense?"

Ambrose's bottomless eyes settled on him. "Everyone must find out for himself," he said. "But I will give you a start. You learned various things in Westgate. To revere the Well, that Captains are always right, that there is a Treaty between men and monsters, that the Manner is the Manner, and that Kyd Murther is Dolphin of Lyonesse in the true line."

"Yes," said Idris impatiently. "What do you mean, I can't go back?"

"I mean that if you show your face you are dead, and your family with you. Now listen while I tell you the things you must know. I expect you think that matters were always arranged as they are now. Control yourself."

Looking into his face, Idris saw not the harsh, ironic Nose Ring, but a man kind and serious and wise. He felt a calm steal over him, an influence generated by Ambrose, he guessed. "I am sorry," he said. "This is a sore trial. Now explain to me the nature of things, kind mage, if you would."

Ambrose bowed, and Idris got the idea that he could tell the effort it was not to weep from homesickness, and respected it. "We will start with the Old King," he said. "Otherwise known as Great Brutus. Great Brutus was a man of deep curiosity. Having conquered the realm, he set about exploring it. In a valley in a wood at the foot of a hoar rock he found a place held by general agreement to be the abode of darkness. It was in the form of a bitter well and was cared for by a stunted tribe dressed in rancid skins. The job of the tribe was to keep the well stopped up with clods of earth. For if left unblocked, the tribe reasoned, the seep of the well would infallibly flood first the valley, then the world, and then the universe.

"The Old King in his curiosity investigated the well, dug it larger, found monsters therein, and caught them and studied them. He observed that it produced more water with the passing years; this being, as he later determined, because the ground was sinking as the water came up. As the sea at the margins of Lyonesse rose higher than the land, the Old King built walls.

85

Or rather he gave land to chosen men, whom he called Knights, on the understanding that for one moon of every thirteen they would send the people who worked their land to see to the raising and mending of the walls. This worked well, except that there soon came men who were not Knights, who dug more wells, and studied the monsters they caught therein, and bred them, and found burners, and made engines for the burners to work. Until there were floods in the land, and dark thoughts planted by monsters, and the Old King said 'Enough!' and banished the Wellers, as they had been known, and stopped up his well, which we now know as the Old Well. The Wellers went to live in High Kernow, where they made towns and became artful in the making of copper and tin and gold and even iron. While in Lyonesse there were no Wellers and little metal, but the land was good, the people happy, and the work lightened by the gentle magic of star and stone. When the Old King passed to his fathers, his son Kyd Goch succeeded, and his son and his son and their sons and sons' sons after them. These were known as the Years of Plenty.

"But in Kernow, the sons of the sons of the Wellers had heard from their grandfathers tales of the riches of an earlier age. They had cut down Kernow's trees and burned them in their furnaces. When they looked from their barren tors across the green woods of Lyonesse, the sight of all that wealth drove them mad with envy. They knew that in the wells of that land there lurked things that burned hotter than trees, with which they could burn stone and make metal run like water.

"It chanced that at this time the King of Lyonesse, who went by the name of Kyd Ploc Ard, lost his wife to a fever. Hearing of this, Bronzefisher Captain of the Wellers hired a mage who bound the King to the birthstar of Slabada, the Captain's daughter, a girl of no great beauty but indomitable will.

"Well, Slabada married Kyd Ploc Ard and bullied the poor man until he allowed the Wellers back into the Valley of Apples. Where they all decided to call themselves Captains, the pompous scum. The scribes of Bronzefisher found their way into the lore-rooms of the Mount, and read of the Old Well and the creatures that came therethrough. And in a short time the Wells were open again, the Treaty written, the Captains growing prosperous, the towers a-building to stop great floods, and the land still sinking. But this time the Captains would have no Wall building, for the levy of Wall builders gave power to the Knights. Instead, they made engines that pumped water out of the land and started the embankments that take the rivers to the sea. The apple trees in the Valley of Apples did not like the new fumes and died, except for some in the Mount. But Lyonesse now lies unflooded thanks to the Captains, and anyone who says different goes unheeded or worse. And for Kyd Murther and the Regent Fisheagle to have a land to rule, they depend on the Captains. But with every pumping of water, the land sinks farther."

"So the Kyd supports the lies he is told, and is thus a lie himself."

"Never mock a liar," said Ambrose. "'Specially one more powerful than you. Work against him if you must. But be secret, for he has spies everywhere, and Fisheagle his mother is a deadly creature who sees through walls as men see through windows, unless they be of iron, like the walls of this room. Their people are the Captains, and their soldiers are the ones who dress in black, and have no hearts, and work for power and money, not loyalty and love. Which brings me," said Ambrose, "to the Manner. What is the Manner?"

"A way of being polite," said Idris, shrugging. "An old-fashioned way of making powerful people feel more powerful."

"That is the mistake the Captains make," said Ambrose. "They ignore the orders of the land. The old orders are Knights in their towers, yeomen in their lands, crafts in their workshops, hunters in their tribes, and serfs in their labors. You would think that a Knight with all his lands has the power. But a Knight who is scorned by yeomen and crafts and hated by his serfs is nothing. So each pays civility to each, and names himself on meeting, so there shall be no doubt. In a world where the Manner exists, the strong look after the weak, and the weak respect the strong, because each knows that without the other they are nothing. The Captains think the Manner is stupid and old-fashioned, and Fisheagle despises it and has taught her son to do likewise. As you saw. They do not mind being hated, for they crush those who hate them."

Idris looked at this picture of a land calm and united, free from cruelty. He said, "Are not people always cruel to people?"

Ambrose sighed, and Idris suddenly saw that the mage was

much older than he had at first seemed. "I remember when it was not so," he said. "When we practiced the old science of star and stone. But that is almost gone." He fell silent. He looked up suddenly, "What do you know of the Treaty between men and monsters?"

"Men use monsters because monsters dry out as they burn and are hotter than wood or charcoal. Monsters allow themselves to be used because they crave the light, even if seeing it means their death. There are other kinds of monsters, shapeshifters and dreamweavers, that can breed with men. But this is unlawful for monsters and for men, and a Cross is not . . . suffered . . . to live." Idris shook his head to blank out the terrible memory of his trial in the Westgate.

"You have taken your lessons to heart," said Ambrose. "You may now forget them. There is no Treaty."

"What?"

"Men use monsters when they can. Monsters use men when they can. Rules are put in the world to console the foolish." Ambrose smiled. "This has been a long lecture. Come and take the air." He led Idris onto the great terrace.

Idris looked out over the towers of the city through the eyes of Kek, awestruck at the size and majesty and dirt of this monument to greed and the absence of rules. On a distant balcony, sun flashed on something. Kek swooped close. A man in a black Mount uniform was watching through the tube of a bringemnear.

"They watch," said Ambrose. "You watch, too."

As Idris walked off the deep rugs into the naked stone of the tower, the flagstones shook under his feet.

During the next moon, Idris spent long days in the dirty classroom, listening to the hoarse drone of Iron Chair. On the twenty-eighth day, the master addressed the class from between the iron wings of his throne. "Now, dear pupils, you know the theory." The voice was raw with sarcasm. "Now you will meet the elements of earth, air, fire, and water. After which there will be the Test. And a golden future." The eyes glowed reddish under the hood. "For those who survive."

SIX

The Earth Tutor had made them draw maps. Now it was the turn of Air. In the Wellvale, air meant towers. The tutor was a thin man with the face of a scornful horse. The pupils stood around him in the Street of Apples with the crowds pouring past them. Over them hung the towerfronts of fretted stone. Behind the towerfronts rose the Wells. Horse Face was neighing about the Parts of the Well.

Idris already knew the Parts of the Well. He allowed his mind to wander. As usual it arrived behind the eyes of Kek the gull, who was sitting on a high pinnacle of the Rambudget, digesting a live rat. Below Kek stood a plain tower, more ancient and fatter than the rest, its stones smoothed by the millions of tons of water that had flowed down its sides: the Old Well. Idris wanted to see more of it, but the rat not being dead was still causing Kek trouble, and he was doing a lot of wing flapping to aid digestion. Absentmindedly Idris told the gull to stop and look harder. He felt a brief resistance, a tug in the mind. Then Kek was looking where Idris wanted him to look: at the top of the ancient Well. Idris found his heart was beating powerfully.

Before, he had used Kek's eyes, looking where the gull wanted to look. Now he had told the gull what to do. Ambrose had been right. His gift of mind was developing.

Horse Face was talking about Welltops. Idris waited for a pause, then said, "Why does the Old Well have a roof over its platform?"

Horse Face looked at him sharply. "Because it is no longer used," he said. "Come."

The Old Well stood at the back of a dark square set to one side of the Street of Apples. In that thronged city, the Old Well Square stood eerily empty. The houses around it were ancient and crumbling, too high to let in the light. The air stank. "Ugh," said Morgan, shivering.

Horse Face advanced toward the porch. "The Well as you see has the usual features, but in a primitive state. The porch is deep and heavily carved and contains a hall. There is no doubling of the walls, merely great thickness of stone laced with tunnels and chambers. It is a holy place, sealed after the madness that followed the flood. Only the Council may enter. Follow!"

The shadow of the ancient tower fell over the group. Morgan shivered. Idris moved closer to her.

"And now," said Horse Face, "the Great Door."

He led the class into the porch. Their feet scuffed loud in the still, dank air. Idris felt a sort of tingle in his mind.

There were carvings around the outer arch of the porch — not the elegant stone fretwork of the newer Wells, but an older, odder carving, of creatures that turned into other creatures and writhed and crawled and devoured one another. The door itself was of a black wood so ancient it was almost stone, strapped and studded with bronze that glowed soft poison green.

"The door, as you will see, is closed," said Horse Face.

The door was indeed closed: not by a lock, but by a bolt with a loop in its handle. Through the loop and a stirrup-shaped hasp had been driven a sword. The lower half of the sword's blade was sunk deep in a stone. The stone was not like any other Idris had seen in Lyonesse. It was smooth as glass, and red as blood, and had in it little green flecks of light that came and went. And it had been carved into the likeness of a pot-bellied monster, all tentacles and teeth.

Idris stood rigid, partly horrified, and partly because he felt a power in this place sending his hand forward to grasp the handle, and he knew deep in him that that would be a very bad idea.

"This is the sword Cutwater, that the Old King drove into the stone when he stopped the Well," said Horse Face. "It cannot be removed." The tutor's eyes had strayed into a corner of the square, where two figures had materialized from the shadows. They were wearing black uniforms with metal breastplates. Over the heart of each gleamed the golden sign of the tower. They were watching the class.

Idris saw them, and so did Morgan and Perce and Kay and Gavin. Dawkins did not; or perhaps he did, but once Dawkins had started to show off he was half mad, and now he was too carried away to pay any attention. "Sword, sword, you're in the road!" he cried, in a false High Kernow accent. Leaping onto the belly of the red-stone monster, he gripped the handle and tugged.

"Down!" roared Horse Face, and his wristwhip flicked, and Dawkins fell off the stone with his hand to his ear, crying. No, Idris realized. Not crying. Laughing. Or both at the same time, hysterical.

"Won't budge!" cried Dawkins. "Can't get in the front way. Must get in the back way!" And he skipped off to the corner of the square, dodged around a Mountman, and started to run down the alley by the side of the tower.

"No," said Morgan, white as a cloud.

Dawkins was small, and mad, and he probably only wanted to play tag. But the Mountmen did not play games. There was the sound of nailed boots running, the slide of a sword drawing, one shriek, then nothing.

Idris started forward. He felt the familiar blanket come down on his thoughts. Ambrose was trying to get into his head. He pushed him angrily away, felt a mental grunt of pain. "What are you going to *do*?" he said, full of rage and horror. "*Do* something!*"

"Do?" neighed Horse Face. "About what?"

"About Dawkins."

"About whom?"

Morgan gripped Idris's arm. He found himself walking across the square.

Muffled by Ambrose, gripped by Morgan, and full of shame. In the deeps of his heart he knew that it was the duty of the strong to protect the weak.

Dawkins had been casually murdered for nothing.

And Idris had failed in his duty.

That night Ambrose was in a workshop, windowless except for ceiling holes, training starlight into a beaker of water. Idris stood there, sullen, watching.

"This was the old science before this stuff of the Captains," said Ambrose. "Star and stone. And we who practice it are mages, though precious few of us remain. Slow it may be, and gentle, but it is potent, potent, needing the heavens to turn, not to be hurried. One day you will come to the Sundeeps, and you will see how things were in the old world." He looked up, hawk-faced and fierce. "What was it that you were doing today at the Old Well?"

"We have studied the porch," said Idris sullenly.

"This you have been taught," said Ambrose. "But what have you learned?"

"That you were right, the Mount watches." Idris felt heavy with grief and anger.

Ambrose said, "You have lived up to my hopes for you when I found you in the Westgate. And also my fears. You battered my mind today. Your gift increases. For perhaps two years it will wax. Then it will be gone. Use it with care. If," said

Ambrose with a skeptical lift of the eyebrow, "you know the meaning of the word."

"They killed *Dawkins*," said Idris. "Dawkins was *funny!*"

"Nothing is funny in the porch of the Old Well," said Ambrose.

"What difference does the Old Well make?"

Ambrose sighed. The beaker on the bench sighed, too, and collapsed into a pool of starlight.

"It would have been honorable to rescue him," said Idris.

Ambrose gave him an odd look. "It is not a rescue if two perish in place of one." He beckoned to a servitor. "Take Master Idris Wouldbemonstergroom back to his chamber," he said. "And watch that he goes straight to his studies and makes no jokes."

This morning, the class was going to do Fire.

Fire was dangerous. Fire was bad. Fire was one of the things through which they must pass to take the Test.

Morgan hated fire.

Not that she would ever have told anyone.

This morning she brushed her teeth with a mint twig and washed her face in the bronze bowl and climbed into her red boiled-leather fire armor and went down with Idris, ordinary, comforting, totally unusual Idris. She was worried that they were drifting apart. Every night he went off down the passage to talk to Ambrose about . . . well, she did not know what. It was not knowing that put her in a bad mood. Could actually get on her nerves, the way someone gets on your nerves when you think they think they are special.

Though Idris definitely was special. And he needed her, whether he knew it or not. And she needed him, because in this deadly world he was the one safe thing. . . .

They had arrived at the iron door.

The gatekeeper was a dwarf, bent and horribly seared. He bowed to Idris — people did nowadays, without knowing why. "Rest of the gentlemen down below," he croaked. As Morgan went past, he touched her hair and said, "Red as fire and will be fire."

"What?" said Morgan, frightened.

"Quiet, halfpint," said Idris. The dwarf took a quick step back.

The stairs were a spiral, winding down a narrow hole in the thickness of the Well wall, full of the scuff of leather armor on stone and the scorched smells rising from below.

Morgan could hear cries and entreaties in her mind — the voices of monsters. If she could hear them, they must be very loud. She glanced at Idris. His face was pale and still. Muffled.

She was terrified of monsters.

Oh.

The stairs had ended. The class had spilled out onto the floor of an enormous chamber, badly lit by little grilles a hundred feet above, their light reflected downward by polished bronze mirrors. Everywhere old was like this, sunk deep in the modern ground.

The room was circular. Through its center rose the huge stone cylinder of the Well. There were tanks of water in the floor. They swirled and eddied among the grid of bars that covered their surface. The catwalks between the tanks were cracked and twisted by the constant earthquakes of the Valley of Apples.

The class was gathered around Iron Chair, who was their Fire Tutor as well as their class teacher. He darted a red glance at the late arrivals. "As I was saying," he said. "These are the monsterstables of the Great Ambrose, who has kindly made them available to us. The monsters will arrive from the Welltop, sliding down the chutes and into their water. There they are kept until it is time for them to be hauled to cutting and thence to their furnaces or engines. But engineering need not worry us now. Hear them."

There was a silence. A silence in the air, that is, but not in the mind. Ever since the iron door, Idris had been muffled. Now he opened, and a tangle of voices poured into his head — old men, young women, reasonable, cajoling, insane. All were different, but all wanted the same thing: to be let out and put somewhere else.

"How they do go on. Grooms, extract," said Iron Chair.

Two figures in boiled-leather armor went to a small empty cage and latched it open. One of them poured fish blood into a trough in the cage. A crane lifted it and swung it into the air.

A minder raised the iron grille covering one of the monster pens and made a signal to the crane. The baited cage was lowered into the monster pen. There was a commotion in the water. An iron door clanged shut. Something screamed. Perce put his hands over his ears, but the scream still sounded inside his head. The cables above the cage grew taut. It began to rise.

There was a thing in the cage, suet-white and shiny, with the odd flicker of Well creatures. The scream had changed to a constant, panicky repetition. *Not dry, not dry, not dry,* it whimpered, dripping.

"This one," said Iron Chair, "we will not let out. Normally it would be lowered into the water cart. If it dries it burns, of course, and is drawn away to cutting, where the surgeons prepare it for the machines. Not today, though. Today we will see a demonstration of its properties."

Good, kind people, the monster was saying. *Be kind to me, do not let me dry, and I will show you darkgardens of the most beautiful —*

"Right-hand side's drying," said Iron Chair, perfectly at ease in this place of torment. "Watch."

A small area of the monster's surface had indeed become dry. From it there had begun to drift a fine white smoke. An acrid smell floated across the gangway. A spot at the root of the smoke had begun to glow brilliant white.

HELP ME, roared the monster.

"Silly creatures," said Iron Chair. "You will see that it is becoming phlogistous."

Toady Benrid asked what "phlogistous" meant, of course.

"Fiery."

"Ah." Benrid asked questions not because he wanted to know the answers but to impress his teachers. Now he stepped forward from the group and peered around the edge of the smoke, so everyone could see he was getting a closer look at the burning monster.

Iron Chair said, "Benrid, will you please —"

He never finished. From the monster's bright patch there shot an arm of white fire. There was a quick stench of burning leather, a short cry, and Benrid rolled away, smoldering. Two monstergrooms threw water over him. Two more carried him away. Idris felt Morgan clutching his hand. He squeezed hers back.

"The rewards of unwisdom," said Iron Chair to his pale and horrified class. "Grooms, slime it. The slime is made of various sea creatures, crushed. We will look into it later."

A monstergroom was pumping a thick gray liquid toward the monster. Where the liquid touched the burning portions they went out. In seconds, the monster was dark again and quiet except for an agonized whimpering. Two hookmen pulled it back into its cage and locked down the iron grille.

"Any questions?" said Iron Chair.

Benrid was the asker of questions. Benrid had gone. There was silence.

"Well," said Iron Chair. "You have had Earth, Air, and Fire. Still to come, Water." The hood bowed. "After Water, the Test. After the Test, you are on your own. If you survive it."

The hood shook a little and emitted a hoarse gasping.

Iron Chair was laughing.

Idris saw Morgan flinch and look away. He gave her hand another squeeze and was warmed by her look of gratitude. Then the class went back to its room and studied the Composition of Slime.

That night, a tap came on Idris's door.

"Enter," he said.

The latch rose and Morgan came in. Her hair hung about her shoulders, and her face was white, with dark smudges under the eyes. He rose and bowed, as was proper. She curtseyed in return. She said, "I wondered would you care for a game of Check?"

Idris was not in the mood for Check. But he caught the need in her voice and said, "Of course."

She smiled at him. He was surprised by the warmth in it. The board was under her arm. She put it down on the table and opened it out. Idris helped put out the pieces.

Morgan put out the seal and the stone, positioning them too carefully. Without looking up, she said, "I think I may not want to be a monstergroom."

"Why not?"

"Too much dying."

Idris had been thinking the same thing. But he said, "The ones who die are the ones who are bigheaded or not concentrating." He was thinking of the plank in the Fort at Westgate. "This is Lyonesse. You can die anywhere."

"But it's not right."

Idris did not answer. Right or wrong, that was the way in Lyonesse.

"And besides," said Morgan, "why do we want to be Captains?"

"To understand how other Captains work," he said. "That's what Ambrose said. He understands. And he's not fat and greedy. And we trust him. Yes?"

"Yes."

"Well, then. So this is going to be very nasty. But when we get through it we will be strong and we will know a lot. So we will get through it. All right?"

Morgan put the castle and two serfs on their squares, not meeting his eye. "It's all right for you," she said. "You were brought up in a rough-and-tough family and if you weren't here you'd be dead."

"True," said Idris, offended, though.

"I came here because Ambrose talked to my parents," she said, putting a bison on the wrong square. "I thought it would be all power and glory. But it's just dirt and fire and agony."

Idris repositioned the bison. He said, "Are you going to give up and go home?"

Morgan shook her head. "I told my parents I'd come back a groom. So I will."

She's tougher than me, thought Idris. He said, "I'll help."

"You!" said Morgan scornfully. "Help? Me?"

Idris realized his enthusiasm had led him into a stupid lack of tact. "Only if you want, that is."

But Morgan had told Idris more than she had meant to, and now she was angry with herself and therefore with him. She slammed the rest of the Check pieces onto the board, trying to think of a way to change the subject. "We have got a really beautiful Check set at home," she said. "Mammoth ivory, red crystal, and two granites. It's a shame to play on anything else really. I'll move." She moved a serf. Then she said, "Perhaps you'd like to come and see it, sometime?"

"I might be too rough and tough," said Idris, in defense of Harpoon and Ector.

Pink rose in Morgan's neck. "That's just nasty," she said.

Idris laughed, then realized that it was the wrong thing to do. But by then Morgan had swept up the Check armies, and the door had slammed, and she had gone to bed.

So Idris went, too, and lay listening to the rumble of monsters being carted to the barge docks by the lake, and thought how unfair it was that Morgan would never actually meet his parents, because she would really like them. And the next morning, when they had breakfast and went down to class, they did not seem to be on speaking terms, and neither of them could think of a way back.

This week, the subject was Water.

The inhabitants of Westgate knew about the tides of the sea. The Wellworld had tides, too, their rhythm subtle, as if driven by water-swimming moons imperceptible in Lyonesse.

Iron Chair embarked on a long and boring lecture about the probable size and weight of these moons. Idris drifted back to the Westgate and smelled the salt wind blowing, and for a moment all was cheerful.

Then he brushed Morgan's mind.

He had been careful not to do this, because it was unfair to pry into the thoughts of your friends. But this morning the unhappiness was so loud it might as well have been written on her forehead. He put his mind closer to hers and was nearly deafened. *NO*, her thoughts shouted, *NOT THE WELL. I DO NOT WANT TO GO THERE IT IS DARK DEEP DANGEROUS AND FULL OF FILTHY THINGS.* Then a picture drifted in, of the Check board she had described last night by a window with spring-green oak leaves in a tower of golden stone. Morgan was thinking of home.

"The meters are being watched," said Iron Chair to the pupils. "When the time comes you will be summoned, and you will descend into the Well."

From the corner of his eye Idris saw Morgan blanch, and he caught another glimpse of green oaks and gold stone. Then her defenses were up.

He hated to see her frightened. But frightened or not, into the Well they must descend.

Idris was in Westgate, playing the after-school game of his last evening at home. He had bounced off the plank, and was up, arms out, and he started to plummet, and the plank was not there, and down he went, down, but this time the water was not blue but black and he roared through it with bubbles in his ears, fast as a spear, and his heart was banging like a fist on a door. . . .

His eyes opened. It was pitch dark. But the thing that was banging like a fist on a door was a fist on the door. "Up!" cried a voice. "Up, up!"

"Wha — ?" said Idris, tangled in the rags of his dream.

"Deep Spring!" said the voice, which belonged to Ambrose's dwarf Cran. "On the Ambrose Welltop in a crow's flap! With gloves!"

Through the cell window he saw the red stars of the Flatfish low in the western sky. He pulled on his boots. There were two hours till dawn. Not that that would matter where they were going. There were butterflies in his stomach. He opened the door and said, "Morgan?"

"Yes." A thin voice, brittle.

"Are you ready?"

Her door opened. "Of course I am." Angry. Nervous.

"Let's go."

Their boots boomed in the empty corridors. There were other boots on the stairs. The air on the Welltop was cold and dank. The class stood shivering on the platform in the bloody light of a pine-knot torch. "All here?" said a tall man in leather.

"I am Sacker. Do as I say and no trouble will befall you, barring accidents."

"What are we going to do?" said Morgan's voice, hard and high.

"Take a peep at the Wellworld," said Sacker. "And come back. If we're lucky."

"But how?" said Morgan.

Sacker's torch roared as he flung it out and over the Well. The pupils craned their necks over the abyss, watching it as it fell. The flame became a spark, shrank to a glimmer, and went out. But not with quenching. With distance.

"But we will not be jumping, ha-ha," said Sacker. "We will be climbing."

Idris heard Morgan make an odd noise somewhere between a gulp and a sob.

"Down rungs on the Wellside," said Sacker. "That's why you've got your gloves. Now we'll get going, because your Deep Spring comes and goes pretty quick, and the tide's slack now. If you lag you drown."

"What is it?" said Idris quietly in Morgan's ear, to let her know he was there.

"Nothing."

"What?"

"Shut up. Oh, bother you, I forgot my gloves and there's no time to go back and get them."

"Have mine."

"No."

"I'm rough and tough. You said so."

Short, guilty silence. Idris felt her smile and knew that she was remembering what he had said. "All right," she said and took the gloves. "Thank you." She headed for the edge.

Idris followed her, hoping he looked more confident than he felt.

He lay on his belly, swung his feet out over the abyss, felt for a rung, grasped another with his hands, and began to descend.

He climbed as fast as he could, keeping his mind away from the awful void below. The rungs were smooth and round. Foot down, hand down, take the step. The Welltop was far above now. The first time he looked up it was the size of a plate. The second time it was the size of a button. His mouth was dry, his knees shaking. Foot down, hand down. A mile below, water sloshed and boomed. On he climbed, Morgan below, Kay above.

Idris's hands began to hurt. The rungs down here must be very ancient, corroded to sharp edges. He managed to pad his palms with the sleeves of his jersey. Even so, the pain got worse, and something was running down his arms to his elbows and he thought it was probably blood. He jammed his teeth together.

Climb.

The sloshing and booming from below were louder now. When he next looked up, the disc of the Welltop was a little gray star. He began to feel suffocated, buried alive.

"Keep moving," said Sacker's voice below. *Moving, moving,* said the echoes. *Slosh, boom,* said the water in the awful gulf, far below, deep as a planet.

Down, down. The wall of the Well began to slope away, as if they had been climbing down the neck of a bottle and were now arriving in the bottle's belly. Idris found more of his weight coming on to his hands. The pain was intense. He called, "Morgan?"

"Yes."

"All right?"

"Do you think there's far to go?" The words punctuated by grunts, step, step.

"Don't know," said Idris.

"It's a long way back up," said Morgan.

The same thought had occurred to Idris. "Always easier on the way home," he said, wondering how his hands would do it.

"Yes."

Step, step. Down, down. The pain was like gripping sword blades.

Then there was the sound of voices from below, and a floor instead of a rung, and he was on a sort of ledge or balcony with a wooden wall and a wooden floor, and there was the tiny glimmer of a lantern that glowed yellow on the faces of the class. Huge sloshings and boomings came from farther down. "All here?" said Sacker.

"Yes," said everyone.

"Right. I am lowering an iron basket into the Wellwater . . . thus," said Sacker. "In it I shall catch some little tiny burners — think of them as Wellworld shrimps."

Idris was standing with his hands resting on the wooden wall that ran around the front of the balcony. It was interesting, despite his agonizing palms. Below all was blackness, except for gleams of red and blue that might have been inside his head. They reminded him of the lights he had seen when he had escaped drowning. . . .

There was the sound of a tiny splash.

The night blazed white.

The class gasped.

The light came from a basket on the end of a cable. The other end of the cable was in Sacker's hand. "You will see," said Sacker's voice, flat and ordinary, "that I have used this here wire basket to scoop up some of the tiny burners that swim under the Well, and now they have dried out, and they are burning." He frowned. "There seem to be a lot of them. Anyone bleeding? Hope not, for their sake, ha-ha. Anyway, there you are."

As his eyes got used to the light, Idris saw that the balcony hung giddily over an enormous cavern. The floor of the cavern was black water, stirred from below as if by powerful creatures that could not be seen. By the fins and tails of monsters. His flesh crawled with horror.

"Behold the edge of the Wellworld," said Sacker. The class gazed down into the abyss, numb and silent, their faces lit bluish in the glare. "We are standing on the watchstep, which is the lowest place man can go. We are in the watchboat." He slapped the wooden side of the balcony. "I've undone the catches. It floats up as the tide comes in. No more climbing, see?" A murmur of relief from the class. "Monstergrooms come down here to take samples and to listen. Ordinary wells may be deep," said Sacker. "But this one is bottomless. It is a portal into another world, a watery one." The water swirled, as if something huge had looked up, turned, gone down again. By the harsh light of the basket Idris saw Sacker frown. "Is someone bleeding?" he said.

Idris looked at his hands on the wooden side of the watchboat. A drop of blood, black in the burnerlight, collected on the end of his finger, swelled, and fell into the void. Instantly the water where the drop had fallen was sucked down into a funnel, and a great black back rolled, like a vast trout taking a fly.

Something came into Idris's mind above the hum and chitter of the shrimp-monsters in the Well. A giant whisper that said, WHO'S THERE? Idris froze. He tried to make his mind small, so it would not be seen.

The watchstep shook underfoot.

"Tide's turning," said Sacker. "We'll be afloat in half a glass. Hold tight."

Idris heard him as if he were far away. The giant voice in his mind was huge and small and quiet and booming all at the same time. There was nowhere to hide. It had found his mind and gotten in and spun it, until he did not know —

"Idris," said Morgan, pulling at his jersey. "*Idris!*"

— what way up he was, and heard Morgan's voice as a far-away whisper, and his head was filling up with darkness, deep green and dark red and ink blue.

"*Idris,*" said Morgan. She put out her gloved hand to grip his arm, saw in the light that his sleeves were soaked with blood. And Sacker looked, too, and saw the blood, and said in a loud, harsh voice. "Don't touch him. It'll have him, nothing you can do." A deep, shaking rumble. "Tide. Hold on."

Morgan looked at her gloves. Idris's gloves. That he had given her.

In Idris's head, the darkness spun into a whirlwind that sucked the stiffening from his knees and the sight from his eyes.

He felt himself dragged forward over the rail of the watchstep.

IDRIS, roared the voice from below in its loud, loud whisper.

He heard Morgan scream.

He fell.

SEVEN

A t the long table in the Great Ambrose's Hall of Session, Ambrose was explaining a new way of moving hills with starlight. Naturally the Captains were shouting at him that it was old-fashioned. Captain Brassfin opened his mouth to speak again when Ambrose put up a hand for silence. He seemed to be listening to something far away.

It took more than a raised hand to stop Brassfin. "Progress," he said, "cannot be *mff.*" For Ambrose had murmured something under his breath and made a curious hopping movement with his hand on the table. And at that moment each of the Captains became convinced that in his mouth was a fluffy live rabbit that made it impossible to talk. Silence fell, furry and unfriendly.

Ambrose's brows drew together over his nose. His eyes closed. There was a feeling that he was *heaving.* Somewhere in a room nearby, there was an enormous crash. Something shot out of a window and howled upward toward the Welltop — something big and heavy, wailing through the air. "I beg your pardon," said Great Ambrose, opening his eyes and making an unhopping move with his hands. "Someone seems to have thrown a chair into my Well. You were saying?"

The shouting broke out again.

WELCOME, IDRIS, shouted the whisper. Not a kind whisper. The sort of whisper spiders used when talking to flies.

Idris felt himself turn over once in the air. He shouted, "GO AWAY!" He felt the message hit the huge voice and hurt it. Then the water smacked him in the head and shoulder, horrible burning water that tore at his throat and eyes. But what was in his mind was not burning water but that thing that had come tearing up the Well his first day at Ambrose's, all teeth and slime. YOUR LOVELY BLOOD, LITTLE ONE, shouted the whisper, and Idris was suddenly terribly aware of his feet, kicking in the surface of that world of water, and the huge teeth below.

Something slid along his leg. It slid and slid and slid, caressing, while he kicked at it. All this kicking was keeping him afloat, and away from the teeth. *Please,* his mind yelled, panicking, *not the teeth.*

The light flickered, as if something had crossed the light from Sacker's brazier of little monsters. Something big crashed into the water three feet from Idris, kicking black spray into his eyes, as if it had fallen from an enormous height.

Like from the top of the Well.

The slime-thing had stopped moving. Idris could feel the horror of muscles bunching under its skin, as if it was getting ready to twist and rip. He lunged away from it. His hand crashed into whatever it was that had fallen from the sky.

The thing was made of wood.

Wood. From a tree. Which grew in light and air.

Idris clasped the wooden thing like a piece of home in a world of enemies.

DEAR ME, said the huge whisper in his mind. He caught impatience, something to do with finishing, ending, and tasted a taste in his mind that no one had ever tasted in the world of light and air.

The wooden thing seemed to be a chair. An enormous chair of carved wood, with huge soggy cushions.

What was it doing here?

SSSS, said the shout-whisper.

High above on the watchstep, the voice of Morgan cried, "Idris! Hold on!"

IDRIS, said the shout-whisper in a horrible mockery of Morgan's affectionate voice. Something took the chair, delicate but powerful. There was a crunching noise. Wood splintered.

Teeth. No. Please.

The world was roaring. Even the water was shaking. Idris paid no attention to it. All he wanted to do was be out of the Well and to have his old, simple, poor life back. Or anyway to keep what was left of this chair between him and the teeth. He clung to it, hammering the creature with his mind: *Go away, let go . . .*

Crunch.

The chair began to spin. Water roiled and eddied. The whisper became the scream of a thing that had left it too late.

The Welltide came in

Idris felt the chair hurtle upward, himself clinging to it, whirling like a leaf in a gale. He banged off a stone wall. He caught a glimpse of something that must have been the watchboat, the white faces of the class, spinning in the currents, rising. Up he went, up and up until the Wellwater around him lightened and there was a roar and another bang and no more water, and he was wedged against something hard. And he could breathe.

He opened his eyes.

His face was jammed into iron railings: the railings around the tower. Below him water fell lazily down the side of the Well into the relief channel, and the long shadows of dawn were creeping over the Wellvale. Above him he heard the cry of a gull.

Kek.

Going into Kek's head was as comfortable as going home. Through his old friend's eyes he saw the platform of the Great Ambrose. He saw himself sitting in a heavily carved chair, jammed against the railings overlooking the city. He saw a wooden box, yes, the watchboat, jammed into the far side, Sacker climbing out, the pupils following, looking shaken and pale. In the railings on the Mountside he saw a monster: not a burner or anything like a burner, but a black serpent of a thing, thick as a whale, with a huge head jagged with teeth and evil eyes both blank and clever. The eyes looked at him. The shape of the monster blurred. Suddenly in its place there lay a baby. The baby was crying. Tears ran down its face. The baby knuckled them away.

Sacker drew his knife, walked across the platform, and drove it into the baby's body. "No!" cried Morgan. The baby screamed and blurred and turned back into the huge black thing. Idris saw it writhe its whale-bulk across the platform. He heard it say, *IDRIS*. He saw it show its dreadful teeth and fall thrashing into the Well. Idris crawled into the middle of the Welltop and sat there shaking.

A shadow fell on him. Sacker said, "What's that?" and pointed.

"Chair," said Idris. "It fell into the Well." But it had not just fallen. Someone had thrown it, and he knew who.

"Fell?" said Sacker, frowning, perhaps suspicious. "That's lucky."

"Master Sacker," said a high, cracked voice.

"What?" said Sacker impatiently.

"Captain, the mage Great Ambrose wishes to see pupil Idris Limpet," said the voice. Looking up, Idris saw Ambrose's dwarf Cran. "Soon. Now."

"Oh," said Sacker. *Ambrose threw it?* said his thought. *Why?* "You had better go, then," he said sulkily.

Behind Sacker's back, Morgan held up a hand with Idris's glove on and made a "sorry" face. Kay's eyes went between them, not liking this understanding. Idris looked down at his palms, cut deeply across. They hurt. A lot. He made himself wink and shrug.

"Come," squawked Cran. "Ambrose busy, you in trouble."

He followed Cran down stone stairs onto carpets and into a new and magnificent part of the Well where he had never been before. Two liveried servitors opened a double door. Down the pillared sides of a great hall, scribes were writing on skins. Slumped on the throne at the far end sat Ambrose. Binding his brow was a gold circlet in the form of an eel devouring its tail, and wedged under the circlet was a cloth soaked, by the look of it, in cool water. "Oh," he said, looking up. "You." He pointed with a languid finger. Against the wall stood a chair of carved and gilded wood with red velvet cushions. "Ever seen one of those before?"

"It is like the one that fell down the Well," said Idris, stopping his jaw from wobbling, but only just.

"They were once a pair. Did it fall or was it pushed?" said Ambrose.

"You threw it. I am grateful," said Idris. "You saved my life, that I put at hazard by rashness."

Ambrose seemed taken aback. "You are learning grace," he said. "Bring a stool, Cran. Sit, Idris. Show me your hands." He sighed. "Idiot. Cran, send a leech, and tell him to come ready to mend cuts."

"Thank you. I don't need one," said Idris. The shock of his escape was leaving him, and in its place came misery, because he knew Ambrose was going to tell him exactly what he had done wrong.

"Well, I do," said Ambrose. "I have a very bad headache, because it is no small thing to root up a valuable and very heavy chair and throw it down a Well. Worse than that, people will look at what I have done, and they will say, why did he bother, when prentices are wasted like sparks from the anvil? Sacker is already wondering. Idris, this knack of drawing attention to yourself will get you killed. Which would not be fair to those who have taken trouble over you."

All this was true and very depressing. Idris bowed his head.

Ambrose said, "So why did you not take your blasted gloves when Sacker told you to take them?"

Idris frowned, muffling. He did not want to get Morgan into trouble.

"Morgan?" said Ambrose.

"Sir?" Idris strove to strengthen the muffle against the mage's powerful mind.

"Tiring child," said Ambrose, pushing aside the muffle. "Let us make a bargain. We will stay out of minds and use speech, and use it truly. Now. How did she make you go bathing in the Well?"

"She had forgotten her gloves. I gave her mine. I insisted," said Idris, lest it be thought that it had been Morgan's idea.

Ambrose sighed. "Blast all women, and the fools they make of men." He thumped Idris gently on the head with his fist. "Soon it will be the Test," he said. "And in the Test I will not be there to help you. Ah," he said. "Here is the leech. Leech, give me willow bark, for my skull is bursting. Then look at the child."

The leech gave Ambrose a greenish liquid from a bottle, then looked at Idris's hands. "There is a cut here that must be nipped," he said. He took from his bag a box. From it he took four large ants. "This will sting," he said. He put the ants beside the cut. Their powerful jaws clamped together, uniting the edges of the wound. Idris's eyes watered with the pain, but he kept his face still.

"That would be the venom," said Ambrose, watching him with some satisfaction. "It will stop the wound from mortifying."

"Oh, good," said Idris, between clenched teeth.

The leech twitched off the ants' bodies, leaving only their heads. He bowed himself out.

"So," said Ambrose. "Your blood is in the Well, and you are known in the Wellworld."

"Known?"

"They read your blood."

"Does that matter?"

"There is a world in the Wells as complicated as our own. There are orders of monsters as there are orders of men. The Captains do not like this known. So you are in danger of being questioned by a court of Captains and thrown back into the Well, from which I shall this time be unable to extract you and in which you will perish. You have been in one court. You did

119

not like it." He took a scroll of lambskin and handed it to Idris. The letters down its side said *Of the Diversitie of Monsters*. "Read this," he said. "It is a description of some of the kinds of monster to be found below the Wells. You will find it interesting at your Test and after."

"But —"

"And I will make it clear to Sacker that you are a clumsy oaf of no breeding."

"But —"

"Be quiet. Thanks to what I shall say to Sacker you will not be questioned by the Court of Captains. You will be free to concentrate on the Test. Which will require all your concentration."

"Yes," said Idris. His hands hurt. Suddenly this world was too hard and bitter for him, and he was lonely. He wanted to talk to someone he trusted entirely. Ambrose was too clever. And it would not be fair to say the things he needed to say to Morgan. She would understand, of course. But she needed to be strong. If he showed her that he felt as lost as she did, it would help neither of them. There was only one source of comfort that he could think of. He said, "Sir. Before I undergo these dangers, may I write to my family?"

Ambrose closed his eyes, then opened them. They were no longer hard and ironic but affectionate, even sorrowful. Idris found himself enveloped in warmth. "No," Ambrose said.

"I would use no name," said Idris, half desperate. "I would disguise where I am."

Ambrose said, "You are all in enough danger already. But accept this. They know you are well, and they are proud of you. Speak of them no more. Yours is a lonely road, but if you follow it boldly, your destiny will take you beyond them."

"My destiny?" said Idris, frowning.

Ambrose laughed, but Idris got the impression he was vexed at himself. "Your path in life, I meant," he said. He rang a little bell. Cran scuttled down the aisle between the desks. "My interview with Master Limpet is closed," said Ambrose. "Now. Admit the Ambassador of the Norns, and I suppose you had better tell the second-best dancing girls to paint their toes pink, for the Ambassador will certainly want to see them perform, drat him."

Idris walked slowly back to his quarters. His hand hurt. He tried to imagine a road that would take him beyond Harpoon and Ector and his brothers and sisters. And he thought he caught a glimpse of something. Something indistinct, that had to do with the dark, cruel world of the Wells, and things so enormous that he could not take them in. A glimpse of great power and terrible pain. Destiny, perhaps?

Well, if that was destiny he did not want it.

Then another thought came. What was it that made Idris Limpet worth saving when others were left to perish?

A destiny was not something you could choose. Destiny was what happened to you whether you wanted it or not.

This was the only road. He must travel it, and survive.

"What are you reading?" said Morgan as she sat in his room that night.

He showed her *Of the Diversitie of Monsters*.

"But it is only the burners that it is lawful to catch. So why bother with the rest?"

"Why are the others unlawful?"

"They just are," said Morgan, shocked.

Idris could see that he was talking not only to his friend, but to her father, and her father's father, and a golden stone tower in the oak wood, built on age-deep foundations of trust and faith. He shrugged. "Perhaps," he said. And reopened *Of the Diversitie of Monsters* with a hand throbbing from the tug of the ant heads, and plunged alone into the unnatural history of the Wells.

"You are, I suppose, as ready as can be expected," rasped Iron Chair in the classroom next morning. "You are each, with the assistance of the others, to secure a license for burnercatching from the Council, catch a burner according to the routines and techniques you have been taught, put it in your master's monsterstables, and care for it until it is ready to be taken to the engines, this to be done within the next moon. The meter rooms are open for inspection so you may calculate your tides. Now I have finished with you. Begone." He rose and stumped out of the room.

"What a kind man," drawled Kay. The others laughed but nervously.

Idris could see how it should be done. "We must help each other," he said. "We can work in teams."

"I'm fine on my own," said sullen Thorpe, with a curl of the lip.

"And me," said Bwrpau, who nowadays spent most of his classes hiding his notes from the others and adding up imaginary sums of coin.

"We could meet at the Wrestler's Elbow," said Kay. "My brother said he used the practice room there before his Test."

The practice room at the Wrestler's Elbow was dirtier even than the classroom but more fun. There was a round table, and cartoons of Iron Chair on the wall drawn by earlier generations of pupils. There was sunapple juice to drink, and blackberry juice from the Stone Downs, and apple madness from High Kernow for anyone who wanted it — nobody did, because it made you sick and sleepy. There was a sort of holiday mood, though there was a darkness behind it, for the Test was the opposite of a holiday. But in this darkness, the prentices looked to one another for light, and Morgan seemed to find comfort in the faces around the table: Kay, less superior nowadays, and stolid Perce, and amusing Gavin, and of course Idris. Idris was quiet, but when he made a suggestion, others followed it, though this did not always please Kay. Morgan could not get rid of the idea that Idris belonged at the head of the table. Except, of course, that it was round.

As the first step in the Test, they secured burner licenses from the Council officials in the offices by the Old Well. Then they walked in a body to the Hall of Meters.

They stood in a room with walls of polished tin covered in pointers. There were depth of Wells, hour of day, height of water, quantity of water admissible, all driven by strings and belts that came along shafts from floats and paddles and feelers sunk under this city of Wells, a mass of information, too much, too much.

Perce had the sharpest mind for numbers, so he made the calculations. "There are good monstertides in two days, three days, and five days," he said. "As far as I can tell. Interesting, though. There are no records for the Old Well. We should see the main meter, really."

A sour-faced clerk looked up from his table by the door. "You do not need the numbers from the Old Well for your silly little Test," he hissed. "And nobody, but *nobody* can see the main meter but the Council, on the orders of the Regent Sea Eagle —"

"Blessings of the Well upon her," murmured the other clerks, who were eavesdropping.

"— blessings indeed. At any other time you would be dragged from here and knocked on the head like a rabbit in a food garden. But most of you will die anyway. So," said the thin man, apparently feeling much better now, "you may now get out of here, and take your Tests, and good riddance."

So away walked the prentices, with their tides ready, pushing confidently through the crush of carts and serfs and shoppers. And Idris looked back in wonder at the dazed child who had made flies turn upside down and gaped timidly at the wonders of the Valley of Apples. Had that been him?

That had been him then. This was him now.

EIGHT

The prentices divided themselves into teams of three, the two waiting to assist at the third's Test on each of the three tides. Idris's co-prentices were Morgan and Kay. They sat on a grassy terrace near a roof that was being retiled after a shaking of the ground. Kay picked up a tile from a heap. The tiles were made of clay pressed into the mold by hand. The pressed side bore thumb marks. "For first catching. Thumbs or plain?"

"Thumbs I go," said Kay.

"Plain," said Idris.

"Plain," said Morgan.

The tile came down thumbs. "I go," said Kay and swallowed nervously. "Big tide."

The first tide was indeed a big one — bigger than the second, but not as big as the third. The third tide was enormous. It would be violent and difficult. Idris hoped Morgan would not get it.

Second tide. The tile went up. "Thumbs I go," said Morgan, in a small, tight voice.

Idris watched the rectangle of baked clay turn in the air, thumbs, plain, thumbs, plain. He could see by the way it was turning that it was going to come down thumbs. He reached out his mind to make sure, then thought: She would not want me to interfere. He withdrew. The tile clattered down, thumbs.

"Thumbs. You go," said Idris.

"Idris gets the big one," said Kay, with the usual needle in his voice.

"Big tide, big monster," said Idris. "Piece of pie."

"Sometimes," said Morgan, "you are so stupid and cocky." And she burst into tears.

So there they were, two days later, the day of Kay's tide, having the catch briefing on the Welltop of the Brassfin Spouter, to which Kay was apprenticed, in the helmets and visors and red boiled-leather armor of monstergrooms. The only way of telling them apart was by their devices: on Kay's breast the barbed squid of Brassfin, and on Idris and Morgan the self-devouring eel of the Great Ambrose. Beside them was the Well's team of mechanics and hookmen. Idris could see them eyeing these green children coldly from behind their visors. It made no sense to be friendly with people who might in the next twenty minutes be fried, or devoured, or thrust into a Well. For a moment Idris felt small and frightened. Then thought, This is the road, and I must travel it. There was a job to do.

Kay was watching the meter. "All right," he said, voice hollow behind his mask. "Idris, stableman."

"Stableman," said Idris. He winked at Morgan. She gave him a false, worried smile.

As he ran down the endless stairs toward his station in the monsterstables at the tower's root, he could feel the rumble of the Welltides in the stone treads.

Through the iron door. Down into the monsterstables. The caged monsters came at him in an unholy choir. *Oh Mr. Limpet,* cried their minds in his mind, *we have heard your blood in the world, what pleasure to see you, let us out and we will lead you to your destiny, which is to rule the world of air with our help, our very powerful help.*

Idris muffled against the flattery.

Concentrate on routine.

"Hookmen!" he cried.

Boots crashed on riven stone. The stable hookmen stood before him, blank in their boiled-leather visors. "Check hooks," he said. The gaffs lowered for his inspection. A sharp hook made life easier for its operator, but it could pierce a monster and cause an early burn. "Hookman two," he said. "Too sharp. File it blunt."

"But —"

"Go."

The man tracked his hook to one of the workbenches under the wall and started scraping with a file.

"Time to tide?"

Another man reached for a sandglass from the rack. "Half a glass."

"Stand by your entry," said Idris.

Another bell, lower in tone.

"Tide." A quick, living shudder animated the ground under Idris's feet. The water under the bars swirled and frothed as the monsters sensed the coming tide.

Then the stable was filled with a booming roar, and the whole Well shuddered as the column of water rushed up its hollow center, and the last grains of sand fell through the glass, and every monster in the stable screamed, and a thin, high bell started to trill.

"Monster on the Welltop," said Idris in a voice artificially calm. "Hooks ready."

"Ready," said the hookmen.

From the fireplace-like hole in the wall there came the sound of shouts, and a voice, Kay's voice, crying, "Monster down!" The echo stopped. A slithering took its place. There was a rush of water from the hole, a crash, a scream, and something was in the entry, something the size of a cow, with half-formed teeth and fins and tentacles that clung to the fireplace sides.

"Hooks!" cried Idris. His heart was really hammering now. There were only eyeblinks to get this right. The monster was drying by the second. It could burn through metal, reduce a tower to ashes of stone —

"Hooks in!" said the hookmen.

"Heave," cried Idris, readying his pole.

The hookmen gave a haul of their long-handle gaffs. The monster screamed, let go its grip in the entry, and began to slither down the chute toward its stall. Idris saw its shape begin to shift, as it started to make legs that would propel it off the end and onto the catwalk and into the body of the stable, drying, starting the burn. It rose on two legs, teetering on the edge of being mobile. As it teetered, Idris placed the pole's iron tip on its upper part and leaned his full weight to it. Off balance, the monster rocked backward and fell through the open stallgate and into the pen.

"Gate down, please," said Idris, in a voice he commanded not to shake. The gate fell. The monster was safe in water behind iron. "Feed them when you're ready."

"'Ssir," said the hookmen, respectful now. "Lively monster, sir."

"Tolerably," said Idris, keeping his voice casual, controlling the urge to whoop and yell. He made himself walk calmly up the four hundred and nine steps to the Welltop. He was pleased to see Morgan looking pink and happy, shake hands all around, then stroll down to the Spouter's hall for the breakfast of salmon, wheatbread, and sunapple provided by Brassfin for Kay, his new-tested groom.

It was a festive breakfast, though Kay was inclined to act superior, as groom to two mere prentices. But a shadow hung behind it.

There were two more Tests to go.

On Morgan's Test day, it was Kay's turn to be down in the stables with the hookmen. Idris and Morgan were on the Ambrose Well in good time before the tide. The bladders hung over the Wellshaft on the crane arm. The blood vat stood to one side, its pipe coiled next to the flinging buckets. Morgan had a pale, distant look.

"Luck," said Idris.

"Luck doesn't come into it," said Morgan, looking at the checklist she had squid-inked, ever efficient, on a whalebone tablet. "Visors." She pulled her visor down. Idris left his up. There was a long wait till the tide, and boiled leather smelled grim. "*Visors*," said Morgan, muffled by the helmet.

"Done," said Idris, making his voice extra cheerful and moving out of her line of sight.

The ground shook. The Initial bulged water, became a geyser, roared. On its Welltop little figures were moving around, as if unsure where to stand. Shouts drifted across the high air. Then the Spouter bulged and bloomed and became a cataract.

Under his feet, the Well shuddered.

Idris stepped back and jammed himself against the railings. The water came up and roared out. The crane engine howled. The monster lay. Idris could feel Morgan's unsureness and so could the monster. *Please*, the monster started to say with its mind. *Help me, help me.* Morgan acted tough, but Idris knew that actually she was kind and loved helping people. That was the wedge the monster would use to get into her mind and lure her back into the void, if it could.

Into Idris's mind came the struggle under the Ambrose watchstep. He had not merely heard the monster. He had . . . *battered* it. Now, he slammed his mind onto the monster's. *Oof*, thought the monster, stunned. And while it was still reeling, the hookmen got it and hauled it to the chute and down it went to where Kay was waiting in the stalls. "There," said Idris, pushing back his visor. "That wasn't so bad, was it?"

"Of course it wasn't," said Morgan, her face lit up with delight. She had not noticed Idris's shove, then. That was good. He grinned at her. He was happy, his mind up with Kek, sailing over the Wells. The relief channels were full, the lake a stinking turmoil. On the Welltops, the men were sweeping up. Except on the Initial. Idris's happiness curdled. On the Initial, the hookmen were standing immobile. There was no monsterslime on the chute mouth. One hookman was standing with his mouth open, gazing down the Well.

Idris felt cold. He closed his eyes. But Kek's stayed open, showing the awful cylinder of the shaft plunging into darkness.

The darkness where money-hungry Bwrpau had been mind-lured, and from which he would not return.

Kek slid away.

"You next," said the new, confident Morgan.

Idris managed a smile. Poor, greedy Bwrpau.

And two days later, there they were again on the Well for Idris's Test. Kek was down in the Westgate, lucky Kek. High, though. Too high to see individual faces. Actually Idris did not like looking at the Westgate nowadays, had not looked closely since he had left. . . .

Concentrate, thought Idris, looking around the Welltop. This is the road, and you walk it alone. Hookmen in place. Kay was there, visor up, looking superior. Bait ready. Blood filled. He moved to the chute. "Ready?" he said.

"Ready," said a hollow version of Morgan's voice rising up the chute from the monsterstables far below. She sounded cheerful and casual.

"Careful," he said.

"Of course," said Morgan, in a don't-teach-Granny-to-pick-crabs sort of way, because she was now a Tower Ambrose monstergroom and had the badge to prove it, and her doubts and fears had blown away, and as far as she was concerned she was senior to Idris. Idris was worried. The stableman had the most difficult job. Sometimes that did not become clear until too late.

"Luck," he said. "Visors." He turned away. The Initial had blown. The Ambrose top had a faint tremor, as if alive.

"Tide, sir," said the foreman Welltop hookman.

The tremor became a shudder. Idris walked to the edge, settled into the railings, and muffled. The crane howled. Huge teeth clashed. There was a terrible screaming beyond the Muffle. *IDRIS*, it howled. *WE KNOW YOUR BLOOD AND YOU*

WILL DIE. Water smashed into him, a great bitter swamp of it on this enormous tide. He heard its thunder in the relief channels. He shouted, "All well?"

"Cor stone me," said the foreman hookman.

Idris turned his visor on the monster.

It should have been a huge gray mass, shining with wet, sliding across the Welltop slabs on a cushion of water.

It was not.

There were the hookmen, standing in a way that made Idris certain their mouths were hanging open inside their visors. There was Kay, shaking his helmet as if he could not believe his eyes. And at the focus of all these people was a child. A remarkably beautiful child, perhaps eight years old, with pale golden hair and tawny eyes. "Thank you," said the child.

"Wha —" said Idris.

"You have rescued me," said the child. "From the . . . Well." Except that when it said "Well" Idris somehow had a feeling that it said "garden" as well, though the words were quite unalike, so the idea was impossible. "Look. Here," said the child, beckoning. "I'll show you." It moved closer to the Well.

Idris's mind went to the *Diversitie.* This was an infant summoner. "Hooks!" he cried.

The hookmen still hesitated. You did not stick hooks into beautiful golden-haired children.

"*Hooks!*"

Still no movement. One of the hookmen was moving toward the Wellshaft in response to the child's beckoning. Idris snatched a hook out of the rack, put it around the man's ankle, and pulled. The man fell over. Idris dragged him away.

The child roared, a huge and terrible roar that wanted to blast Idris's brain out of his ears. Then it flickered and became the biggest monster Idris had ever seen. A monster that lay there with no hooks in it and was starting to thrash back toward the Well edge, shouting with its mind, *FOLLOW ME, IDRIS, COWARD, FIGHT LIKE A MAN.*

"Chute it!" roared Idris.

Never! roared the monster in his mind. Its tail swept around like a flail, trying to thrash him into the Well. Idris jumped, felt the wind of it as it passed under him. *SILENCE,* he roared, felt the thought thud into the monster's mind, felt the mind stagger under the blow, felt his own power. And in that instant, he had his hook in and was leaning back with all his weight, setting it sliding for the chute, and now the other hookmen had their irons in, too. As it slid, it started to revive. And he knew that Morgan, Morgan standing all smug and casual down there with the stable hookmen, was not going to be able to pole this monster, this truly enormous monster, into its stall. The monster slid down on him. The teeth clashed a hand's breadth from his head. The body slid past him, high as a cliff, endless, the mind roaring and shrieking. And he knew what he was going to have to do to put it safely in its stall, and pass the Test, and save Morgan from being bitten in half or burned to vapor. So at the moment when he should have twitched the hook from the monster's hide, he left it there, and jumped on its back, his boot nails gripping the slime, his body leaned back against the anchorage of the hook.

The monster slid into the chute with Idris riding it like a Bretan charioteer. *NO*, roared the monster. *I'M SCRAPING. I'LL BURN.*

Shut up and behave, said Idris, falling, for the first part of the chute was a vertical shaft.

Bang. His knees gave, but he kept his boot nails in the monster, jets of fire coming from their punctures now. They were no longer falling but sliding, down a tunnel lit with little green and blue lights from the monster's skin, Idris hanging on to the hook for dear life, the tunnel curving so he realized it was built corkscrew-fashion into the Well walls, the boot-nail wounds burning now, hot feet, thick white smoke lit blue and green, the monster gabbling, *Take me away from this and I will show you my garden of red and blue darknesses, where the fishes swim —*

And out they crashed, into the dim light of the ramp in the monsterstables of the Great Ambrose. There was Morgan's voice, too high, telling the grooms to get the hooks in. There were the grooms, staring, so that he guessed that they were not seeing a five-ton mass of teeth and slime, but a little blond child with amber eyes. And there were the ramps leading down to the open stall door, and beyond them Morgan, white-faced, holding a pole that trembled in her hand.

The monster rippled and jerked, sending sour smoke over the water from its burning spots. "Push!" said Idris.

"Idris?" said Morgan, frowning.

"Push, idiot!" said Idris.

"There is no need to shout —"

"PUSH!" shouted Idris. He could feel the monster's mind again, strengthened by panic. But he could also see his hook, still lodged in a part of it that was burning now. Any minute now the hook would be burned through, his boots would catch, and all the lessons might as well never have happened, because they would have failed the Test, but it would not matter, because —

BURN, roared the monster.

— they would be a puff of ash.

"PUSH," shouted Idris and leaped onto the grilles over the monster cages, still holding the handle of his hook. The monster wriggled into a half turn, snapping. He heaved on the hook handle, trying to unbalance the creature. Other monsters writhed and snapped at his feet on the bars. Morgan jammed the pole on the monster's front half and pushed. Out of water it was clumsy, off balance. *NOOO*, cried a great voice in Idris's mind. Then the beast fell sideways with a titanic splash, and the door clanged down, and the stable of the Great Ambrose was quiet except for the slosh of water and the echo of alien thoughts.

"I thought you were doing the Welltop," said Morgan, put out by his interference, bless her.

"I fell down the chute," said Idris.

"And saved your bum, miss," said one of the hookmen, made over-frank by relief. "You don't often see a summoner as big as that. Highly dangerous, they are. If Master Idris hadn't —"

"Enough," said Morgan, very red.

Idris hid his pleasure. "Thank you, hookman," he said. "Mistress Morgan, thank you for your help."

Morgan went even redder and seemed about to say something about Idris not being so superior. Then she changed her mind. "Sir," she said and bowed. "I thank you, and give you my own congratulations, in the name of the Well."

"In the name of the Well," said Idris and caught an echo of monster thoughts from the stalls, *well, well, well.*

"And now," she said, "will you take breakfast, monstergroom?" And she grinned and hugged him.

"Monstergroom," said Idris, "I will." He pulled off his helmet, and flung it against the wall, and grabbed Morgan's hand, and they danced around in circles. After which, they went for breakfast, three grooms, very superior; and if Kay was the most superior of all, well, that was just Kay.

·PART TWO·

Oh, the beauty of darkness, red and blue flecks swimming, the Helpers drifting in the slow spirals of the tides toward the pillars of light that lanced into the world from the Wells.

When her mind was down here in the cool and lovely dark, she could hear the babel from above. The thoughts of men were like the thoughts of babies: eat, grab, sleep, laughably plain. Men were energetic, of course. They could make things. But they thought that making things was an end in itself. And they never asked themselves why they were doing it, and why the creatures who burned in their machines should submit to that horror. They were too full of themselves for that.

Of course there were men who could see outside the desires of their race. But there were few of them, and they were imperfect. One in particular there was. Not truly dangerous, though. More awkward, like one of their stones in one of their shoes. He would be watched, and brushed away, in his time. And there would be only quiet drifting in lovely darkness. A greater darkness, spread into the world of men.

The darkness would cover them, and she would cease her strife, and her line would continue in her darling boy.

There would be death. Much death.

But what was that to her?

Out of the darkgarden her mind flew, into the pillar of light, until she rose through the Well and the tunnels and into her tower, the bronze shutters closed tight against the light of Lyonesse. And her mind roved over the land. . . .

If she had had a face like other faces, she might have frowned. For where there had been one stone in the shoe, she felt the beginning of another: not even a stone yet — a grain of sand, perhaps. A grain that in the end she would crush to dust, or perhaps turn into a pearl so she could play with it before she dissolved it, screaming, in strong acid.

No. There was nothing to frown at. She could lie down and rejoice in her child, and feel the waters rising, and the land sinking, and that all was proceeding as she desired.

NINE

Now that the Test was out of the way, the grooms' quarters were made more comfortable. Morgan managed to get hold of some bright curtains and a part-worn carpet, on which she kept house. Idris found in the storerooms of the Great Ambrose a family tree of the Kings of Lyonesse, curiously squid-inked and illuminated with knots and beasts in shell-purple and fine gold. Something in the lists of names drew at his heart. He brought it up and hung it on his wall.

Ambrose had congratulated him and Morgan on their Tests and handed out the enamel devouring eel badges that in grooms replaced the embroidered versions worn by mere prentices. He had seemed in a hurry. Idris had been disappointed, hoping for more talk. But the mage had left on a journey, nobody knew where.

One night, Idris was reading in the Great Ambrose library, deep in a padded chair. After a while, something made him look up. An old man stood before him. Something about him seemed familiar, though Idris could not tell what.

"Sir," said Idris, displeased at the disturbance, but rising as the Manner dictated.

"Idris Limpet," said the man.

Idris was surprised. Now that he was Idris House Ambrose, he had not realized how nearly he had forgotten his old name. The man turned toward him. Idris drew his breath in a gasp. "You have grown," said Master Omnium, the schoolmaster of the Westgate.

Idris opened his mouth to return the compliment with another. He could not.

Master Omnium's face had been handsome and clever and compact. Now, it looked as if it had been raked with monsterhooks. One of the eyes was gone. The lid of the other sagged over a red and weeping orb. The mouth had been torn open at one corner, and the skull was out of shape, as if it had been pressed.

"It is good to see you here," said Idris, concealing his horror. "You are welcome."

"I am not," said Master Omnium, in a hoarse parody of his old, clear voice. "I live by the charity of my old friend Great Ambrose. And if I can tell you anything, you will find me here in the library."

Idris bowed, horrified. He would have liked to take his eyes off the ruined face. Instead, he made himself look firmly in the one good eye and said, "Master, I find you changed."

Something like a smile lifted the corner of the mouth. "And I you," said Omnium. "For the better; I am grateful that you do not merely look away. Since you are wondering, Captain Ironhorse and his masters . . . put to me the question as to your whereabouts. To which I made no answer. You, though, I will gladly answer, on any subject. Now you have done your duty, and you may go."

Idris bowed and left.

In the next few days he was busy, standing his watches, gaining experience.

One night, he was supposed to be keeping night watch. Instead, he was dreaming.

He was in the Westgate, and he was on the Wall with the whole family, and he was trying to stop the ears of the Precious Stones against the sound of someone Captain Ironhorse was torturing in the school —

Someone was shaking his shoulder. He saw red hair and green eyes in the candlelight.

"Why are you asleep? You're on watch. Something's loose," said Morgan.

Before the words were out, Idris had heard it for himself. He swung his legs out of bed. He had his clothes on — monstergrooms did not undress on night watch (nor did they put their heads on the pillow, not even for a tiny moment).

By the Well, thought Idris, I am a fool.

He found himself stumbling onto the landing. He could hear the voice in his head now, even through the iron door. It was the cage nine burner, a nice burner as Idris understood burners nowadays, a bit of a shapeshifter, one of the rare funny ones, but not, of course, to be trusted.

He pulled his boiled-leather suit over his jersey and fumbled at the buttons. "Here, let me," said Morgan.

"Go back to bed," said Idris.

"Are you sure you can manage?" said Morgan, mostly to annoy him.

"Quite sure," said Idris, impatient. Then, attacked by guilt, "Thank you for waking me."

"Be careful," said Morgan, still being annoying.

Idris marched forth to do his duty.

When he opened the iron door to the stables he heard a shuffle and a squelch from below. The voice in his mind was louder now. *Here you come*, said the voice. *Here you are, my noble young friend, my hero, who will lead me to freedom out of pure goodness of heart.*

"How did you get out?" said Idris aloud. He had come to realize monsters were creatures, not things. Every creature needed a way of protecting itself. All you had to do was understand it.

Take me to the Well, it cooed in his head.

"Back in your cage," said Idris. "Where do you think you're going?"

To the Colony.

"What's that?" said Idris, humoring it.

Where my friends live, beyond your lake.

Idris sighed. "Back in the cage."

Won't, said the monster. The voice between Idris's ears sounded like warm syrup. *Let me lead you to my darkgarden, deepest green, where the little fish sing —*

Idris came off the stairs and into the monsterstable. Halfway down the causeway on the right-hand side one of the pen grilles was hinged open.

"Oh, go on, back in," said Idris wearily, pulling down his visor.

The thing standing on the causeway had found a useful shape. Well, not standing, exactly. More *being,* on three stubs that might have been legs if they had been longer and if they had ended in anything like feet, or hooves, or claws, or anything but these stumpy little tree trunks each fringed with something that might have been a fin.

At this point, Idris was meant to muffle and use force. But he knew that his mind was stronger than most monsters' now. Besides, he preferred persuasion. There was enough pain in burner lives.

"Oi," he said. "Milking stool. In. By the Treaty."

The monster raised what was possibly a finger in what was certainly a rude sign. *Don't give me Treaty,* said the voice in his head, more like vinegar than honey now. *We know you. Your blood is in the Well. The Treaty is nonsense.*

Idris found himself frowning. This was not normal. They read minds, he told himself, and use the weaknesses they find. But he merely said, "Look, you're starting." Smoke was rising from the monster's shoulder. It was drying out.

The monster started to stump toward Idris with a rolling three-legged gait. The smoke from its shoulder stung Idris's eyes behind his visor. A patch of blue-white was growing there, very bright in the gray of predawn.

"Last warning," said Idris. "Back or slime." Why was this creature ready to burn before its time?

Because I must prove to you that what I say is true.

Again, Idris should have muffled. But as usual his curiosity got the better of him. "Know what?" he said.

That you are destined to change all this. Look at the main meter. Ask in the Colony.

Then the voice became a roar of agony and rage, and smoke poured from it in a thick white cloud, and it glowed blue and pink, throwing the shadows of the hoists onto the vault. Idris could feel the heat of it even through his visor. The stone went glassy under its feet as it thumped toward him, screaming.

Idris sighed. He picked up a shield and dropped to one knee. He jammed the base of the shield into the shield slot on the causeway. He engaged the nozzle of the slimehurl with the shield orifice and squeezed the bag. The slime shot out of the hurl in a green lump. For a moment, it seemed to pause in front of the glowing monster like a cloud before a setting sun. Then it made contact, locked with the burning fabric of the creature, settled and spread, eating the fire, until the monster's light went out and it cooled.

"Now if you please, honorable creature of the Well," said Idris, using the formal words prescribed in the useless Treaty, "return to your quarters and wait patiently for what may next befall, in accordance with the agreements between our rulers."

This can change, said the voice in his mind, no more than a whimper now and a feeling of struggle.

He prodded the monster back into its cage and locked it down, wondering all the while how it had escaped. He kept his eyes about him as he went over to the hoppers to get the monsters' breakfast. Sure enough, there beside a fish bin was a serf, hiding his eyes behind his hands as if by not seeing he could avoid being seen.

"Good morning," said Idris, polite as a gateguard's son, not arrogant like a monstergroom.

"Dunna kill me, young master," said the serf, peering between his fingers at the figure in the scorched flame suit. "It made me loose it. Dunna kill me."

"No chance," said Idris. "What did it tell you?"

"It?" said the serf, both his teeth chattering. "It said it would give me a big royal spread of food for me childrens. You get terrible money on the barges. I was working on the furnaces night shift hammerin' clinker for extra. It called me in. Dirty monster brute." The serf spat into the nearest monstertank. Something swirled and ate the gobbet.

"Your name?" said Idris.

"Wayncull Hedger."

Idris fumbled open his boiled-leather tunic, felt in a pocket, and found a silver. He pushed it into Wayncull's hand, hustled him up the stairs, and opened the little wicket in the loading gate. The serf scuttled off into the misty street, heading for the streets of hovels by the barge-quays on the lakeshore. Idris went back to the hagfish hoppers, hooked one up, and hauled it out onto the rails above the tanks. The monsters stirred in their cages. As the hopper crossed the cages, Idris pulled the release line. The hagfish cascaded into the cells. Absently Idris watched one coil around a bar, then slide away, pulled violently loose by the thing below the water.

The monster had puzzled him.

Burners always talked to monstergrooms about dark-gardens, and to Knights about hunting, and to serfs about food. So it was no surprise that it had talked to Idris about the Treaty.

But what was this about the main meter and the Colony?

The main meter was taboo, like the Old Well. No surprise that a monster was trying to cause trouble there. But what was the Colony? He would have asked Ambrose, but Ambrose was gone. Into his mind came the wrecked visage of Master Omnium.

But now the grooms of the day watch were clattering down the stairs. "Handing over," he said to his relief. "In the name of the Well."

"In the name of the Well," said the relief.

150

As he was changing out of his flame suit, Morgan stuck her red head around the door. "Couldn't sleep," she said. "Oh! It hurt you."

"Really?" said Idris, squinting vaguely at a patch of burned skin on his arm above the elbow.

"You need some balm of bladderwrack on that," said Morgan, banging out of the door to the medicine cupboard. She came back. "Hold still," she said, smearing. "Oh, by the way, happy birthday." She handed him a parcel.

"I had forgotten," said Idris. He smiled at her, unwrapping. "A Wolf Rock pie," he said.

"My parents sent it. They say happy birthday, too." She smiled. "This time, you know what it is."

Idris pretended to swat her around the ear. He thanked her. It was truly good to have a friend. They ate the pie together. Then it was time for her duty.

Reflecting alone in his cell, Idris remembered his last birthday, at home in the Westgate with his family. Being suddenly twelve did not make you less lonely. Thinking of the Westgate led his thoughts again to Master Omnium.

He walked to the library. Master Omnium sat twisted in a deep chair by the fire. "Excuse me, Master," said Idris, steeling himself for the sight of the hideous face. "I have a question."

"Then I am glad you came," said Omnium, with a gratitude in his voice that went straight to Idris's heart.

"A monster spoke to me," said Idris. "It told me that I am known in the Well. It told me I should consult the main meter and speak to the Colony, whatever that is. Master, I believed this monster. Am I a fool?"

Master Omnium's ruined face twitched. "You should ask yourself, not me," he said. "And these are the questions you should ask. Why did anyone bother to save me from Westgate, where I was lowly among the lowly? Why was I singled out for training by Great Ambrose? Why was I saved from a Well when others were let perish? Why do I hate Captains, despise the Dolphin, but love the Realm? If I wish to see the main meter, why do I not walk from the check machines to the meter, and knock upon the door? And if I wish to speak to the creatures of the Colony, why do I not keep my mind open next time I am in the Poison Ground?" He wheezed a laugh. "It is the job of a teacher to put questions in minds, not answers. It is questions that will draw you along the road you must travel."

Idris sat for a moment gazing at the golden ruin of the ashes in the library fire. To protect him, this man had suffered agony. Anything he said was not a monsterdream, but truth.

Next day Idris was off watch in the late morning. It was a slack time, with small tides in the Wells and no monstercatching worth speaking of. He took nuncheon with Morgan and Kay at the Wrestler's Elbow. Morgan and Kay talked of Knightly pleasures, green leaves and gold stone and the joys of hunting, and how they longed for air untainted by Wellwater. Idris longed for it, too. But he kept quiet, because he did not think the other two would be interested in his small life as a Westgate Limpet. Also, he was nerving himself to carry out the plan he had made for that afternoon.

When they had finished eating, he left them talking and went into the street. He picked his way through monstercarts carrying tanks to the barge-wharves and a group of pack cattle slung with ingots of silver from the Southgate. He threaded the woven awnings of the market stalls in Cheap Street and came at last to the square over which loomed the granite portico of the Hall of Meters. The Mountmen on either side of the door looked at the enamel devouring eel on his shoulder and let him through. So did the inner guards. Idris passed by the check machines and went straight for the Hall of Clerks. "Can I help you?" said a clerk, looking down his nose at this child.

"I wish to consult the records," said Idris.

The clerk took time to squeeze a pimple in a bronze mirror. "For what purpose?"

"I am monstergroom of the Great Ambrose," said Idris, making himself stay humble in the face of this lack of Manner. "I seek to oblige my honored master with a new system of predicting the Welltides."

"Oh, I see," said the clerk, examining the results of his pimple squeezing. "So you have, what, eleven summers?"

"Twelve," said Idris. There was a difference, and he and Morgan had marked it with a pie.

"Ten thousand pardons," said the clerk, dripping with sarcasm. "In that case, O wise one, I will give you the skins you require. And I look forward to hearing what in your wisdom you may discover. Bring a basket." He led Idris over to a room of shelves and started pulling down armfuls of skins and stuffing them into the basket. "There," he said. "There will not be above thirty or forty more basketfuls that deal with the last five years. Beyond that, well, they are as the stars in the sky, but for one of your wisdom and skill that will be no worry. When you are finished with these I shall give you the next lot."

Idris made his eyes big and round and innocent. "I thank you, brother clerk," he said. "I am lucky to have met one who takes joy in explaining complicated matters to simple people."

The clerk took this flattery as his due. He led Idris down a passage to a windowless room with a desk, lit a fish-oil lamp, and said, "Good luck, brat."

The door closed.

Idris waited until the clerk's shuffling footsteps died away. Then he got up, opened the door, and put out his head. The corridor stretched in both directions, old, twisted by tremors. But empty.

He swallowed. It was time to be as ignorant and stupid as the clerk had expected him to be. He shoveled the papers back into the basket, picked it up, walked out of the cell and turned left, away from the Hall of Clerks, making himself step firmly, as if he knew where he was going.

A new corridor ran across the end of the one he was in. Nailed feet tramped its quake-cracked flagstones. Idris let his mind steal out, caught a hint of hard, soldierly thoughts.

Mountmen. Into the military mind he crept, and dropped an idea: *main meter.*

The footsteps halted. He stepped back into a doorway, heart hammering. Overconfident. Fool.

"What?" said a Mount-harsh voice.

"Something in my head," said another. "Monster, feels like. Search the — whoa!"

The ground under Idris's feet twitched and shuddered with a Well-tremor. Lumps of stone fell out of the ceiling and crashed onto the corridor flags. "Ow!" said one of the Mountmen voices.

"One of these days it'll all fall down," said the other. "We'll find you a leech." The feet tramped off, one set limping slightly.

Idris stayed in his doorway, faint with relief.

Before the Mountman had felt Idris poking at his mind, Idris had seen a picture there. A corridor, with various turnings and a flight of stairs. And at the end of the corridor at the stairtop a chamber of vaulted stone. And in that chamber, a meter. *Two* meters. And to get into that chamber, a sequence of stones outside that must be pushed, turned, weighted, and unweighted in a careful sequence.

But how would he walk unseen down hundreds of yards of passages?

BONG, said a bell somewhere. The floor trembled again. A dim roar of voices sounded in the Hall of Meters.

It was the Hour of Thanks.

Idris had been brought up in a world slung around the regular silence of the Hour of Thanks, the silence that let him thank the Well, and examine his heart for things he had done, and to hear the great slow pulse of the land in stillness and peace.

But something was wrong with the heart of the world, and something in Idris was telling him that only he could find what it was.

Flying in the face of custom, habit, and Manner, Idris began to run.

TEN

Down the corridor he ran, his feet beating the flagstones over the muted sounds of the Hour. He turned right at the end, then left up a curling stair, along a corridor lined with the worn escutcheons of forgotten Captains, following what he had glimpsed in the Mountman's mind. And all of a sudden he was at the blind end of a passage, standing in front of a blank wall.

The floor on which he stood bore the device of a battlemented tower, sign of the Old Well. Normally the tower was shown sealed. Here, it was spouting. This place and its machinery must be as old as the Old King, who had dug and capped the Old Well. Idris shivered with awe.

But the Hour of Thanks was passing fast. He made himself stay calm, moving his fingers in the sequence of shifts and presses he had seen in the Mountman's mind.

The wall remained gray, slablike, immobile. He began to panic. He was where he should not be.

His heart was beating loud enough to hurt his ears. He looked down. The door in the center of the Old Well symbol was made of a different stone from the rest of the tower. A voice inside him, like Master Omnium's but somehow deep and ancient, said, *If I wish to see the main meter, shall I not knock upon the door?*

Automatically he trusted the voice. He put his foot on the door and pressed.

The wall in front of him slid aside. He took three steps forward.

He was in the presence of the main meter.

It was a dial with a single hand, made of ancient bronze, surrounded by signs in a script strange to him. Beside it was another dial.

He felt a thrumming of the stone under his feet. At first he paid no attention to it; the ground in the Valley of Apples was usually thrumming, or creaking, or shuddering. But this was different, like the running of a river. Except that there were no rivers in the Valley of Apples.

He examined the meter. The bronze pointer was up, shaking, as if measuring a flow of water. But there was no tide, no water to measure. How could this be? In the middle of the green and ancient dial of the meter next to it was the device of the Old Well. The Old Well, blocked and stopped these seven hundred years.

So why was the pointer on the Old Well up and trembling, too?

There was a rack of skin scrolls in an alcove by the meter, each in its bronze tube. The Hour of Thanks was almost done.

Idris took a tube at random from the bottom of the rack, pulled out the skin, and stuffed it among the other skins in the basket. Then he started to walk swiftly back the way he had come, pressing the skin lower as he went. Behind him, the door of the main meter slid shut.

BONG, said a great bell somewhere in the building.

The Hour of Thanks was over.

Suddenly the corridors were rustling to the scuff of feet and the murmur of voices. Idris kept walking. Feet sounded ahead of him. A Captain came around the corner, rolls of stomach bulging his crimson robe, talking to someone who looked like a scribe. His small, cunning eyes rested briefly on Idris. Idris bowed low, passed him, and walked on, trying to make himself shrink to ant size. It's working, he thought. Ten steps, fifteen. He had gotten away with it.

The footsteps behind him stopped. "I say," said a voice, high and petulant. "You. Groom."

Idris turned. The Captain and the scribe were looking at him. He bowed obsequiously. "Sir?" he said.

The piggy eyes went to the eel badge on his shoulder. "What is one of the grooms of Ambrose doing in here?"

"Research, sir."

"Into?"

"The tides, sir."

"You are far from the Hall of Clerks."

"Am I, sir?" Idris did not dare unmuffle, but he supposed that the Captain would feel a powerful scorn for everyone except himself. "Oh, dear, silly me, I am lost, alas. Would you mind telling me which way I should go?"

"Do I look like a signpost?" said the Captain.

Actually he looked like a fat bullock. Idris bowed again to hide his grin. The scribe said, "Back, brat. First sinister. Straight ahead. Ask your master for a beating."

"Sir. Your honor," said Idris. He hunched over his basket, clutching the handle with both hands, and scuttled away around the corner, full of wild inward laughter. He shut the door of the cell behind him and took deep breaths to still the thump of his heart. Then he took the lambskins out of the basket and laid them on the desk.

The lambskin he had taken from the chamber of the main meter was dated Year 2 of the Cycle of the Gull, Hay Moon. He went back to the Hall of Clerks, bowed to the clerk, who ignored him, and took from the shelves Year 2 of the Cycle of the Gull, Hay Moon. Then he went back to the cell and spread the lambskins on the table next to one another and compared the results.

All laughter left him, and his mind filled with a great and dreadful silence.

The skin from the Hall of Clerks recorded that in the Hay Moon of that year, twenty-one dam feet of water had been admitted to Lyonesse.

The skin from the chamber of the main meter recorded that in the Hay Moon of that year, one thousand two hundred and nine dam feet had been admitted into Lyonesse.

The ground trembled under Idris's feet, and the writing on the skin blurred with the table's shudder.

To cope with that much Wellwater, the Council would have had to issue more than three thousand burner licenses in a single month. According to the skin from the Hall of Clerks, they had issued forty.

Someone was letting in enough water to flood the land of Lyonesse. Or at the very least to spread the Poison Ground.

Very carefully, Idris folded the main meter skin. He put his hand outside the bars and stuffed the skin into one of the deep cracks in the masonry, where nobody would find it until the building fell down. Then he packed the other skins carefully into the basket and carried them back into the hall.

At zupper that night, Morgan looked at him, frowning. "Are you all right?" she said.

"Pass the nutdust, would you?" said Idris.

Morgan passed it. "What's happening?" she said.

"Thank you," said Idris.

"Your nose is blue," said Morgan.

"Oh," said Idris, eating.

"And your ears are green."

"Exactly," said Idris. "Excuse me, would you?"

Morgan watched the door shut behind him. The food was bustard leg and sea kale, very delicious. But she pushed it around her plate, suddenly not hungry. Being a monstergroom was all very well. But it was lonely up here in this tower, and it was even lonelier when Idris did not want to talk.

She pushed away the bustard. Well, she would just have to make him listen. Stop him wandering away in his head like that. It was probably because he was lonely, too. It must be terrible, having a family but not being able to see them. All that stuff with Captains and drowning cells in Westgate. Horrible. He needed looking after, properly. . . .

Then Morgan had an idea.

I know exactly what to do to cheer us both up, she thought.

Pulling gullquill and squidink toward her, she smoothed a blank lambskin and began to write a letter.

The library was a big, dark universe splashed with pools of lamplight. As Idris approached the third lamp, he saw the smashed remains of Master Omnium's face. "Master," he said, sitting down. "I have a question. If more water was coming into Lyonesse than was declared by the Council, what would that mean?"

Omnium's single eye was a pit of shadow. "That someone was cheating," he said. "That things were being done that the Council wishes to hide from the people. Perhaps the Council wishes to please the Regent. Enough. Go."

But why, thought Idris as he walked back to his quarters, would a poison river running into Lyonesse please the Council or the Regent?

In his cell he sat on his bed and tried to make sense of it all. Think as he would, it made none. Suddenly the door opened. Morgan put her head around it. She looked cheerful. "Listen," she said. "I've written to my parents. They'll ask Ambrose if I can go home for the New Deer next moon. It's the first day of the deer hunting, such fun. Why don't you come with me?"

Idris nearly said, No, go away, I'm thinking. Then he thought, Actually the New Deer is the great festival of the Knights, a time when families get together in a private way. It is a great kindness that Morgan has asked me to the Wolf Rock. I can as easily think there as here. He said, "That would be very good!"

"Hooray!" she said, pink and delighted at the success of her scheme. "We'll get some fresh air and I can show you my father's country." She started to bounce and became a new, excited, rather homesick Morgan, going on about her dog that had had puppies, which would be quite big by now, and the frieze in her room that her mother was doing in special pink shells from the Fal Mouth, and the cousins who would be at the New Deer revels.

"And we'll put you in the Sea Room," said Morgan. "It's got tapestries in shell-blue and Tyrian purple, with merboys and mergirls and corsairs a-dancing 'round the salt fires of the Lower Sea. You'll absolutely love it!"

Idris saw a vision of green leaves and golden stone, a place far from filthy rivers and crooked councils. It was a long time since he had been anywhere bright and happy. "I certainly will," he said.

The morning Idris and Morgan set out for the Wolf Rock the horses pranced in the street outside the Ambrose, catching the excitement of their riders. They rode side by side through the crush of carts and people, showed their passes at the gate, and came out on to the Great Road. "Lambert!" shouted Morgan, standing up in her stirrups.

A bandy, curly-headed squire was waiting in front of the traveler's inn by the gate. Now he turned toward her, grinning hugely, and spurred his horse to her side.

Morgan introduced Idris. "Stinks here," said Lambert, who seemed deeply suspicious of all things cityish. "Shall we go?"

Off they trotted, down the road out of the Valley of Apples, past the barges carrying cut monsters over the lake, around the dam, and into the Poison Ground. Soon the poisoned lands lay about them, fading into a dark-brown haze. They threaded the river embankments and poison pools; Idris thought he heard the voices of monsters. At nightfall they came to the ruins on the mound, where they had stayed all that time ago on their way to the Valley of Apples. The little blackened people recognized them and stood on tiptoe to slap them on the back and greeted them in their hoarse little voices.

As Idris lay in the dark, waiting for sleep, he heard voices. Not the voices of his companions, or the little people of the mound — monster voices, in his head. *Happy*, they said. *Happy, in the Colony.*

And Idris knew beyond a doubt what the Colony was, and where in Lyonesse the river that flowed through the Old Well had its issue. He slept.

Next day they woke early, with sore throats and smarting eyes, Kek coughing on the wall of the ruined barbican. All day they rode. Around sunset they saw the first green bush, with a yellowhammer bouncing over it. As night crept over the land from the east, the harsh smell of the Ground was driven away by the smell of thick green woods, and Morgan began humming a small, happy tune, and Idris felt happier than he had been since he left the Westgate, excited at the prospect of clear air and kind people and a holiday. And finally, under a moon lopsided with the days remaining before the feast of New Deer, their hooves clattered up the hairpin road to the Wolf Rock.

Last time he had been here, Idris had been dazed with worry and exhaustion. Now, he was able to see that the Wolf Rock was more than a simple tower. A curtain wall enclosed a couple of fields. At one corner stood a set of stables and a great hall, from the end of which rose a lofty square tower. It must have been built for defense. But arrowslits had been enlarged into windows, and the portcullis had become a beautifully wrought gate of bronze wolves howling at a copper moon, so now it was a big, comfortable house whose windows overlooked league upon league of forest and farm.

"Mother and Father, I name Idris House Ambrose, Monstergroom," said Morgan in the moonlit courtyard.

The father bowed and said, "He is already known." Then the mother, the beautiful, powdery, sweet-smelling Lady Nena, kissed him on the face. "Welcome back, Squire Idris," she said. "Morgan tells us you have been a true friend to her."

In they went and ate zupper in a room clad in tapestries, and Idris was shown to the Sea Room, which was indeed beautiful, and whose bed wrapped him like a cloud. He stretched, luxuriating in the linen sheets. Last time I came here, he thought, I felt small and terrified, and I had never even seen a meat pie before. Now, six moons later, I feel that this tower is the right size and shape for me. This is destiny at work.

At which point he went to sleep.

When he awoke, someone was drawing the curtains, and sun was pouring through the window. "Up," said Morgan's voice, full of the confidence of being home.

But Idris lay a moment in the cloud-soft bed and rejoiced that today he did not have to quarrel with monsters in the stink of poison.

"Come *on*," said Morgan, extremely brisk. "We are going to teach you to ride."

"I already can."

"Not the way we mean riding," said Morgan.

"We?"

"Knights. It's the New Deer. It means hunting. There are some clothes on the chair."

Idris washed in the giant clamshell built into the wall. The clothes fitted well: a tunic of greenish cloth smelling of sunshine, not Wellstink; trousers; and long boots of soft leather infinitely comfortable after the clumpers that were issued to monstergrooms. After breakfast, Lambert was waiting with the horses in the yard.

"Well," said Lambert. "We'll pop out and see, will we?" He led his pupils and their horses on to the Bleaching Green, a big flat ledge, grassy and set with rocks, on which the tower's linen was spread to dry after the wash.

Morgan went around first. Her pony was light, with pointed toes that floated it over the rocks while she balanced in the saddle like a Kernow wave rider. "Not bad," said Lambert, when she came back. "Now then. Idris."

Idris clambered onto his horse. He could ride for a journey, but this jumping looked nothing short of dangerous. With his mind, he said to the horse, *Excuse me, but this will be embarrassing for both of us.*

The horse's mind was wild and proud and unclear, but Idris thought he heard it say, *For you, maybe.* He felt its muscles bunch under him. It thundered up to a boulder, launched itself into the air, came down with a quadruple thump, changed direction, floated over another boulder, and came down with another thump.

After the first leap, Idris had landed hanging on to the horse's mane, trying to look casual. After the second he was still trying to look casual, but with less success, because he had come off the horse and was lying winded on the short turf.

"Huh," said Lambert, while Morgan hid her laughter behind her hand.

Idris lay and watched late swallows hawking for insects in the high blue and tried to remember how to breathe.

The horse rolled its eye, whinnying.

Peace, sent Idris.

For you, maybe, sent the horse.

Idris got to his feet and tried again.

And again.

"No," said Morgan, after the fifth fall.

"Let him," said Lambert, who now had an odd expression on his face. For Idris was falling, but he was learning, too. Learning fast.

"That's enough for now," said Lambert, after Idris had made his first circuit, jumping all the boulders. He led the horse away. Idris tried to look disappointed, though actually he had taken enough battering for one day.

"Pretty good," said Morgan.

"Not as good as you."

"I learned when I was three," said Morgan. "Have a bath. There's some balm of stinket. It'll unbruise you." She picked a bow from a rack. "I'm going to do some shooting." She sighed. "It is so good to be home."

Idris felt the pang of one with no home of his own. But he was glad to see her happy. As he climbed painfully up the steps to the bathhouse, he sent his mind looking for Kek. The gull was descending rapidly toward a cliff, on what must have been High Kernow. The shapes became hounds, and men on horses. At the foot of the cliff something bloody struggled among boulders, then became still.

Kek cheered hoarsely and swooped toward it. Idris felt a shadow fall over the world. He shivered and withdrew.

The moon was not yet full, but the New Deer were falling.

The hunting season had begun.

"So," said Uther Wolf Rock, setting his humorous eyes on Idris and draining a glass of Iber wine. "Apparently you learn pretty fast."

They were at zupper around a long table in the bright hall of the Wolf Rock. Morgan's family had made Idris feel completely at home. Now he bowed. "They say it takes thirty falls to become a horseman. I'm not even halfway there."

"Hmph," said Uther, with an oddly searching glance. "Anyway. It seems you are advancing toward Captaincy. You don't sound selfish enough to be much of a Captain, though. From what Morgan and Ambrose and now Lambert tell me, you have the makings of a Knight. Well, let me tell you, there's not much future in Knighthood these days. Which is why

Morgan is in that ghastly Well place. That horrible fishy Regent woman —"

"Uther," said his wife sharply.

Uther said, "I am talking to Idris like this because he has been a good friend to Morgan and Ambrose trusts him and I trust Ambrose. Idris, you know and I know that if this goes any further there will be trouble, but this is one of the only places in the land that isn't heaving with spies. Fact is, they don't like us on the Mount. They like Captains and their horrible stinks. And my silly ancestor was pleased when they said he didn't have to provide a lot of serfs to labor on the Walls anymore, and they'd pump it out with their ghastly monsters instead. And now the land's sinking, and do they care? If you ask me —"

"*Uther!*" hissed Lady Nena.

"— if you ask me," Uther plowed on, "it is too late now and the land's too low and the Poison Ground is spreading, and the only saving of the land will be if we get more Knights and fewer fat-bottomed Captains, but if you tell anyone this and the Mount hears about it, it's off to the dungeons and out with the crushing hammers —"

"Uther!" cried Nena. "Do shut up. What about the other thing?"

"Oh," said Uther. "Sorry. Got carried away." He went to a chest and brought out a bundle. "Now look here," he said. "As I was saying, you've been jolly nice to Morgan. And we heard you didn't have much of a birthday."

"I had a very good pie," said Idris, with total sincerity. "It really cheered us up."

"Good," said Uther, while Nena directed her beautiful smile upon Idris. "Well, we've got something else for you." And he handed the bundle to Idris.

It was long and narrow, wrapped in a black cloth.

"Unwrap it," said Morgan, excited. "Go on."

It was a dagger, with a handle of black stone and a blade two handspans long. The blade was razor sharp and shone silver, beautiful and deadly in the window light.

"Just an old thing. Been lying around for years," said Uther. "Centuries, actually. It is beastbane. Iron, you know. We hope you find it useful."

Idris bowed. This was a truly valuable present. He was deeply moved. "It is a royal gift," he said. "If the Rock needs defense, you may call upon me and it." This was the Manner, but he found he meant it, from the bottom of his heart.

"Oh, well, thank you," said Uther, with a laugh. "Learn to use it, and use it wisely."

"Well!" cried Lady Nena briskly, rising from the table in a clatter of silver necklaces. "Busy day tomorrow. There's Caum the harper by the fire. Then bed!"

Next day was the New Deer. It was scarcely light when Idris staggered downstairs, stiff and sore from his many falls. Still he seemed to be late for breakfast — instead of the usual spread of bread and fruit and meat and salt cheese, all that remained was a single loaf, much torn at, and some butter. A servitor was perched halfway up the stone tracery of the window, polishing panes in the first gleam of sun. Two more were scrubbing the flagstones. The air was full of the clammy smell of scouring ash. "They're getting ready for the New Deer feast tonight," said Morgan, putting her head around the door. She was dressed, Idris noted gloomily, for riding. "I thought you wouldn't want to go hunting. The whole tower is upside down, so we'll go for a ride instead. Come on!"

So there was Idris strapping on his new blade, hobbling into the stables, saddling up his horse with fingers that somehow knew what to do, and trotting down the road behind Morgan, every muscle in his body yelling that it would rather be on a nice soft cushion. He hoped the ride would be a short one. But on Morgan rode, bow slung on her shoulder, through a rolling green forest, past streams, the land trending downward until they came to a flat, grassy meadow. A couple of hundred yards away a herd of aurochs was grazing, the smallest of them twice the size of the horses. A river flowed through the meadow, a slow river, winding. Across it someone had built a weir of woven sticks. Big silver fish were hurling themselves at the bend of the water over the wattle barrier.

"What's this?" said Idris.

"The salmon weir. They're going upstream to lay their eggs."

Idris lay down on the bank and put his head over the edge, watching the huge fish waving in the jewel-green deeps of the pool. "Better than monsters," he said.

"Much."

They fell silent.

It was one of those days you get before leaf-fall, a day that feels like summer still, but a day when the birds are getting ready for winter, too busy to sing. The world was green, greener than green, drenched in thick golden light. Swallows swam in that light: a whirling tower of swallows, sucking in other swallows ready for the great pilgrimage across the sea. So huge and pregnant was the silence that Idris did not even want to think, for fear of disturbing it. He lay and watched the fish, bathing in the peace.

Of course the silence was not a real silence. There was the rustle of leaves, the tick of insects in the grass, the mew of a buzzard over the woods.

And the baying of hounds.

Idris sat up.

There seemed a depth to the sound, a wildness not quite like ordinary hounds. It was coming closer.

Morgan was sitting up, too. Her face was pale. She was looking at the edge of the forest, where the trees came down to the meadow. Something gray and glistening lolloped out of the trees. Idris leaned forward then rose to his feet. "Impossible," he said.

"What is?"

Across the river the bull aurochs put its enormous nose in the air, stamped a hoof the size of a tree stump, and tossed its horns. The noise of hounds was much closer. The bull aurochs put himself between the noise and his cows.

"It's a monster," said Idris. There could be no mistake; he had seen it in the *Diversitie*. "A slimehare. Coated in stuff like snot, so it won't burn in air. Fast, too."

"It can't be."

With a crash of hound music the hunt burst out of the trees.

"Oh," said Morgan and turned white.

The hounds were the biggest Idris had ever seen. They were the size of ponies, and their muzzles dripped greenish foam, and even a bowshot away their eyes could be seen to glare red fire.

"This is *disgusting!*" said Morgan. "What are they?"

Idris's mind was still in the *Diversitie of Monsters*. "Halfhounds," he said. "They come of breeding deerhounds with the monsters known as shriekets. Crosses, in effect. Good on a scent, and ferocious —"

"But who hunts monsters with halfhounds? On the New Deer?"

A group of horsemen burst in to view, horns shrill, yodeling cries. "They do," said Idris grimly.

The slimehare was galloping across the meadow, leaving a trail of flattened grass. It shrieked in Idris's mind with the terror of pursuit, drowning the buzzards and the alarm calls of blackbirds.

"You! Serfs!" cried a high, angry voice. "Stop that dragon or you die!"

Idris had been moving forward to cut the slimehare off from the river, hand going to the hilt of his new iron dagger. The voice brought on a sudden attack of stubbornness. He looked at Morgan. Morgan looked back at him, unslinging her bow. She looked as rebellious as he felt. Her head moved, a finger's breadth right, a finger's breadth left. He turned to the man who had shouted and called, "It's not a dragon, it's a slimehare."

The slimehare tumbled into the river. The halfhounds came to the riverbank and stood shrieking at the rolling wake the monster left as it powered away downstream.

The hunters approached. The horse in front was a beautiful black mare with a boy on her back. The boy was about twelve. He wore black breeches and tunic, and a hat of black fur pulled down over a big white face. A liver-colored mouth said in the high, cross voice, "They spoiled it! Someone kill them. Will *nobody* kill them?"

Idris drew his dagger.

"*Well?*" said the boy, his hot black eyes slithering over Idris and landing on Morgan, standing with arrow nocked. Even if Idris had not recognized the face, he would have known that he was in the presence of Kyd Murther, Dolphin of the Realm. He knew that the threat was real and terrible. But he could not feel afraid. Instead he felt a great, weary sadness that the peace of the world had been ripped apart, and that this nasty creature, so ugly, so powerful, had crawled through the hole.

Into his mind there came a sudden, surprising thought: *Something will have to be done about this person.*

Where did that come from? he thought, pushing it quickly away. For behind the spoiled brat with his huntsmen he could feel something else: a presence, watchful, protective, savage as beak and claws. The brat's mother . . .

Idris took a deep breath. He bowed, his hand on the pommel of his iron dagger. "We were watching the fish," he said.

"I don't care what you were doing. You are going to die. Slowly. Huntsman, put the dogs on them," said the boy.

Idris bowed low, taking his time, feeling cool and confident as if the open air was his element, not this Dolphin's. "It was just that we did not know you were talking to us, for you seemed to be addressing serfs," he said. "Permit me to name myself. I am Idris House Ambrose, Great Ambrosegroom."

"And I am Morgan Wolf Rock House Ambrose, Great Ambrosegroom," said Morgan.

The youth's savage look gave way to something sulkier. "Oh. Well," he said. "Whip those brutes away!" he yelled at the huntsman, who was now approaching with his creatures. "Find me something else to kill. I want to *kill* something."

"My lord Dolphin," said the huntsman, bowing deeply.

"Shut up or I will have your children throttled," said the Dolphin absently. He was staring very hard at Morgan, his tongue running around his mouth. "Yes. Miss, ah, er. I bid you come to the Mount at Darksolsticetide. You have found favor in my eyes, and I grant you this boon and another should you ask one."

"Dolphin, you do me too much honor," said Morgan, bowing low. The white face smirked. "As for your boon, I beg I may bring my friend and brother Idris with me."

The smirk vanished. "Yes. Well. Let him come," hissed the Kyd between his teeth.

"Your graciousness is as a healing rain," said Morgan sweetly. "Now would you tell your huntsman to call off the hounds before I have to shoot one? Only I fear they will kill my father's aurochs."

The Kyd's purple lip jutted, and his eyes were full of sulky rage. "Huntsman, your children will die in torment unless you control your pack and find me something to kill."

The huntsman glanced at the hounds. He must have talked to them with his mind, for they yelped as if scorched and cast around, noses down. "Darksolstice, then, Morgan and er," said the Kyd.

A hound shrieked; others joined in. "Ground sloth!" cried the huntsman.

"Kill!" shrieked the horsemen. The hunt rode away after their savage quarry, which ate only grass and whose top speed was a slow walk.

"Splendid sportsmen," said Idris. "How do burners get into the woods?"

"They don't. They must have brought this one from a Well and let it go so they could hunt it."

Idris's thoughts were following the slimehare. "Where does the river go?"

"Across the Poison Ground on a causeway. Then into the Fal."

The slimehare would not thrive in the sea. But it would be happy in the bitter waters of the Poison Ground.

With the rest of the Colony.

"Bad luck to the lot of them," said Morgan, pulling her horse's head around. "Come on, I'll show you a longtooth cat's den."

The den she showed him, and other marvels, which filled him with the joy of the land and put thoughts of monsters and the Dolphin out of his mind. That evening he gathered with the Wolf Rock family in the great hall and waited for the guests to arrive for the New Deer feastings.

"So," said Uther from his deep chair in front of the huge fire of logs. His normally benign features wore a look of sly pleasure. "That nasty little Dolphin. I heard it was a bag monster, meanin' he brought it with him to hunt, dashed unsporting. Hunting a deer gets you food, gives you a ride, and the deer's got a chance. Huntin' monsters is pure waste."

"Uther," said Nena sharply.

Her husband bowed, and the subject was changed. But later, when Nena was talking with her ladies, he returned to Idris. "Those halfhounds," he said. "I mean, what's the breedin' of a hound like that?"

"Mastiff and shrieket," said Idris.

"And how many shriekets do you catch in the Great Ambrose?"

"None," said Idris. "Nothing but burners."

"So you tell me," said Uther. "Where are they coming from, them and that slimehare thing? If it was me young again, I'd be asking. Dear me yes. A Cross is a Cross, and none too legal, they tell me. Glass o' beer?" It was lightly said. But Idris knew that it was proof of a deep trust between him and Uther. No Captain would have said something to put his life in danger merely because he loved the land. Uther was a man ready to stake his life on honesty, and of course Idris would do the same.

"Sunapple, please," he said. "And I can promise you that I will be asking."

Uther filled Idris's glass and raised his own. "Here's demnition to monsters and their men, what?"

"Demnition to monsters and their men."

They drank. Uther gazed upon Idris with those deceptively lazy eyes. "Now look here," he said. "Old Ambrose said that there was a bit of difficulty about you seeing your family. Morgan says you're a good chap and I agree. So Nena and I had a chat. And, well, if you need a family, not that you will, age you are, bright lad, but if you ever do, well, here we are. All right?"

Idris felt a great warmth. He rose to his feet and bowed, as the Manner dictated. "Sir," he said, "you have paid me the compliment of kinship, and I take honor in it and accept it gladly."

"Welcome aboard, then," said Uther, pleased. "You'll have to take us as you find us, rough and ready. First off, we'd better get you taught to use a sword and have the rest of your thirty falls off a horse. Eh, what?"

Idris looked around the hall at the kind faces, the worn hangings in their richness, the gleam of candles on precious metals worn with centuries' polishing. "Thank you," he said.

"Ah," said Uther. "Band's tunin' up."

They ate mightily. Then they danced Mending the Walls and Weave the Basket, local squires and tall Knight girls. It was a very good evening. At the end of it Idris sat with Morgan on a balcony in the tower, looking west over forests and downs over which the New Deer Moon hung vast and silver. The New Deer was a time for thinking of the future.

"Will we be grooms, and rich, and wreck your Captain Ironhorse?" said Morgan.

Idris pointed to a metal gleam far on the horizon. "Or perhaps we can leave the stinking valley and I shall take you to sea."

"To far, hot lands," said Morgan.

And nothing passed over Idris: no chill of augury, no cold breath from the future.

So the rest of the evening passed in joy and amusement, and the days that followed in the learning of swordsmanship and the arts of battle, and (grievously) more horsemanship. And at the last quarter of the New Deer Moon, the monster-grooms of Great Ambrose returned to the Valley of Apples.

ELEVEN

W ell," said Ambrose, in his iron room on the third evening after the return. "I hear that you had an exciting New Deer." He leaned back in his chair. He had a scorched look, as if he had been traveling in places closer to the sun than Lyonesse.

Idris said modestly, "The people of the Wolf Rock were kind enough to take me into their kinweb."

"That is pleasant," said Ambrose with annoying casualness. "But I heard that you have been tripping up the Dolphin of the Realm, and chasing slimehares."

"Not at all," said Idris, shocked. "At least not like that."

"And nearly gotten yourself killed in the process. May already have gotten yourself killed."

"I *beg* your pardon?" said Idris.

Ambrose sighed. "Why, pray, Idris Ambrosegroom, do we meet in an iron room?"

"All are watched. This you have said."

"Our thoughts as well as our actions," said Ambrose. "You are no longer a useless child. You have become dangerous."

Idris felt his heart swell with pride. "This is good," he said. "For I feel my destiny."

"Oh?" said Ambrose wearily. "Do tell me about it."

"It is a simple thing," said Idris. "To lead an honest life. To hunt honestly, not with halfhounds of unholy breeding. To do battle with the quarry in single combat. To conduct myself as a member of the family of Knights now mine by adoption. And to help care for the kingdom of Lyonesse, its people, and its land, and to fight those who make war on it."

Ambrose's eyebrows were dark arches, and his eyes had an icy glitter. Six months ago, Idris would have been terrified. Not anymore. "Really?" he said.

"The main meter readings are falsified. A river of Wellwater runs, I believe, into the Poison Ground. The creatures of the Well plan to make all Lyonesse a Poison Ground, and the Captains will help them without knowing it or perhaps without caring."

"And suppose you are right," said Ambrose. "How will anything you can do make any difference?"

"It is my destiny," he said. "I feel it."

Ambrose shook his head. Idris heard the words he had just spoken. He had meant them and they were true. But at the same time they were the words of a child, spoken in a child's voice. "Uther Wolf Rock is a delightful man," said Ambrose patiently. "It is reasonable that you should admire him, but not that you should imitate him. Knights depend on their wealth, and you have none, and their skill at arms, and you have a dagger. And even the wealth and valor of the Knights is no defense against the Regent and the Council and the rest of the rabble in the Old Well." Ambrose pursed his lips, as if he had said too much. "But I ramble," he said. "Before you decide to conquer the land, give some thought to what befell Master Omnium, poor man. Now get along with you."

Idris rose, bowed humbly, and walked from the iron room. Ambrose did not ramble.

Once again, he had been given a hint.

Next day there were watches to stand and monsters to catch. In the afternoon a thin autumnal rain moved in from the west. Idris ate zupper with Kay and Morgan at the Wrestler's Elbow. Kay was being sarcastic about Idris's learning to ride, probably because he was jealous that Morgan had asked Idris and not him to the Wolf Rock. As soon as he had finished eating, Idris slipped away.

The rain had become heavier, and the streets were almost empty. He went to a tavern on the corner of the Old Well Square, a dingy spot, favored by the landless serfs who labored on the monsterwharves by the lake. In his dingy cloak and monster-burned trousers, Idris fitted in well. He ordered sunapple juice, found a table by a window, pulled aside the blackened cobwebs to give himself a slanting view of the Old Well, and settled down to watch.

The squat, plain tower crouched at the end of its square. Few people came here, and those that did paused only to bow to the Well, then went on their way. Once a cross-eyed man with a bottle in each hand did a dance and dropped the bottles. Almost immediately, a couple of Mountmen appeared from nowhere and hustled him away. It was interesting that the Mountmen had appeared so quickly. The Council did not seem to be meeting; there were no lights in the tower. What was there in a blocked Well important enough to need guarding, and by Mountmen, not Town Guardians?

It was cold out there, and lonely. It would also be very dangerous. But he was the one who had been talking about his destiny. He had a feeling that this was a moment that would show him whether it had been childish bragging or the grown-up truth.

As if in answer to the thought, the tavern floor shuddered under his feet. High in the Old Well, a slot window turned from black to dirty yellow, then to black again, as if someone had let fall a curtain.

There was someone there.

Why?

Idris took a deep breath. He got up, paid the surly host for his untouched sunapple juice, and walked across the wet, lonely square to the front of the Well. Deep in the porch the great doors were still in place, locked by the sword through their hasps. Idris bowed, as the other passersby had bowed. He looked around him. There was no one in the square. He began to walk around the Well.

A narrow passage led out of the square, curving around the tower's wall. Once it would have been the tide channel, to take away the water from monstercatchings. Now it was a dry, smelly tunnel crossed by other ancient buildings linking to the tower's sides. Idris walked on, head deep in his hood. *The Council and the rest of the rabble in the Old Well,* Ambrose had said.

It was dark. From around the stone bulge ahead came the sound of two voices, one educated, the other harsh and violent.

"The Deep," said harsh and violent.

"And all that therein swims, bless the Well," drawled the other voice.

"Why bless it?"

"An angler blesses the increase of the water." A yawn.

"Pass, Captain, Master." A door opened. A door closed.

Idris swallowed. This must be the exact spot on which Dawkins had been killed like a rabbit. He took a deep breath and walked around the wall.

In front of him was a turreted porch, smaller than the one on the square. Above the door a pine-knot torch sputtered in a sconce. The red flames glinted on the helmet and breastplate of a black Mountman.

"The Deep," said the Mountman, in the harsh and violent voice. Idris thought he saw a sarcastic glint in the eye.

"And all that therein swims, bless the Well," said Idris, doing his best to sound relaxed and drawling, though his voice was too high, and he could hardly hear it over the thump of his heart.

"But," said the Mountman, with an unpleasant smile, "how do I know you wasn't waiting 'round the corner listening?"

"Don't be stupid," said Idris, his voice going even higher. He knew he had made a terrible mistake. They had killed Dawkins. They would certainly kill him. If he tried to explain . . . well, he had no explanation. If he ran away, the Mountman would have time to take careful aim and put a flung sword in his back. There was only one way out.

"So," said the Mountman. "What is your name? And let us have a look at your — *oof!*"

Idris dived forward between the guard's legs. He felt his head hit something, and the guard grabbed at his cloak, but Idris wrenched out of his grip and started to run. Over the pant of his breath he heard the squinch of the guard's boot nails on the granite as he staggered to his feet and started after him. A whistle blew. Then more boot nails on the pavement, giving chase.

Idris knew he was dead. He also knew that he was going to die running. He carried on around the Well, keeping the wall on his left.

He came out of the passage. The square stretched before him, wide and dark and empty. The rain was lashing down now. He put out a foot to take the first step across the square. Then ahead of him he saw a bloody radiance of pine-knot torches in the rain, and heard harsh orders, and he knew that all roads away from the Old Well were blocked.

But the feet at the far side of the square were marching in time. There was no shouting.

They had not heard the whistle. They had not seen him. They were merely a squad marching to change watches. But there were feet behind him now. A whistle would blow again. Rain roared on the cobbles. He found he was edging around the front of the Well. Edging fast, beyond hope now, just wanting to stay out of the hands of the Mountmen for an extra heartbeat.

One step. Two. Twenty. Suddenly the rain stopped battering his head. He was under the cornice of the porch of the Great Door. The runoff from the roof bounced up from the paving in front of him, making a curtain that got in his nose and mouth, but which would hide him for some more heartbeats. Some of the very few he had left. Idris squelched into the darkness of the porch. He wanted to weep. This had been such a stupid, *childish* idea. If only the Well doors would open. But the doors were sealed with the Old King's sword Cutwater, driven half its blade-length into stone.

Something dug into his ribs. Lightning flickered death-blue. In its cold light he saw that what was digging into him was the hilt of the sword Cutwater. That was keeping the door shut. The sword that none might shift.

Idris put a hand on the sword.

Something happened.

Suddenly he was no longer a frightened child taking his last few breaths. He was a person who would soon be a man. He could feel other men standing with him, dead now, but brave men, noble, simple, loyal to the land they owned and which owned them. Men of House Draco, joined to their families and to Lyonesse by love and loyalty.

And he saw that the Mountmen in their black uniforms were little bullies in fancy dress, and Fisheagle and Kyd Murther were spoiled brats, and the Captains were stupid and vicious, and all of them were drenched in terror of their own shadows.

Idris had escaped Hell's Throat, and fought monsters in their Colony, and defied the halfhounds of Kyd Murther. Now he saw that these things were mere annoyances on the road to this moment.

He heard the nailed feet tramping toward the porch from left and right and straight ahead.

He felt the power of the land flow through him. He grasped the hilt of the sword Cutwater and lifted.

The sword came out of the stone like a spoon from a cup.

The doors of the Old Well sighed open. Idris, Swordbearer of Lyonesse, stepped inside.

He stood inside the door for a moment with the sword in his hand. It felt light but powerful, warm and well balanced. He felt the stones of the land firm under his feet, his mind keen and strong. Somewhere, an Idris was saying, *Attack, run.* But that was an old Idris. Since his hand had closed on the hilt, there was a new Idris, filled with the strength of the land in which he was born. Caution, thought this new Idris. Discretion. The hour is not yet come.

Thunder crashed. Rain roared on the flagstones outside.

There was a hole in the door exactly big enough for him to push the sword out and maneuver it back through the hasps and into the stone. The blade sank easily into the rock. He drew back his hand and watched through the hole. A pair of Mountmen peered into the porch. "Nothing," one of them said above the roar of falling water.

"I saw something," said his companion. In the lightning he had a wide, flat face and sharp black eyes. "By the Great Door."

"'Course you did," said the first Mountman with intense sarcasm. "Like he just pulled out the sword and went inside. I should pull it out myself and go after him, if I were you."

"Yeah," said his partner. "Well." Idris stepped back into the dark. He heard footsteps as the man walked up to the door. He heard him put his hands on the swordhilt, grunt as he heaved. The sword did not move.

"Now if you have finished your work as one of the 'eroes of 'istory," said the first Mountman, "perhaps we can get out of this rain before us armor greens up solid? Nasty spooky monstrous place."

"Aye, aye." They tramped away into the rain.

But a patrol remained in the square. The men were hunched, miserable and streaming water, but their eyes were sharp and moving. No way out, thought Idris.

He was cold now, shivering. And he felt very strange. He saw the world frozen in a blue flash of lightning, felt the enormous power that had flowed into him as the sword came out of the stone. Goodness knew what kind of mechanism the sword must have, if he had been able to pull it out and the guard not. Some sort of time lock? wondered the old Idris.

The new Idris was not interested in time locks. The new Idris had felt the power of the land flow through him. The new Idris felt a strange silence, as if destiny were holding its breath, ready to blow warmth and life into him.

But this was not the time to try to think things out. This was the time to survive. First things first, said Idris to himself. There was no way out.

So he must find a way in.

He began to feel his way around the walls. Their stone was smooth and dampish. His hands came to a corner. He moved his foot forward and found a wall. Not a wall. A step. The stairway out of the hall. He started to climb.

Idris knew how Wells worked, and this was the Well on which all later Wells had been based. At ground level you had the grand entrance, and inside the grand entrance the hall, with iron doors leading to the cutting rooms and monsterstables. On the first floor were the rooms of the Captains. It was in the window of one of these rooms that he had seen from the tavern the glow of candlelight, swiftly veiled.

The stairs had the soft, gritty feel of deep dust. Above him there had come into being a faint glow. Beyond the turns of the staircase someone had lit a candle. No, candles, for the light was bright.

It got brighter.

Idris arrived on a landing. There was a curtain here, a heavy drape of what felt under his fingers like corsair carpet. One of the curtain's sides was not drawn fully to. Around it light poured, white and brilliant. From behind it came the sound of voices and the sharp, dirty smell of Wellwater.

Idris grasped a fold of curtain between finger and thumb. Very carefully, he pulled it a hand's-breadth aside.

And felt the air cool in his open mouth.

He was looking into a huge, round room. Normally the shaft of the Well would have occupied most of its center. But there was no shaft. Instead there was a circular pool of water, a good stone's throw across. Around the pool were benches upholstered in red leather intricately patterned with gold tooling. Scattered on the benches were a half-dozen men wearing the crimson robes and triple crowns of Captaincy. Each of the half-dozen held a long pole of red yew wood bound with rings of gold. Each was intent on a brightly colored float that bobbed on the black water. Girls moved among them, unnaturally beautiful girls with bare middles and gauzy skirts and braceleted ankles above feet painted pink for dancing. The light came from an apparatus hung from the ceiling. It was not candles. It was a great globe of rarest glass, the biggest piece of glass Idris had ever seen, suspended by chains. Inside it something struggled and glared. By the roar of pain that battered his mind,

Idris knew it to be a burner. For a moment, there was no room in his brain for anything but shock. A *burner!* To light a *room!* What luxury! And (said another voice, very like Harpoon's) what *waste!*

One of the Captains shouted and stood up. The pole in his hand was jerking and bouncing. Two big men Idris had not noticed came out of a side door, grasped the pole, and heaved. He saw that a line went from the pole's end into the pool. The line looked tight, as if something was struggling on its far end. The men groped in the water with hooks, found something heavy, and hauled. The heavy thing slid onto the paving. It was a woman, dark-haired, beautiful, dripping. *Oh, thank you for rescuing me, kind and handsome man,* said a voice in Idris's head.

The Captain's triple crown had become crooked in the struggle. He straightened it, looking cross. "Take it away," he said. "Put it with the breeding stock." The hookmen dragged it across the floor to . . . a *monsterchute.* Idris knew what he would see. Down the woman's back from shoulders to heels ran two spiny fins. An eelhag, according to the *Diversitie,* used in the making of Crosses. She hissed, showing pointed teeth. The chute swallowed her. There was a fading howl. She was gone.

Idris took a step back. He was horribly shocked. These were Captains, who formed the Council, that made the rules. And they were catching monsters that were not burners, which was not lawful. For . . . *breeding?* And not on the tides, as was lawful, but in a Well converted to be a pool in a perpetual river of Wellwater that flowed out of the Wellworld and into Lyonesse.

No wonder the main meter readings were so huge. No wonder Lyonesse was sinking.

These men were drowning it.

Idris felt a deep anger. He moved back to the curtain and looked long and hard at the fishermen. Two of them had their backs to him. But there was Brassfin of the Spouter, and Gradrock of the Initial, and Zincrack of the Reliable Perpetual, crouched over the roiling water, watching their floats with greedy intensity. Also watching, but not fishing, was a man lounging on a padded bench with his back to Idris. He was tall and thin, and he was wearing a deep-red hooded cloak like the one Ambrose wore. And on his hand was a devouring eel ring, like the one Ambrose wore.

Very like. For the man in the red cloak was Ambrose.

The breath stuck in Idris's throat. What was Ambrose doing here?

Betraying the land. The land whose love and power had flowed into Idris when he grasped the sword Cutwater.

How *dare* he?

The figure in the hood became still, as if it had heard the thought. It began to turn.

Idris faded back from the curtain and crept down the stairs the way he had come.

There was treachery in the Wellroom, and Mountmen in the square, and only damp, dirty darkness in the entrance porch of the Old Well. What other abominations lurked at the bottom of the chutes where the eelhag had gone?

He found himself in the entrance chamber. He patted his way around the walls. From stone, his hands passed on to iron: the door of the monsterstables.

He should take himself back to the Great Ambrose and hope he escaped with his life. So said the old Idris.

But the new Idris had felt the power of the land flow from the hilt of the sword.

The new Idris opened the iron door and passed through.

A monsterclamor roared over him. He was descending a staircase, spiral, deep, deep into a world darker than the darkest cellar, filled with voices.

I am a plate of steak and bread, more delicious than you have ever eaten, said a voice. *Take me out of here and I will assuage your hunger.*

No, thank you, thought Idris, though his mouth was watering.

Idris, said a voice. *How lovely to see you. Dear me, we have missed you. The Precious Stones keep asking and asking where you are. You never wrote. We're so worried!*

A wave of grief drowned Idris. He sat down on the steps, gasping. It was the voice of Harpoon of the Fishers, with the cat whiskers tattooed around her eyes, in her dark-blue dress. Idris could feel his heart breaking. . . .

No. It was an illusion. But an illusion of awful power.

— and your dad, well, he's so lonely since you left —

"Shut up," said Idris.

We don't understand why you went —

The grief swamped him again. He had been snatched away from everyone who loved him and put in this cold world of stink and power and no love. And his dear family was miserable without him, and there was no one to tell them he was safe and well, and no one to love him. . . .

His hand fell to his waist. It touched something round and smooth. The pommel of the dagger Uther had given him. The iron dagger, given him by his new family. Made of iron, beastbane.

The voice in his head was a cheap puppet version of Harpoon. How dare they use her so? He sent his mind out to the voice. He went through it like an arrow through lambskin and slammed into another mind behind it, this one a huge thing, dark and savage and completely alien. *There's no call for —* oof! cried the voice of his mother, breaking and shredding and becoming the shriek of the beast.

Idris dried his eyes on his sleeve and took a deep breath. With his mind he said, *Shut up, all of you. I am here to make an inspection.*

The voices faded. There was a feeling of worry and satisfaction, as if some of the more sensible monsters thought this was long overdue. Idris felt his way to the tool bench, found flint and steel, knocked them together, made sparks, then flame, and lit a torch.

The monsterstables of the Old Well looked as if they had survived many earthquakes, but only just. The walkways between the grilled monstertanks sloped crazily away into dirty water. Some of the grilles were burst and twisted, whether by earthquake or pressure from below it was hard to tell.

Idris, started another voice, Ector Gateguard's this time. *No call to talk to your mum like that —*

"Ah, be quiet," said still another voice: a weird voice, thin and tinny but oddly friendly. "This is Idris. If you try to bend his mind, he'll bend yours, innit, Idris?"

"True," said Idris, before he could stop himself.

"Lot of timewasters," said the tinny voice. "Oops, sorry. I should introduce myself. Name of Digby. Fourth cage along, row C."

"Greetings, creature," said Idris.

"Come and have a look," said Digby. "As the blind man said to the deaf man, ha-ha."

"Ha," said Idris, puzzled. Bad as the joke was, there was no mention of anything like this in the *Diversitie.* Idris's professional interest was aroused. He picked up an iron-shod pole and walked along the gangway. Wild faces looked up from among the red reflections on the water: a beautiful woman, Ector with tentacles, even Morgan, as the monsters dug in his mind and used what they found. He muffled against them, swiped with his pole at a tentacle that snaked onto the catwalk. It withdrew, hissing. When he got to 4C he paused. "Digby," he said.

There was a slight commotion in the water. And there standing on the bars was a small, scaly object that looked like a one-eyed melon with fins and a single leg.

"I expect you're rather surprised," said the object.

"Not at all," lied Idris politely.

"Well, I admire your coolness, yes indeed, highly creditable," said the thing called Digby, "Because I was. Surprised, that is. I mean it's always surprising to be caught, and uncomfortable, too, when you are minding your own business in a darkgarden. But then to find yourself in a menagerie with a manhag who can kill trees by looking at them, some slimehares, a couple of succubi, and goodness knows what else."

"No," said Idris, caught thoroughly off guard by the no-nonsense cheeriness of the creature.

"Modesty. Charming quality," said Digby. "They make things called Crosses, apparently. Mixtures of dogs and shriekets. Even succubi and humans. They breed them, you know."

Idris had already worked this out, but that did not prevent it from being one of the worst things he had ever heard. But he was dealing with a monster. He pulled up the muffle and told himself he was a trained monstergroom. "So what," he asked, "is your talent?"

"Nothing in particular," said Digby modestly. "I can live out of water, of course. Otherwise, I get by."

"Except that you do not seem to be in your cage."

"Oh, that," said Digby, and there was a distinct tinge of embarrassment to the remark. "I do a little shapechanging, nothing dramatic, just enough to squeeze between bar and bar and keep my distance from the nasty iron, aha."

"Aha," said Idris. "Well, it is time you shapechanged right back into your tank." The lancet windows a bowshot above were gray now. The rain must have stopped. It was time to go. *Kek*, he called in his mind. *KEK!*

The monsters stirred in their tanks, pricked by the power of the thought. *Go away. Not dawn. Sleep*, thought the gull.

Idris imagined a dead eel among the Welltowers and sent the idea to the gull. He saw the world spin far below as Kek came instantly awake, tumbled out of his roost, and glided across the Old Well and its square. The square was empty.

"You off?" said Digby.

"Yes."

"Can I come, too?"

"Of course not," answered Idris. "Back in your cage." He drove Digby back into the pen and laid a double grille on his bars.

"*Most* disappointing," said Digby, wounded.

Idris found himself actually warming to this very peculiar creature. But a monster was a monster. He turned away, headed for the stairs, and started to climb. The monsters were quiet, sullen in their cages. Very quietly he opened the iron door.

All the monsters shrieked at once. *HELP*, howled the voices, rushing past him through the open door. *ESCAPE! HE'S GETTING AWAY. A TRESPASSER. LOOK IN HIS POCKETS.*

Idris leaped into the hall and slammed the door, cutting off the voices. There was silence. He drew in a breath.

A bell started clanging.

"Oops," said a voice in his pocket. "There goes the alarm. That would have been me. Sorry about that."

Idris put his hand into his pocket and drew it back sharply. There was something in there. Something round and cold and scaly.

"It's all right," said the voice. "I don't bite. Much."

There were feet and voices in the upper parts of the Well. Idris strode across the gatechamber, stamped out the torch, reached through the door, found the swordhilt, and pulled the sword out of the hasps. He opened the door, sidled out, closed the door behind him and slid the sword back into the stone. Inside, muffled feet slapped on flagstones. The rain had stopped. Beyond the porch the Old Well Square lay silver-wet and empty under the waning moon.

"Ahem," said the voice from his pocket. "I think we'd better, you know, hurry?"

"Quiet," said Idris, so cool and calm he amazed himself. Kek was sitting on a turret. Having been let down over the dead eel promise, he was losing interest in everything but sleep. Through the gull's eyes Idris caught a fleeting glimpse of a patrol of a half-dozen Mountmen coming up from the direction of the Great Road. Then a wing covered his gull-vision and the picture went out. Idris flitted through the empty streets to the Ambrose, tiptoed past the snoring night guard and into the Well. "Is this the Ambrose?" said Digby, in his pocket. "This is wonderful! I've always wanted to see the famous —"

"Hush," said Idris. The effect of the sword was wearing off, and he was nervous again. Harboring a monster was an offense punishable by death in the Well. He would find a way to put Digby back in the morning.

In his room, he hung the tunic on his chair with Digby still in the pocket. He pulled off his breeches and sat on his bed. The events of the night rolled past him in a jagged parade. What if he had been recognized? What had Ambrose been doing with all those Captains?

He found his head was on his pillow. He must stay alert, think his way through this deadly maze.

His eyelids were heavy as iron doors. He slept.

Idris saw a woman in blue with a man in gateguard's uniform. The man was Ector. The woman looked like Harpoon, from behind. But when she turned, her face was wrong. She had *fangs*. And she came at Idris, gripped him, and shook him. And Idris was weeping and shouting, "No, you're wrong — "

"No, I'm right," said a voice: a man's voice.

Idris opened his eyes to cold morning light. And in the light a face: eyes pits of shadow on either side of the cruel hook nose, cheeks sunken, brow lofty. Ambrose.

"What have you done now?" said Ambrose.

Idris was still tangled in his dream. "Done?" The events of last night came back. He started to be worried.

Ambrose sighed. "What were you doing last night?"

Into Idris's mind came the notion that Ambrose was no longer to be trusted. He decided on a half-truth. "Studying." He muffled his mind.

"Studying what? Speak."

"The *Diversitie*."

"Perhaps you were," said Ambrose. He strode across the cell and began opening cupboards, hauling out clothes, and going through the pockets. "The reason I am here," said Ambrose, "is that someone seems to have stolen a monster."

"From where?" said Idris in a strangled croak.

"Never you mind," said Ambrose, rummaging through Idris's fire armor. "Idris, you are in trouble."

Hypocrite, thought Idris, seeking refuge from fear in defiance. You fish with Captains who breed Crosses and drown the land for their amusement.

Ambrose had finished with the cupboards. His eyes landed on the chair over which Idris had hung the tunic in whose pocket he had left Digby.

Ambrose picked up the tunic. His hand dived into the Digby pocket. Idris opened his mouth, though he did not yet know what he was going to say. Then the hand was coming out again, and Ambrose's shoulders were shrugging, and he marched out of the room, slamming the door behind him.

Idris closed his eyes. He lay listening to the feet receding on the stone stairs. Perhaps last night had been a dream.

"Close call, eh?" said a voice, inside or outside his mind, he could not tell. "Did you sleep well?"

Idris opened his eyes. Digby was standing in a shaft of morning sun, bouncing on his single leg, and surveying him brightly with his single eye. "Until I was woken up," he said.

"That's awful."

"Which was your fault."

"Sorry," said Digby, looking quite penitent, for a one-eyed, one-legged, scaly melon with fins.

"Where were you hiding?" said Idris. It was hard to think of Digby as a monster, unless you were looking at him. Impossible, actually.

"Sort of around," said Digby. "I come and go a bit. You're angry, aren't you? I can sing," said Digby hopefully. "And dance. The singing," he said with charming frankness, "is better than the dancing." Idris heard a burst of beautiful music. Digby hopped around on his foot, roughly in time. "See?" he said.

"I see," said Idris. Ambrose would not stop investigating until he found out the truth. He put some thoughts around the monster to bind it captive. "Well, you just hang around here and I'll think what's to be done."

"How kind," said Digby. Then, "Hey. Hey! Let *go*!"

"Sorry," said Idris. "Can't take any chances. You're bound."

"Bound, schmound!" cried Digby. Idris felt him struggle, and fail. "Who taught you to do that?"

"It comes naturally," said Idris. "What do you eat?"

"Fish," said Digby reproachfully. "I'm a monster. Though I have always felt a little out of place."

"You're still a monster."

"What do you think you look like to me?" said Digby. "There's a little bit of monster in everyone." He turned it into a song, with a pleasing rhythm and a large orchestra of instruments Idris had never heard before.

"I'll get the fish," said Idris.

He got Digby a mackerel fillet in gooseberry sauce. The monster ate the fish and spat the sauce all over the walls. Idris found himself laughing in spite of the load on his mind. Then it was time for him to stand watch in a stable of burners. Morgan was sharing the watch. Idris was tired, and he kept thinking of Ambrose and the sword.

"What's *wrong* with you?" said Morgan, after he had dropped a hagfish into her boot.

"Nothing," said Idris.

"I heard your door in the middle of the night."

"Bad stomach," said Idris.

"And I heard music."

"Probably singing," said Idris as casually as possible.

"To your bad stomach."

"Trying to keep my mind off it."

"Oh," said Morgan, pulling an order peg out of the board. The cranemen swung the baited cage over a pen, sprang the grille, and lowered the cage. The monster came out of the water, dripping and roaring.

"Drop."

Morgan pulled the handle that dropped the monster into the water cart. The cart rumbled up to the cutting rooms. She said, "You might as well tell me. What is it?"

Idris would have loved to tell her. But if he did, she would be his accomplice in assault, trespass, and monstertheft. As good as dead. He shivered. "Nothing."

She squeezed his hand. "You're still not well. I'll give you some mixture."

Morgan's mixture was a vile fluid she brought from home, where it was made up by her ancient nurse. Idris had gotten on the mixture list since his adoption by the Wolf Rock. After the watch he had a spoonful, to please her.

"Cor," said Digby, when Idris returned to his room after swallowing the awful draught. "Your breath smells like dung."

He is taking what is in my mind and using it to charm me, thought Idris. "Listen. I've been thinking. I've got to take you back."

"*What*?" shrieked the monster. "Me? Back? But I thought you *liked* me!"

"I do," said Idris, finding he meant it. "But —"

"I thought you picked me out because we had something in *common!*"

"You are a monster. You stowed away in my pocket," said Idris patiently. "And tonight I am going to take you back to the Old Well, because if you are found here I will be drowned alive and so will my friend, and you will be crushed or given to the cutters."

"The cutters?" said Digby, in a tiny voice.

"They cut monsters," said Idris. "To trim them for the machines, or to find out how they work."

"Oh," said Digby.

"So it is better that I take you back."

"Oh," said Digby.

"I'll bring you some more fish. Any preference?"

"Hagfish," said Digby, with the deepest sarcasm. "The kind you feed your slave burners. Should be good enough for me. Mere brute reptile that I am."

Idris bowed. "Digby," he said, "I think you are a very nice creature and I would love to have you by me." A burst of celestial harmony from Digby. "But the law is that after zupper I must take you back where you belong and not get caught. Now what would you really like to eat?"

"Anything but hagfish," said Digby. "And if you could tell them not to singe it or smear it with that disgusting paste?"

"Raw fish, no gooseberry sauce," said Idris. "Coming up."

He went down to zupper in the refectory. Morgan cast a disgusted eye at his plate. "Raw *squid*?"

"Westgate speciality."

"I thought you had a bad stomach," she said.

"The mixture," said Idris.

She brightened. "I told you."

Later in Idris's cell, Digby grew a set of frightful fangs and ate his squid. When he had finished, Idris buttoned him into his pocket. "Keep quiet," he said. "Or it is drowning for me and cutting for you."

"Oh," said Digby.

Idris walked down the stairs and into the street.

The sun had gone down, and there was a cold wind blowing from the north as he hurried down the Great Road. The lights of the tavern on the corner of the square glowed dim orange through its filthy windows. There were a couple of Mountmen in front of the Old Well. Idris stood by the tavern door for a moment. The patrol walked away down an alley. The square stood dark and empty under the stars. Idris put his mind up to Kek, wheeling over the valley. Kek's eye picked up the Mountmen on their patrol, another, bigger group at ease. Idris said, "Here we go."

"Can't wait," said Digby gloomily.

Idris started to walk swiftly across the empty square. His feet sounded horribly loud. After what seemed like hours, he was in the Old Well porch. He put his mind up to Kek. Still no Mountmen. Stealthily Idris drew the sword from the door hasps. The door sighed open, oddly smooth after seven hundred years. Again he felt firmness, resolve, the power of the land in him. He said in a low voice, "Digby, it has been nice knowing you."

There was no reply.

Probably sulking, thought Idris. He slid into the hall, replaced the sword, passed through the iron door and down the stair around the monsterstable wall, to the tool bench for a torch and then to the crazy-tilted stable grilles, black in the pine-resin's flicker. The ill-smelling water sloshed nastily. The monsters, drowsy, put out thoughts that said *rescue, meat, love.* He opened 4C and reached into his pocket for Digby.

The pocket was empty.

"Digby," he hissed.

Digby, Digby, Digby, echoed the monsters in the tanks, stirring as they fed on his fear. He put his mind up to Kek. The square was still empty, but the Mountman on the small door was saluting, as if someone had just passed in to the Old Well. A monstergroom, come to tend the stables? What if they found him here?

Idris panicked. He ran up the stairs. The sound of his feet boomed in the great vaults, and his fear stimulated the monsters so they howled in his mind. Why had he come back? He was a fool. Digby could look after himself. Had already looked after himself.

The red light of his torch glared on the iron door at the stairtop. Idris hurled it into the void. It flared, shrank, and winked out in a monstercage. Darkness fell, black as velvet. He pushed open the iron and passed through. He groped toward the Well doors, reached through the hole, gripped the hilt of the sword, and drew it from the stone, feeling again the strength pour through his being. He put out his hand to pull the door open.

He expected his hand to meet wood.

It met another hand.

TWELVE

The other hand was slender but very, very strong. It folded around Idris's hand and it would not let go. Idris thought: I am caught and it is dark and I am going to be thrown into a Well and I will never see my family again and never grow up, I wish I had never come here never met Digby never trained as a monstergroom never met Morgan or Ambrose.

All this passed through his mind in the splinter of a second. Then it ran against the feeling Idris had when he was holding the sword and evaporated. I am a power in the land, he thought, and the land is a power in me. As for all that, if none of those things had happened, I would have been drowned like a seal in a net in a tunnel under the Westgate. Furthermore, while my right hand is gripped in the hand of my adversary, my left hand holds an ancient and beautifully balanced sword, that I can run into this person who is holding my hand. But I am Idris Limpet of the Westgate and the Wolf Rock, not a murderer in the dark.

He said, "Unhand me, or I strike."

His adversary grunted. Suddenly a yellow sphere was floating in the air, casting a soft but brilliant light over the carvings of the gates, the black iron of the stables door, the arch leading to the staircase, and the fishing chamber above. . . .

And a man with a crimson hood hiding his face.

The man pushed back his hood. "Idris," said Ambrose, "you are in very big trouble."

The old Idris squirreled around for an excuse. None came. What actually came was something else. He heard himself say, "I am defending this green Realm against those who would destroy it. Including you, who carouse with Captains as they catch monsters forbidden."

"Oh, that," said Ambrose, with a trace of his old drawl. "Who will keep an eye on those dirty Captains if not me?" His eyes traveled to the sword in Idris's hand and grew wide. He opened his mouth to speak, then seemed to change his mind. He said in a new, hushed voice, "Let us go outside."

Idris put his hand to the doors, which seemed to open more by mental intention than muscular effort. They stepped out into the porch. The doors closed. "Now," said Ambrose quietly. "Put the sword back. If you would."

Idris reversed his grip on the sword. He slid it through the hasps and into the stone. For the first time he noticed that the hole where the sword fitted seemed to have healed up. But it sank in easily.

"Wait there," said Ambrose.

Idris waited. Feet departed. Feet returned. Back came Ambrose. And Idris's heart turned to stone in his chest. For in Ambrose's wake strode a huge man in black uniform. A Mountman.

Ambrose had betrayed him.

Dully, he wondered why Ambrose had gone to the trouble of rescuing him from the Westgate if he was just going to let him be slung down a Well. Perhaps the mage had seen something in him, but that something had been snuffed out by this dreadful act of trespass, and he was tired of him.

So why was he not frightened?

Idris stood and watched his doom approach.

Ambrose said, "Sergeant, pull the sword out of the stone."

"Can't be done," said the Mountman.

"Try."

The Mountman grabbed the hilt of the sword and gave a mighty heave. Nothing happened.

"Harder," said Ambrose.

"It's stuck in," said the guard. "Everyone knows."

"Pull," said Ambrose.

The Mountman pulled again. Idris saw a vein stand blue on his temple. "Nah," said the Mountman. "Not with a team of whales."

"Thank you," said Ambrose. "You may return to your duties."

"Now you," said Ambrose to Idris, when the Mountman was gone.

"Me?"

"Pull it out."

Idris took the pommel of the sword between his thumb and forefinger and lifted it delicately upward. The point of the blade came clear of the rock. "I don't really understand," he said, turning back to Ambrose. "It's pretty easy really . . . What?"

For Ambrose had fallen to his knees. In a quiet voice, he said, "All Hail Kyd Idris, Draco's son, of the Vanished Children, King of Lyonesse and the Lands in the Sea."

"For goodness' sake get *up*," said Idris, deeply embarrassed. "What are you *talking* about?" He put out his hand to help the mage.

Ambrose took the hand, pressed it to his brow, his lips, and his heart. Then he rose. "It was in the hope of this that I found you and brought you here," he said. "But I thought you would be longer in discovering yourself. Now if your majesty will permit me to make a suggestion, he could replace the sword?"

"Talk properly," said Idris, confused almost to tears.

"Yes," said Ambrose, extinguishing his light. "Your maj — that is, put the sword back, and we will go back to the Ambrose, and later I will explain to your maj — that is, explain some things that need explaining. We must be secret yet a while. Already you have enemies. If they find out what you have done now, they will be deadly. Now muffle, and we go."

Idris slid the sword into the stone. When he turned his back on it, he felt a curious reluctance, as if he were leaving part of himself behind. But he put up the muffle and stepped into the square.

"Listen," said Ambrose, "and I will tell you the thing that must not on pain of death or worse be spoken. The Old King set the sword Cutwater in the stone at the time of the Blocking of the Well. None could draw it but the descendant of kings, king himself, who would save the kingdom from its enemies — wait!"

The world held its breath for a moment. Then something smashed into Idris's mind: a thing like a beam of cold darkness, probing, horribly powerful, sharp as talons. It swept over his muffle and went on. "Fisheagle," said Ambrose. "She feels something. She will be on her guard, as well she may be, for you are her doom."

Idris stood for a moment cold with fear. Then the power of the land returned, and he thought: So this is the destiny I have been feeling.

Then another thought came into his mind.

Just *wait* till I tell Morgan!

"Not yet," said Ambrose, divining it. "You are in great danger, and so is any you tell. Console yourself with this: You are the rightful King of Lyonesse for the rest of your life. Be it long. Or," said Ambrose, "be it short."

Later, Idris was playing Check with Morgan. "Mate," she said, moving her barn. "You're miles away. What's wrong with you?"

"You've outplayed me. You always do."

She had opened her mouth to accuse him of flattery when there was a knock at the door. "Sir," said the dwarf Cran. "You are to have zupper with the master in the Iron Room." He left, slamming the door.

The dinner was an excellent pie of rock sheep. To Idris's relief Ambrose seemed to have gotten over his attack of reverence. "Now," said the mage, after the servitors had cleared away the remains. "I have not asked you here for eating only. I must tell you the story of Kyd Draco, Angharad, the Vanished Children, and the Troubles of the Realm."

"By all means," said Idris.

"Meaning yes?" said Ambrose, leading Idris to blush dark red at his own pomposity. "All right, then." His eyes hooded, as if he was looking at pictures unfolding in his mind. "I have told you of Great Brutus, whom men call the Old King, who came to the land of Lyonesse in a barbarous age, when men lived in holes in the ground and worshipped the weather. I have told you of the rise of the Captains, and the fall of the Knights, and the bullying of Kyd Ploc Ard by Slabada of the Wellers, that brought the Captains back to Lyonesse. But I have not told you what followed. For the knowledge of this can bring swift and horrible death.

"So. With the arrival of the Captains hard times came to Lyonesse. Under the Knights the world had been powered by a sense that work was a duty but also a joy, and people lived hard but cheerful lives, harnessed by the Manner, lightened by a kind magic of star and stone. The Captains showed everyone a life of luxury, but one built on the burning backs of screaming monsters. So the long years passed, and the land sank, and the engines pumped, and the towers grew. Now hear this, Idris. Kyd Ploc Ard was the ancestor of Kyd Lumsden, who married Drwsla of the Captains, a most unpleasant woman. She was too proud to walk, so she must ride in a litter. This made her horribly fat, for which she blamed her husband, though that is a different story. And their son was Kyd Draco, who was a man in the old and noble mold, and he married Angharad of the Knights, who was brave, kind, and beautiful, and loved the land and her husband. And, when she arrived, her daughter.

"But it must be remembered that Kyd Draco had in him the blood of Captains, and strange blood it was, come from who knew where. And while Angharad yet lived, his eyes fell on another woman, a daughter of a minor Captain."

"How, strange?" said Idris.

"The person who caught the eye of Kyd Draco," said Ambrose, "was a woman of great beauty, but hard as a bird's talons. She called herself after the greatest of birds, big as a meadow, cruel as death, the Sea Eagle. But there was something chilly about her, and skills that called to mind the power of monsters, so people called her the Fisheagle. With this woman Kyd Draco talked far into the night, many nights. And after one of those talks he let her visit Angharad of the Knights, Angharad being in childbed, and the Sea Eagle having persuaded Kyd Draco to let her attend Angharad and lighten her labor with secret art. The Sea Eagle sent out the wise women, and they heard Angharad's cries through the door. And one wise woman, a friend of Angharad, burst in, and found Angharad dead, and the baby boy who was heir to Lyonesse facedown in a bowl of water, and the Sea Eagle gone, and an arras over a secret door blowing in the dirty wind from the Valley of Apples.

"And the rest of the story is this," said Ambrose. "It was noticed in the land that Kyd Draco paid little attention to the loss of his wife and his child. He had them burned on the usual pyre though he himself did not attend, and there were rumors that Angharad burned alone, the dead child having been stolen away. Kyd Draco seemed entirely in thrall to the woman Fisheagle, whom he married with great pomp after the shortest permitted period of mourning. The little girl was sent away. Fisheagle soon afterward bore a son, the child we now know as Kyd Murther. But when Kyd Murther was two, at the feast of his moving from babyhood to childom, a mage spoke to Kyd Draco in a powerful way; and Kyd Draco said in a speech to the assembled Knights of Lyonesse that he regretted the death of Angharad, and the loss of his children, and the passing of the old magic of star and stone, and the coming of the Captains with their machines, and he was of a mind to restore what was lost. Upon which the Knights became happy, but the Captains drew together in a great fat mass and laid their plans for clinging to power.

"At the Childom Feast that followed, Fisheagle wore robes of black gold covered with rubies. She fed Kyd Draco, king of

Lyonesse, with her own hands, and handed him a cup of metheglin fashioned from a single block of crystal. That night, Kyd Draco was taken by pains in his belly and died. So Kyd Murther in his childom was the king, and Fisheagle the child's mother was the Regent, who would rule until his coming of age.

"Some said Kyd Draco had been poisoned. But Fisheagle had a piercing mind for thought watching. And she brought in men from High Kernow who had no roots in the land and gave them black uniforms, and bade them reinforce the Town Guardians and kill trouble before it reached her. So pretty soon the Valley of Apples was full of Mountmen. And the mind of Fisheagle wormed into the crannies of people's thoughts, until people decided it was better to stop thinking.

"But remember the serving woman at the death of Angharad and her newborn son. The serving woman had staying with her a cousin, a Fisher," said Ambrose. "With the cat-whisker tattoos at her eye corners. Being of the Fishers, the cousin used her arts to take the water from the infant's lungs, so that it —"

"He," said Idris.

"— very well, *he* breathed. And she took him away. To the town where she lived. Which was —"

"The Westgate," said Idris. "So I am the child of Angharad and Kyd Draco, and the nurse's cousin was Harpoon of the Fishers, who is not my mother, and my mother is dead."

A silence fell over the room. Idris hung his head and felt the crumbling of everything that had kept him warm and safe in the world.

But little by little, shock turned to grief. And at the same time as the grief there came that feeling of power that had touched him when he gripped the hilt of Cutwater. He was filled with his duty to the stones of Lyonesse and scorn for the false Captains and murdering Regent who had caused him this grief. And most of all, by a burning resolve to right these terrible wrongs.

He rose, and to Ambrose it seemed that the boy had grown taller. In that silence, he heard himself say, "Thank you for your explanation of my ancestry." Vaguely he noticed that Ambrose had stood up, too. "It seems to me that if anyone finds out that I am who I am, we will all be thrown down a Well."

"Correct," said Ambrose.

"So for the moment we shall pretend that nothing has happened. Good night."

He walked dazed along the passages and stairways. He opened the heavy door of his room. He sat down on the bed and felt love and gratitude for Harpoon and Ector, who, at awful risk, had reared him as their own —

"Penny for yer thoughts," said a bright, chirpy voice.

"Argh," said Idris, jumping a foot in the air. When he landed, he observed a scaly boulder examining him with a single eye. "Digby! What are you doing here?"

"Those stables," said Digby. "Boring boring *boring.*"

"But if anyone finds you —"

"I don't know if you've noticed," said Digby. "But I'm quite good at not being found if I don't want to be."

"Yes," said Idris.

"And as for all that stuff with the sword at the Old Well," said Digby, "I'm sure it'll all work out in the end."

A chill seized Idris's heart. "You were watching?"

"Don't worry," said Digby. "My lips are sealed."

"You haven't got any."

"Oops," said Digby, growing an awful pink mouth and blowing Idris a kiss. "But if someone locks me up I might lose my mind and babble."

"I see," said Idris. There was the scuff of feet on the stairs. The feet came straight to his door. Knuckles rapped. "It would be discreet to hide," he said, with forced politeness. Then, louder. "Come in!"

Morgan came in. She said, "What did you eat? We had badger ham, sooo smelly —" She frowned. "Is something the matter?"

Idris said, "Matter?" How to seem normal?

Then he heard Morgan gasp and looked around. Digby had not hidden. He was standing on the windowsill, and Morgan was staring at him with eyes that had grown large and disc-shaped. "What's *that*?" she said.

He said, "Digby, this is my friend Morgan. Morgan, this is Digby. A monster," he said, unnecessarily. He was grateful to Digby for distracting Morgan. But she really hated monsters, and she was not going to like the idea of one being in his room. "Er . . ." he started.

"Isn't she *sweet!*" said Morgan. Idris stood with his mouth hanging open.

"He, actually. Do you really think so?" said Digby, who was still wearing the lips. He leaped in the air, formed himself into a flying saucer, and sailed across the room onto Morgan's shoulder. He said, "You're nice, Morgan."

"Aah," said Morgan, turning pink.

"He brought me for you," lied Digby.

"Thank you, *thank* you!" cried Morgan.

"Oh. Not at all. If you will excuse me," said Idris, who had had enough of this very complicated day, "I think I should be getting to bed."

"Yes," said Morgan absently, patting Digby on his scaly head. "Us, too."

"He eats fish," said Idris. "His table manners are disgusting."

"How sweet," said Morgan, totally under the influence. As she left, Digby was lying on her head in the form of a green hat, talking into her ear.

Idris took off his clothes very slowly. He folded them very slowly. He lay down and pulled the furs over him. He kept his hands by his sides and his feet together and gazed up at the ceiling like the Knights on the tombs in the ruins in Old Westgate; or like a King, going to sleep in a Well where he was working as a monstergroom. He closed his eyes, and for the first time looked for thoughts that would be harmless if overheard by Fisheagle.

He thought of his family in Westgate: Harpoon's crab stew, the Boys and the Precious Stones, and the glitter of mica in the air, and the stamp of boot irons as Dad came back from watch on the Wall —

As not-Dad came back from watch on the Wall. For real Dad was a King he had never met who had died of poison, and real Mum was a tall, smart woman with dark hair and blue eyes, dead when he was born. And Murther, white-faced, liver-lipped, cruel Murther, was his half brother.

And for even thinking this, he was instantly in danger.

He cried, quiet and savage, so the tears ran out of his open eyes and into his ears. And after a bit, he was too tired to think about the difference between real families and unreal families, or anything but love. So his mind slid back to Harpoon and Ector. In the warmth those thoughts brought, he drifted away into sleep.

And woke into a new world.

·PART THREE·

The drift in darkness, cool, lovely, the darkgardens brushing with their slippery colors. Floating, floating —

She stopped. Through the immense dark volumes of the world there thrilled a vibration. A tiny vibration, but needle-pointed, stabbing the delicate nerve web she kept spread over the land, a web that took the vibrations from huts and palaces and those parts of Wells not protected by iron . . .

Someone had moved something. Something that acted as a pivot for everything that kept the land as the land should be. If the pivot was moved, control could slip away. And she needed control, absolute control, if the course of darkness was to stay steady until it burst forth to flood the bright world.

She took herself away from the caress of the slimehands. She drifted, faster than the drift of the Helpers in the spirals that brought them ever closer to the light shafts from the Wells. Into the Well she put herself, up, where living rock became built stone, and stone became secret passage and air and dazzle, until she was once again in her chamber, high above the land.

It was dark in the chamber. She could feel the sleep of her child nearby. The beautiful child who would be in danger, unless she made the sacrifice that must be made.

She sighed, entering the body, feeling the poor weak air fill the things called lungs and drive the wet blood around the billows and hollows. She flicked the catch; the bronze shutters wheezed open. The black eyes opened. There below lay the land, agonizingly bright under the cutting blade of a quarter-moon.

She steeled herself. Then she let the power of her mind scorch out, burning into every chink and fissure.

Nothing. Whatever she had felt was gone. Her child slept. The land was in subjection.

But from now on, she would be watching.

THIRTEEN

The first thing in Idris's new world was Ambrose's voice in his mind very early the next day. *You will report to Orbach and learn the arts of Knighthood,* it said. *Your watches have been reallocated. Go muffled. You will be sought.*

Idris lit the lamp. On his chair someone had laid out a red tunic bearing an enamel devouring eel, good leather boots instead of the monstergroom clumpers, red breeches, a sword (not, of course, Cutwater), and a round shield.

Orbach was a large black-haired man with a heavily battered face and the presence of a thundercloud. He had spent his days in the lamplit metal of the Tower Ambrose armory, alongside the cutting rooms on the entrance floor. "Morning," he said. "They tell me that you can do them monstergroom mind tricks. But them mind tricks stop working when your beard starts to grow, so we'll have none of them, thankee. As far as I am concerned, you are an ordinary squire and will be treated like one. Now. We are leaving this valley."

"Very well. I will say good-bye."

"The Knight leaves instantly, without delay." Orbach threw him a garment. "Your cloak."

Idris slung the cloak around him. "I am not yet a Knight," he said and ran to Morgan's room. She was a lump under the covers, topped with a tousle of red hair. "What a horrible cloak," she said, blearing at him.

"I'm going away," said Idris.

"Away?"

"Back for Darksolstice at the Mount. Be careful."

"I'll look after her," said a cheery voice from the windowsill.

"What are you doing here?"

"Guarding my princess."

"Oh Digby, you are so silly," said Morgan fondly. "Be careful." She reached out a hand and touched Idris's. "I'll miss you."

And down went Idris, feeling lonely and foolish to be jealous of a monster, to where the horses were stamping and blowing in the dark before the dawn.

As they cantered down the road beside the lake, he looked back. The eastern sky was light. Against it the towers of the Mount stood up like broken teeth. In the Kyd Tower a window glowed poison green. Idris shivered. He turned his head away and dug in his heels. The horses trotted down the Great Road and turned west.

It was full daylight when they rode over the top of the dam and climbed the rise of land that controlled the northern margin of the Poison Ground. It was a poor road, winding past little granite farms where goats shared the houses with people.

Drifts of woodcock settled into gorsey hillsides, and an eagle floated over high ground in the distance. The air freshened with a hint of salt that made Idris think of Harpoon and Ector and brought the tears pricking to his eyes.

They rode for two days, Kek sailing high above and a little in front. In the loping rhythm of the pony's canter, the things Ambrose had told him settled in his mind.

It was almost as if he had expected something like this. He searched himself for astonishment and confusion and found no trace of either. It was as if he was a river that had found its valley, or a bird that had found its air. He had been born a King, and it was a natural state, and he would do what he must to fulfill his destiny and save the land of Lyonesse.

At dusk on the third night, they ate and changed horses at an inn at the foot of the first great heathery sweep of the moors. By the time they reached the first crest, the sun was down. Orbach led him to a standing stone, black against the sky.

A small, keen wind soughed out of the ink-blue void. "The Flake of Mica rises," said Orbach. And there in a narrow band of clear sky between the horizon and the cloud-roof stood a pale star that winked like a mica flake turning in the light.

"Watch the stones," said Orbach.

"What stones?" said Idris. The darkness stretched away under the sky; endless heather and bog, pathless, without lights.

Orbach laughed and extended a dark arm. "Here," he said. On the hand, Idris saw something glow the same gray-silver as the star. He felt something pressed into his palm. A ring. He put it on his finger, but it was too big, so he pulled it off and put it on his thumb.

"Hold it to the star," said Orbach.

Idris held up his fist. The stone in the ring caught the light of the star.

Suddenly the black hills were no longer black. Across the world ahead there had appeared little rods of light, arranged in a line, hilltop to hilltop. Idris's heart filled with wonder. This must be the old magic of which Ambrose had spoken: the magic of star and stone.

Orbach spurred his horse. Idris's mount caught its stable-mate's eagerness and bounced forward with a spring that almost unseated him. Off they thundered at a breathless gallop across the drumming turf, freezing air parting on Idris's nose, tors and cairns drifting past against the stars, tearing along the road that was no road but at the same time a perfect road, outlined by gnarled wands of silver.

Deeper in the moors other standing stones went by, ice blue and blood-red, and once a herd of mammoths half lit by a dolmen that glowed pale buttercup yellow. The exhilaration of the ride became weariness, and the smell of hot horse, and the wet slap of muzzle-foam on Idris's face. And at last they crested a rise, and the horses speeded up from a grudging trot to a sure-footed canter, and bucketed down a double silver line of stones to something low and dark and bulky from which no lights shone.

Then there was an arch through a massive wall, and a courtyard, and the creak and clang of an iron portcullis. A torch flared in the heaving flanks of the horses and the armor of serving men in a wide courtyard with a well at its middle. And a voice said, "Welcome to Castle Ambrose."

And finally Idris slept, on a thin straw mattress in a thick moorland silence broken only by the yodel of the last of the year's curlews.

He did not dream. This was partly because he was tired. And it was partly because of the appearance of that green window in the Kyd Tower. Behind the window, he was sure, Fisheagle sat watching the minds of Lyonesse.

Having seen that window, it seemed to Idris that even dreaming was no longer safe.

By daylight, Castle Ambrose was a heavy mound of dark rock crouched on a low green hill. It was an ancient place, built for war, not splendor. The first day, what there was of it after Idris had woken, he spent exploring its maze of rooms, gloomy but exciting, stacked with enough weapons for an army and enough stores for a siege. On the second morning he woke to the smell of frost and an autumn-blue sky through the glassless arrow slit that did duty as a window. There was a tray at his side, bearing weedwater and dry bread. He felt brisk and full of energy. He ate breakfast and trotted into the yard.

Orbach was sitting on the mounting block. "Now," he said, "we refine the Knightly arts."

Winter arrived. Snow fell. The training proceeded.

The days started with Idris's eyes snapping open in his cell, feeling Orbach awake. A knife might clatter on the stone stairs, or a boulder fall from an arch, or poison lurk in the coarse bread or the rank fish. Idris learned to feel it coming and evade. He acquired hurts and scars but escaped sore mischief.

So much for defense, then. There was also the matter of attack. If the lessons at the Wolf Rock had been a school, this was a university. For this purpose, Idris learned the use of the staff, spear, buckler, bow, horse-lance, sling, throwstone, and of course sword: the sword being the principal weapon of Knighthood, the rest merely useful.

One morning, the sixty-first after his arrival, the sky was high and blue. So Idris went to the topmost tower of the castle and looked around. In the far west, the tangled crags of the Sundeeps sat under their piled-up clouds. To the east the moors rolled away, billow on billow. On the horizon of the first hill stood a horseman, dressed with a green cloak that blew from him in the cutting breeze.

Idris went up to Kek. As the gull swooped low he saw the blazon of the Brassfin on the tunic, the longsword strapped to the horse's withers. He saw the light hair and whitish face.

"Kay!" cried Idris as the horseman cantered into the yard.

Kay was very pale, and his eyelids seemed too heavy for him to hold up. "I bring a letter," he said, swaying with exhaustion. He handed a skin packet to Idris.

Idris took the letter, bowed as the Manner dictated, and waved over a servitor. "Show his lordship a bed," he said.

The servitor bowed low. Kay's eyes moved between the servitor and Idris. Idris was aware of a small spike in Kay's thoughts: anger? Not quite. More like jealousy. That was Kay for you. He was tired, though, and that would be making him short-tempered. Idris opened the letter.

We command our subject Idris House Ambrose to attend us on the Mount on the occasion of the Darksolstice, read the note. There was a lot of courtly waffle. The sign-name next to the royal seal was a jagged maze of squid ink on which gold dust had been scattered. The translation clerkwritten under it said *Sea Eagle, Regent of Lyonesse.* There was a further scrawl, in the same spiky hand as the sign-name. *The Dolphin tells me he met you at the New Deer and you took to each other famously,* read the scrawl.

Idris frowned. He did not remember anything of the sort. What he did remember was the sulky jut of the Kyd's lower lip and the hot, resentful eyes the Dolphin had cast in his direction when Morgan had practically twisted his arm to invite Idris to the Mount.

His mind turned to the poison-green window that had appeared in the Kyd Tower as he had left the Valley of Apples. This was an invitation into the jaws of death. But the Manner was precise. Invitations from the Mount were royal commands. Royal commands were not to be defied, on pain of death. Of course Idris would have to go.

As Idris folded the letter he was aware of a feeling of excitement in the pit of his stomach. He would see the home of his ancestors and the throne from which he would one day rule, and meet the people from whom he would seize that throne.

Oh, yes. He was looking forward to it.

Kay slept. Later Idris showed him the castle, remembering the day Kay had showed him the Well, missing Morgan. "Quite good," said Kay at zupper. "Bit old and drafty." Idris caught the spike of jealousy again.

"Is something wrong?" he said.

"No," said Kay. His pale face reddened. "Well, yes. Here you are, getting plenty of fighting and fresh air while we're hooking monsters around in the stink. What's going on?"

"It's Ambrose's idea. How is everyone?" said Idris, to change the subject.

"Morgan reads all the time and talks to herself," said Kay. Or to Digby, thought Idris. "Ambrose has gone off somewhere. The other grooms, well, we're grooms, we work." Idris saw he had been wrong this morning. This was no passing tetchiness. It was a hard, deep anger. He said, knowing it would do no good, "That's the way to become a Captain."

"So they say." Kay pushed his plate away. "But what we all want to know is . . . d'you mind if I'm frank?"

"Do I have a choice?"

"What we all want to know," said Kay, "is, why does Ambrose think you're so special? I mean, you came from nowhere. But you get little chats in the evenings. And when you fell down the Well someone threw you a chair and we all knew it had to be him. Dawkins was no stupider than you, but he got killed. And now here you are in this castle with servitors everywhere. What's going on?"

Idris would have liked to tell Kay the truth. But that would put him in danger from Kay's jealous fits and Kay in danger from the Mount. Perhaps if he showed Kay what his life was really like, his jealousy would abate. "Tell you what," he said. "Come and train with me."

Kay looked up. "When?"

"Now, if you want."

"That would be good."

After the servitors took away the cheese and apples, Idris led Kay through the stone passages to the Sword Hall.

Kay brought his longsword. It was too big and heavy for him, and he used it from vanity, not wisdom. Idris picked his usual weapon, short, useful, well balanced. They pulled on padded coats, bronze helmets with cheek guards and eyepieces, greaves to protect their shins. They moved to the middle of the floor. Kay said, "Ready? Go!"

He said it quickly, and by the time he said *go*, his blade was running under Idris's guard at his chest padding. But Idris had been expecting this or something like it. The world slowed down, and Kay's blade slid past as Idris swayed to one side, and the weight of Kay's stupidly too-big blade carried him on past Idris, and Idris tonked him on the helmet with the pommel as he went by, and down he went on the flagstones. "Cheat!" hissed Kay.

"I beg your pardon?"

Kay scrambled to his feet. "I wasn't ready." As he said *ready*, he swiped heavily at Idris. Idris stepped aside, tapping Kay on the shoulder with his blade. Kay turned again. The visible parts of his face were red, and he was sobbing for breath. "Come on," he said.

Idris made a lunge, purposely easy. Kay batted it aside. "Have to do better than that," he said.

But what can I do? thought Idris. If I stop fighting, he'll call me a coward, and according to the Manner we shall have to fight to the death, which would be just stupid. And if I beat him he'll go on fighting until I have to hurt him, which will be stupid, too. What I would like to do is keep him as a friend.

Since Kay would never admit he was beaten, there was only one way of doing this. Idris gritted his teeth, preparing himself. He saw Kay's sword come over in a clumsy arc. He put up his own blade to parry. But instead of beating Kay's blade aside he turned the hilt of his sword sideways, so Kay's blade did not lock but bounced onto his arm, where it sliced a long red mouth that welled and dripped on to the floor. "Touched!" cried Idris, in the congratulatory voice prescribed by the Manner. "Blood. I yield!"

"Huh," said Kay, pulling off his helmet before it suffocated him. "That wasn't much of a fight."

Idris smiled inwardly, in spite of the pain. Nobody was as ungracious in victory as Kay. "A victory, though."

Kay shrugged, trying not to look too pleased. Back in the Valley he would mention that he had bested Idris, and people would privately conclude that Idris was not much of a fighter and dismiss him from their minds. So it had been a wound worth getting.

"What were you playing at?" said Orbach later as he closed Idris's wound with nipper ants.

"There are fights in which you do not use swords."

"They're not called fights," said Orbach. "They're called wars."

Kay left Castle Ambrose next morning, on the long road to the Valley of Apples, carrying with him Idris's letter accepting the invitation for the Darksolstice gathering ten days from this and a useful quantity of scornful gossip. Idris waved him good-bye, but he was not sorry to see him go. Then he went to Orbach. "I must talk to Ambrose," he said.

"He'll be in the Sundeeps," said Orbach. "I'll take you there."

"I shall ride alone," said Idris.

"You be careful, then," said Orbach. "Funny sort of place, the Sundeeps. We can have everything ready by noon."

As the sun climbed the last hand's breadth to the zenith, Idris slung his saddlebags, checked his weapons, mounted his pony, passed under the gate arch, and turned west, toward the horizon, where the crags of the Sundeeps loomed under their clouds.

All that day and the two that followed he rode west over the bare flanks of the moors. At night he rolled himself in the skin of a cave bear and made sure he did not dream. The air smelled salty. When he looked over his shoulder, the peaks of High Kernow floated snowcapped just above the far horizon. Ahead the Sundeeps themselves rose ever higher, cliffs, and above the cliffs grassy slopes climbing through veils of vapor, then more cliffs and ridges and cairns around which dark clouds oozed and billowed.

Where are you? said Idris in his mind.

No answer.

The moors rolled up to the very cliffs of the Sundeeps. Late on the third day, Idris stopped at the foot of the first, made a fire of briar roots, boiled a kettle, and brewed weedwater. The silence was thick.

"Kek," said a voice. And there on the brownish grass stood his gull, smart white with gray wing covers and brilliant yellow beak and feet.

Normally Kek did not come anywhere near Idris. But now he stood watching him first with one yellow eye, then the other. Gulls have few thoughts beyond food. But Idris got the distinct impression that Kek had no desire to enter the mountains towering into the mist above their heads. "Come on," he said and threw the gull a lump of bread. Kek swallowed it in one, spread his sickle wings, and jumped into the sky.

Idris watched him spiraling upward with a feeling that he had persuaded the gull to do something against its will. A ridiculous feeling, he told himself, for gulls are simple creatures, with no will to speak of. The person who was worried was him. He had a question to ask Ambrose, which was how he, Idris Limpet of the Westgate, could at the Darksolstice dismantle the reign of the usurpers Fisheagle and Kyd Murther before they found him and had him killed.

Idris finished eating. He cleared up the remains of his meal, hid every trace of his fire, and began to lead the pony up the winding path into the first steeps. The moors faded below him as he climbed. His mind was far away. It was a dizzy, dangerous path, but nowhere near as dangerous as the one waiting for him in the Valley of Apples. . . .

There was no warning, only a roar of wind in feathers, and something that might have been a yellow ax slamming past his head. The pony screamed. He got his back to a rock wall and saw that the yellow ax was not an ax but the beak of an enormous bird, and that it had missed his head because it had not been aiming for him but for his pony. The pony was slithering down the scree slope, shrieking and pawing at the rocks, crimson blood welling from a long cut in her flank. And flapping over the pony, blotting out the view with its enormous wings, was a huge gull, white below, black above: a gull with a body the size of an adult seal, an eye as big as a goose's egg, a great yellow beak now open, ready to rend. A greatgull, long gone elsewhere in Lyonesse. A creature from ancient stories. And the Sundeeps.

All this flashed through Idris's mind as he pulled the Wolf Rock dagger from its sheath, aimed, and flung. The bright blade thumped into the greatgull's thigh. It screamed and flopped away from the pony, its dreadful eyes seeking Idris. They found him. He drew his sword, but the hilt slid from his fingers and clattered on the stones. The greatgull labored toward him, screaming as it came. Idris groped on the ground for his sword, knowing it was going to be too late. The greatgull drew back its head for the beak-chop that would take Idris's own head clean off.

And it screamed again. Not greedy and furious like last time, but in a new way, full of surprise and pain. Idris caught a glimpse of one of its eye sockets welling blood. It writhed in the air, beating at the thing that had swooped out of the sky at it. The small thing, white, with gray wings and yellow eyes.

"Kek!" cried Idris.

"Kek!" cried Kek. Then the greatgull's wing caught him, and he spun away, a little sickle of white against the gray granite and the cold blue sky, and landed with a thud on a patch of turf, and stayed there, motionless. The greatgull flapped around to attack Idris. But Idris had used the time brave Kek had won him to pick up his sword. The bird swooped for the kill. Idris took a step forward and drove the blade into the huge white breast. The creature came down with an earthshaking thump.

Idris did not even look at it. He was kneeling by Kek, companion of his childhood, broken on the wild green turf.

"Kek," he said.

"Kek," said Kek faintly. The yellow eye, half an hour ago so bright and curious, was dull and filmy. Blood stained the smooth white feathers. Idris could feel the gull's mind shrinking and darkening.

"Don't die," said Idris.

But there was more shrinking, more dark: and a hint of an odd feeling that might have been pride, and a vision of . . . eggs?

"Kek!" said Idris.

"Kek," said Kek, scarcely more than a breath.

And died.

Idris wept.

The tears streamed down his face, and his vision became a gray curtain of salty rain, and he put his face in his hands and sobbed hard enough to shake himself loose from the rock on which he stood.

Then something soft and warm was pushing at the side of his head. He looked up. It was the pony.

"Yes," he said. He got up. The greatgull was sprawled over the rocks down the slope. "We'll fix you up," he said. "And we will finish what we have started."

So he took nipper ants from the box and put them on the gash on the pony's flank and talked to it soothingly while its eyes rolled at the sting of the venom. Then he took back his dagger from the greatgull's corpse. Finally, he lifted the body of poor Kek, small and light in death, and carried it to the top of the slope, and buried it under a cairn of big stones on a granite crag with an all-around view of land and sea, of the kind the gull would have been used to in life. As he laid on the last stone he remembered his foreboding at the cliff-foot and was sorry. And suddenly felt as if he were high, high above, watching a boy laying a great stone on a pile of great stones. And when he looked up, the boy looked up, and it was him, so he was looking up at himself. It lasted an eyeblink, no more. Then Idris was Idris, and in the high blue a white sickle hung, faded, and was gone.

Idris poured out a cup of the greatgull's blood on the cairn. Then he took the pony by the head and followed the path into the Sundeeps.

The way wound up wooded valleys, then slopes of wind-stunted grass that gave on to other valleys. At the head of a final valley of naked rock was a notch from which the path sloped downward. Idris paused there to catch his breath.

At his feet the Sundeeps spread seaward, a maze of woods and crags. Their far edge must have been five leagues away, in this terrain a day's march for boy and pony. Along that far edge ran the Wall, built into the crags. And to north and south the Wall stretched away, with the dun land on its inside and the shifting blue on its outside. He felt a great pride that it should have been built by one whose blood ran in his veins. That was the kind of thing that Kings were meant to do.

Idris knew he was a twelve-year-old boy who had pulled a sword from a stone. And seven days from now was Darksolstice, the day on which he meant to take back his kingdom.

It was a huge task, as big as the Wall. Suddenly he was full of doubt.

The pony began to trudge along the path downhill. A salt wind was in Idris's face, and clouds were rolling up from the sea. Three leagues away was a wood of dark trees and the gleam of water beyond it. And in the water, if he was not mistaken, a tower. The tower was the only sign of human habitation. Ambrose's, perhaps.

A cloud swept over, trailing black fringes of rain. Wet fog wrapped the land. Soaked and shivering, Idris trudged on, leading the poor wounded pony, through cold gray mist among crags half seen on either side. Somewhere beyond the clouds, night was beginning to fall.

Soon there was darkness — darkness thick, black, and invincible, full of whips of rain.

Almost immediately he knew he had lost the path. If he could lose a path this easily, how much more easily could he lose a kingdom?

There seemed to be trees around him, pressing in. He fell. The pony twitched the reins from his fingers and was gone. The rain was falling too hard for flint and iron and tinder. He told himself that this was only a wood, and that nights came to an end, and that sleeping in the rain might be uncomfortable, but it was not the end of the world. But he felt young, and foolish, and powerless. And frightened.

The wood was in the Sundeeps, abode of the Old Magic. Who could say whether nights here ended? And whether this was normal rain, or something much worse, that would wash your life away and leave your bones for the greatgulls? Nonsense, thought Idris. Keep walking downhill, and you could not go wrong. He walked. Ahead, in a chink between trees, he saw the glow of a fire.

He wrapped his cloak around him and broke into a trot. It occurred to him that a fire in the Sundeeps woods was not necessarily a comforting thing. But he caught a glimpse of stars among the treetops and found he was heading in the right direction. So he trotted on.

The trees stopped. The fire seemed to be a bonfire, with a huge standing stone at each side of it, gilded by the flames. Beyond it was water, flat and black. Far out on the water there rose a pale tower. The tower must be his destination. But Idris did not altogether like the feeling of this place. It was unpleasantly like an arena, made for battle.

He eased his sword in its scabbard. The rain had stopped now, and the clouds had rolled away, and the sky was a bottomless pit of stars. By their light and the fireglow, Idris saw what looked like a man standing still by the stone. It was not the usual kind of man. He bore springing from his brow a great set of antlers. As Idris eyed him, he pawed the ground with his foot and roared like a stag in the breeding season.

Another roar came from the eaves of the wood. When Idris looked around he saw another stagman and next to him another. Mistletoe was twined in their antlers, its white berries turned to blood drops by the ruddy firelight. And in the right hand of each were blades made of chipped stone, long and heavy and hooked, of the kind men use to hack saplings to make hedges. Idris sent out his mind to listen and wished he had not. For behind the firelit eyes only one word thundered like a huge, slow drum.

Sacrifice.

Behind Idris and to his left and right, curved like the arms of a bow, were the stagmen with their billhooks. In front of him, closing off his escape as a string closes a bow, was the fire.

Sacrifice.

Idris held the mind. It buffeted him, but he hung on. He said to it, slowly, *I am your King.*

There was silence, blank, amazed.

No, said a voice. *Sacrifice.*

Part of Idris wanted to run away. But there was something else in him now. These creatures were part of the land, an ancient part, from the time of star and stone, before the Wells and their poison. He must show them who he was, and claim them for his own.

He turned to face them. They came toward him, slowly. He could feel the heat of the fire on his back, see its glow gilding the blades and faces and antlers of these his subjects.

Sacrifice.

Idris raised his arms, fingers outspread. The fire glow cast his shadow far over the turf, the finger shadows like antlers, playing over the chests of the stagmen.

They stopped moving.

Look, said Idris and opened his mind to them, a mere chink, but enough for them to feel the stones of Lyonesse in him.

The stagmen fell on their faces. *King*, boomed their minds. *All hail. Welcome.*

Idris walked through the prostrate bodies, past the fire, and onto the beach. Beyond the beach the stars shone clear and bright and double, reflected in the glassy lake. In the middle of the lake something pale floated. Something tall, and serene, and noble. A tower, starlit, with a warm yellow window halfway up its flank, over its perfect reflection. Idris knew without thinking that here was Ambrose.

As he sheathed his sword he felt on his thumb the ring Orbach had given him. He looked up and saw, hanging over a craggy ridge like a pale, winking eye, the Flake of Mica.

He raised his hand above his head so the ring's stone could catch the starlight.

All across the black lakewater a line of stars came up, brighter than the others.

He began to walk, arm upraised, along that line. The water hardly covered his shoes. Behind him the stagmen knelt roaring back and forth, exulting that they had met their King.

With joy in his heart, Idris followed the road of stars across the water to the island on which stood the tower of mortarless stone. He opened the white wicket gate and walked up to the door. The door opened, and there was Ambrose, one black eyebrow up. "Ah," said Ambrose. "I have been waiting for you. And so, by the sound of it, have your people."

FOURTEEN

Idris woke to a bright, cold day with big clouds sailing in on a breeze that had the ducks skidding over their reed-beds. He felt excited and energetic. A pretty housekeeper gave him breakfast in a room on the towertop with a view of the lake, with gnarled yews and granite crags beyond. After breakfast she sent him to the tower's watergate. Beside the quay was a sort of boat — not much of a boat, for one whose eye was accustomed to the seagoing craft of the Westgate; more of a punt, really, square at each end, with two chairs made of polished tree branches. Ambrose was sitting on one of the chairs, staring into the middle distance, thinking. "Good morning yourself," he said, when Idris greeted him. "Come aboard and sit down."

Idris sat, looking around him for oars and sails and seeing none.

"Off we go," said Ambrose.

The boat moved sideways from the quay and began to glide across the lake. "Star and stone," said Ambrose, watching Idris's face. "Powerful stuff."

The surface of the lake was dark, ruffled by the wind. Something slid across the water ahead, making a V-shaped wake. Idris's hand went to his iron dagger. He said, "Is that a monster?"

"A dragon," said Ambrose. "Entirely different. Born in this world, not the Wellworld. Two of them live here. The last two anywhere, as far as I know. Caradoc, of the Red Dragons. Enys, of the White." Idris gasped. Another wake had joined the first. Two triangles the size of boats' sails rose from the dark surface of the lake. One was the color of blood, the other the color of ivory. They circled each other, as if playing.

"This is the last lake of the old world," said Ambrose. "Lyonesse as it was in the days before the Wells, when magic happened through the movement of star over stone, not screaming machines. My world."

"Yet you fish for monsters with the Captains."

Ambrose said, "The monsters are of another world. The Regent and the Dolphin have one foot in that world, and they would drag the Captains there with them, and Lyonesse after them, and turn the land into a Poison Ground. I need to know all that they know, so I can do battle with them." He made a wry face. "Of course I am only human, so I must admit that there is pleasure in knowledge for its own sake. As you yourself know, Idris of Lyonesse, meter reader, sword tugger, spy." His face became serious again, his eyes black and bottomless. "Now. Tell me why you have come."

"I seek advice," said Idris. "The Regent Fisheagle has called me to Darksolstice. I think she knows she is threatened. I think she means to destroy me and turn the land over to monsters. I cannot let this happen. So at Darksolstice I must take my kingdom, and I do not know how." He waited for Ambrose to laugh him to scorn.

But Ambrose did not laugh. He said, "Fisheagle knows that something is stirring in the land; I have felt her mind, and so have you, I think. But she may not know that the thing that is stirring is a twelve-year-old groom, and you must give her no reason to suspect this. It is written that when the Old King's heir returns, the servitors will send up a great white smoke from Tower Ambrose after Darksolstice, at which point all Knights will rise in his support. Fisheagle has certainly read this and has plans for a smoke of her own when Murther comes of age. Many Knights have read it, too, and most of them would welcome any heir but Murther, though many other Knights have grown fat and useless these past years. If you wish, my dwarf Cran will make you a white smoke, and perhaps the Knights will rise and slay Fisheagle and Murther and put you in the Mount. Or perhaps they will not. You are the King. It is for you to choose.

"There is another way. You can take the sword Cutwater as a token of your kingship, and travel across sea to Ar Mor, and speak with King Mark in his city of Ys. He is a dangerous man, but a true one, and no friend to monsters. I built his stonefields, which bring him the force of the stars to help him with his health and his farms. Perhaps you can persuade him to bring his armies to fight with you, and with them his allies the Duke of Eytgard and the Overlord. They all see the power of monsters growing and would like to show the Fisheagles of the world that what comes from other universes should go back there. But you will have to persuade these men. Not an easy thing for a boy, and by the time it is done, you will be almost a man. I will set you on that road, if you choose to follow it.

"Whether you choose the quick smoke or the slow raising of armies, you must block the Wells before they flood the land and give the monsters power over all." He fingered his chin, looking at the dragon fins slicing the lake. "It is for you to decide. Study your enemy. Particularly his feet."

"Feet?" said Idris.

"Look!" cried Ambrose, ignoring him. "The Lady!"

The boat was lying on black water at the foot of a lofty cliff. On the cliff was engraved the device of the eel devouring its tail. The water in front of the device seemed to be boiling. From the turmoil rose an arm: a woman's arm, sinuous and beautiful, tattooed with an intricate pattern of mistletoe berries that ended at the wrist with another encircling eel. The hand was clenched and bore a long object, many-colored against the somber rock.

Idris strained his eyes to see what the object might be. The pull of his eyes seemed to make the boat move, so that it slid alongside the arm. The hand was fine-boned and beautiful, with tapered fingers. An eel ring encircled the third. The fingers opened, offering Idris the thing they held. He grasped it. The arm sank away into the deep.

The thing in his hand was a scabbard, apparently made of gold, but much lighter than gold. It was warm and instantly dry. Touching it filled him with a sense of happiness and well-being. There were ten tiny splashes in the water alongside the boat. What had made the splashes were the heads of the nipper ants holding Kay's sword-slash together. The wound itself had become a pink line, which faded into the brown of his arm as he watched.

"This is the scabbard Holdwater, made before the Old King for the sword Cutwater. He who wears it cannot be wounded and may cure others who are hurt. Though not," said Ambrose, reading his mind, "a gull who is already dead. Now. It is time for you to go. Look upward. Call me when you need me. For now, farewell. Oh, yes. Look up."

Idris looked where Ambrose had directed. A white bird rode up there in the blue, resting confidently on the breeze. He sent up his mind, glimpsed a world of air and vapor, a planet spread below, a lake, woods, crags, built into the Wall that separated the blue from the green —

"We will talk soon," said Ambrose and stepped over the boat's side. The water closed over his head, and he sank away. Idris cried out, looking overboard. The mage smiled up at him, held up a hand, and faded into the deep. The boat was drifting along the cliff, as if drawn by a current. The banks drew together. The lake became a river, then an estuary that wound, fringed with reeds, toward the sea. The boat grounded on a shingly beach. Clutching the scabbard Holdwater in his hand, Idris stepped ashore.

Above him a gull hung on the wind. He remembered the last glimpse of Kek's mind before death had swamped it. There had been a vision of eggs.

"Kek," said the gull high in the air, mentioning its name.

Kek, the child of Kek, second of the hereditary gulls of the rightful King of Lyonesse.

Idris felt brisk, and happy, and no longer alone.

There was a whinny farther down the slope. "Pony!" he cried.

The pony looked up. It gave Idris a look as if it was wondering what all the fuss was about, and trotted up to him. Idris patted its nose, slung a leg over its back, and turned its head eastward along the road that skirted the Sundeeps to the south, to where the standing stones stood like little teeth on the moors, and his destiny awaited him at Darksolstice in the Kyd Tower of the Mount.

He rode back into the Valley of Apples five days later, weary and saddlesore. Nobody even glanced at him as he trotted through the crowds in the streets, just another mud-stained traveler. He gave the reins to a servitor outside the porch of the Great Ambrose and ran up the steep steps leading to his cell.

And found the door closed and locked, and upon it a folded skin nailed, bearing the address Idris Wolf Rock in squid ink evaporated to a luxurious midnight black. He tore it down.

"What?" said a voice at his shoulder. He turned his head, saw Morgan, and forgot about the skin because he was busy giving her a very large hug. After the hug she stepped back and ran her eyes up and down him. "What have you been *doing?*" she said.

"Training," said Idris.

"Certainly looks like it." She sounded excited to see him. "You're all brown and dangerous, and what's that ring on your thumb? Kay said he beat you in a sword fight, but I don't believe him. Come in, come in, I've got some apples from home." They went and sat on the wooden bench in her room and chewed Wolf Rock apples that were getting sweeter as the year went on, and Idris unfolded the note from his door.

"Well?" said Morgan, when he looked up from reading.

"I have been moved," he said. "To rooms on the third level." Actually the note also said "more fitting to your rank." But he did not want to go into that just now.

"The third level?" said Morgan. "I've seen the rooms. They're called the Goldfinch Chambers, apparently. Lovely, lovely. Kay will be furious. Lucky you!"

"Yes," said Idris. He shouldered his bundle. He followed Morgan away from damp stone and the whisper of captive monsters, back to the world of corsair carpets and sweet smokes. Strangely enough, he found he was sorry to leave.

But not for long.

The Goldfinch Chambers were full of sun, with devices of bright birds and men in battle and corsair ships done on the walls in cunning work of copper and stone. There were two bedrooms, a dayroom, and a balcony hanging like a swallow's nest over an interestingly busy street. On the table was a large dish of melted seal cheese on three-grain bread, aurochs fillet, three kinds of fruit, and honeycomb. "What have you done to deserve this?" cried Morgan.

Idris did not answer. He was looking at the chair by the table. It was a heavy chair of carved and gilded wood, with cushions of red velvet. Someone had replaced the front right-hand leg. It was the chair that had saved him from the Well. A chill fell on him. Behind all this luxury lurked the stink of the Well, and darkness, and war.

Morgan sat down with a thump and reached for a melted cheeser. "So what happened after Kay left?"

Idris told her, leaving out anything about rightful Kings, which would have been dangerous.

"Well!" she said breathlessly, when he had finished. "All that fighting, poor Kek, the stagmen, how horrid!"

"Frightfully brave," said another voice. It was mildly sarcastic and seemed to belong to Morgan's bracelet.

"Language," said Morgan to the bracelet, which hopped off her wrist and turned into Digby.

"Yes, well," said Digby. "What I want to know is, all this food is very nice for gasfaces, but where's the fish?"

"Gasface?"

"It's what Digby calls anyone who doesn't live in dirty water. I haven't had anyone much to talk to except Kay, and he gets tiring after a bit, so Digby and I know each other pretty well now. Go away, Digby."

"Sorry I'm sure," said Digby, with a sniff remarkably convincing in one with no nose.

"And I must go, too. I've got a watch," said Morgan.

"Yes." It really was good to see Morgan again. "There's a spare room here," said Idris. "Why don't you move your stuff down?"

"But I can't! They won't let us!"

"They will," said Idris.

Morgan opened her mouth to argue. Then she closed it and gave him a strange look. She said, "You've changed. What happened?"

"I'll tell you someday," said Idris. "Not now."

And Morgan knew that that was all she was going to get out of this new, tougher, better Idris.

After she had gone, Idris took the scabbard Holdwater and laid it reverently in an enamel chest.

Holdwater, he said to the thing in the chest: Your time will come, and mine with it. At Darksolstice. And after.

If we survive.

As soon as Kay heard of the move to the Goldfinch Chambers, he came to visit. He admired the rooms, of course, but Idris caught the old spike of jealousy and noticed that his eyes were sharp and cold. Idris let Kay talk to Morgan and kept himself apart, though he saw that Kay noticed that, too. It was just another thing to be careful about — there seemed to be more and more. When he walked in the streets he went constantly muffled. Everywhere he felt eyes watching, and ears listening, and thoughts probing. Or perhaps he was only imagining it. Whatever the case, it was best to stay in the Goldfinch Chambers, behind whose mosaic walls was a skin of thought-proof iron. To stay inside and brood hour after hour on whether to declare his kingship with white smoke, or bide his time and raise armies.

On Darksolstice Eve he was standing with Morgan on the top of the Well. It was noon. Morgan pointed at the Mount and the shadow it cast on the Dark Tor, first of the mountains of Kernow. "Tomorrow the Mount shadow touches the Tor Cairn," she said. "Then the sun has sunk to its lowest, and the Dolphin must sacrifice a bull and a burner to bring it up again."

Idris was pretty sure that the sun would come up anyway. He remembered the whey-faced Murther on the green meadow at New Deer, at odds with his people, greedy for death. The death of bulls and burners was the kind of thing that would truly delight him. "Why did he ask us, do you think?" he said.

"He thinks I'm pretty, of course," said Morgan. "You he couldn't get out of. You're rather sullen today, you know. It's only a rite and a party. Kay's brother went two years ago. We go up to the Mount and someone introduces us to Fisheagle, only we have to call her Sea Eagle, Regent of the Realm, and then to Kyd Murther, Dolphin of the Realm —"

"We've already been introduced."

"But not written on the skin. All Knights and Ladies have to be written to be in the court. And don't worry, you get written, too, because my father has taken you into the family. So we visit the Dolphin while he is dressing to show that we are his very close friends and then we get written and we drink to his health, and then the sun touches the tor and the Dolphin comes down into the town. To the Old Well. In a procession. It's lovely: uniforms, acrobats, public rejoicing. He pulls at the sword and nothing happens, of course, and the procession goes back to the Mount and that's that."

"Oh," said Idris. Unless he told the dwarf Cran to put up a white smoke.

He was coming around to the white smoke.

He would put out a general thought, in explanation. The young Knights would be assembled for the writing. The smoke

256

would rise, and so would the Knights. The people would rise behind them, and cast off the yoke of Murther and Fisheagle and the Captains. Quick, and clean, and surprising. If he did not do it and Fisheagle recognized him, they would kill him out of hand, and he would not have time to raise armies. He could not risk the delay.

That was it.

Idris felt the excitement rising in his breast. The smoke would rise. He would go to the Old Well and draw Cutwater. By tomorrow's zupper, Kyd Idris would sit on the throne of Lyonesse, with Ambrose his Regent.

If only he was a little more certain.

Morgan was up early on Darksolstice. The sun was a mere glow in the east as she laid out her dress and her shoes and wrote a letter to her mother — she had promised a letter: Winter life on the Wolf Rock was boring, high above the wind-sigh in the leafless oaks. Morgan was excited. But there was a darkness behind the excitement. If she had been a farseer, she would have thought it was a premonition. But she was an ordinary monster-groom of Knightly family, with the power of Hearing, now developed, but nothing otherwise special, so she put it down to not quite enough sleep. She leaned back from the skin on which she had just squid-inked the last of her letter and reread the ending: *Dear Mother and dear Father, whatever may befall, remember always that you have had the most loving of daughters, who will think of*

you for as long as she is capable of thinking. She smiled, imagining her mother opening the letter in the bedchamber that got the morning sun. She would read it to her father. They would laugh fondly at the dutiful sentiments, and be proud of the daughter making her way in the world.

She folded the letter. She sealed it. She left it on her table and went to have a bath and get ready for the day. She would give it to the messenger later.

But in small matters as in great, it is one thing to make a plan and quite another to carry it out.

Idris was in the Well again. There was black water all around him, and he could feel the swirl of monster eddies bouncing against his naked legs, and he knew there were teeth down there, seeking to kill him. . . .

"Oh, for goodness' *sake*," said a voice by his ear. And he realized he was looking at Digby, who had been jumping up and down on the pillow next to his head.

"Get off," he said. "Stop bouncing."

"I am basically a monopod, you know," said Digby. "How else am I supposed to get around?"

"Go away," said Idris. A beam of light was lancing through a chink in the window hangings. It was Darksolstice morning.

"Up!" cried Morgan from the door.

Idris sat up, trying to get rid of the last shreds of the dream.

"Bath's drawn!" said Morgan.

"Bath?"

She grabbed him by the foot and dragged him to the bathroom. He sat in the water and tried to forget the dream, a worrying dream this morning of all mornings, but not a surprising one.

For he had decided. It would be the white smoke.

He washed and put on his tunic and breeches of dark-red wool, gold-edged cloak, the ceremonial helm of the monster-groom, scarlet boiled-leather and gilt with earpieces, worn shoved back on the head. Last of all was the enamel monster-groom badge, the self-devouring eel of House Ambrose. This was the last time he would wear another's badge. By the end of the day the smoke would have risen, and he would carry the sword Cutwater and wear the crown of Lyonesse. He had trouble with the pin, for his fingers were shaking. He strapped on his Wolf Rock dagger and the scabbard Holdwater. Into the scabbard he slid his Castle Ambrose sword. Then he walked into the daychamber.

Morgan was waiting. She made him a half-ironic curtsy. She was wearing the long dress of Tower Ambrose, with tunic and eel badge. Her hair was swept back, and she wore a short dagger through the bun to keep it in place. "You look very pretty," said Idris, managing a smile.

"The ponies are waiting," said Morgan, blushing slightly. "We must go." The excitement of the day suddenly left her. Her earlier darkness and apprehension returned. She knew the feeling was spreading from Idris. He was muffled and silent now, his face pale and rigid. She wished he would tell her whatever it was that was on his mind. But she knew it would do no good to ask.

They went downstairs, mounted, and rode up the highway to the Mount. Morgan tried to chatter. Idris gave short answers, his mind elsewhere. As the road steepened in the wood leading up to the Mount, even that small conversation dried up.

The Wargate of the Mount was not encouraging.

It was not meant to be.

Looking around him, Idris turned sick.

The road led steeply uphill to the gate along the bottom of a steep-sided gulley. At the top of the gulley the walls rose high and sheer and glassy, pocked with arrow slits and spouts for hot oil. The gulley was thronged with riders and carts and fat Captains in chairs borne by sweating serfs. It should have been a festive crowd, but the killing ground robbed it of joy. Nobody could wait to get through the gates and into the Mount.

There were eighteen gates, as it turned out, one inside the other, gates of stone and spiked iron, gates that hinged and flapped and slid in grooves, the spaces between each watched by more arrow slits and spouts and cage-grilles from which burners could be flung blazing and shrieking among the attackers.

"Has anyone ever attacked this place?" asked Idris. He felt very small. How would you do it, with all the Knights in Lyonesse?

"Of course not," said Morgan, giving him a startled look.

"Only, if everyone loves the Regent and the Dolphin, it is odd that the Regent and the Dolphin have to defend themselves with all this." Morgan heard something like contempt in his voice. She found an echo of it in her own mind and muffled hastily. Her worry deepened.

"Names?" said a Mountman on the eighteenth gate.

They gave their names. The Mountman checked a list. "Pass, then. Ponies over there," he said, looking over their heads and yawning uncovered. Idris and Morgan passed, Idris filled with cold anger, for in Lyonesse nobody treated a dog with such want of Manner.

They gave the ponies to a groom and passed through the final gate. Morgan stopped, gasping, her hand on Idris's arm.

They were in the garden at the base of the Kyd Tower. Apple trees stood leafless around the walls, and a fountain played in the middle. In the fountain sat a creature with the upper part of a woman and the lower part of a fish. The creature looked at Idris with sea-green eyes and smiled. *Welcome*, said a voice in his mind.

This is wrong, thought Idris, shocked into unmuffling. *You are a monster.*

It is by order of the Regent Sea Eagle, said the voice. *How can it be wrong?*

A horn blew by Idris's ear. He slammed his mind shut. Someone was shouting their names: a herald, no doubt. They walked across the garden and in at the great door of the Kyd Tower, pointed-arched, carved with biting beasts. They waited in a line of people until a man in a black tin hat that covered his eyes conducted them up a staircase of black stone. He had a thin white face and a drip on the end of his nose. "The chamberlain," mouthed Morgan. Idris nodded, dry-mouthed.

"Enter and kneel," hissed the chamberlain and threw open the doors of a chamber.

The drip fell. A new one formed. Idris stepped into the chamber. He did not kneel. He looked to the top of a short flight of steps. On top of the steps was a big chair of blood-red stone. In the chair, clad in black robes that shimmered with wondrous light but failed to hide his white puffiness, sat Kyd Murther, pulling at his lower lip. A pair of boots stood at his side, so he would appear to be dressing, at ease with his subjects. Behind Kyd Murther stood a woman with a beak of a nose, long, narrow eyes of purest darkness, and a mouth painted the same red as the throne. On her head was a close-fitting hood, crowned with a spiked fin like a mullet's dorsal. The red mouth was a little open, the thin lower lip dented by a pair of sharp yellow canines. *Sea Eagle*, Idris remembered to think behind his muffle.

"Kyd Murther, Dolphin of the Realm," chanted the chamberlain. "And his glorious mother, the Regent Sea Eagle." Then, hissing, "*Kneel!*"

Idris could feel the mind of the creature that was Fisheagle reveling in the slavishness of the Darksolstice crowd. He despised it. He would not kneel to the creature. But this was the Red

Throne of Lyonesse. The throne was worthy of respect, and the Manner obliged even its rightful occupant to respect it. So Idris removed his helmet, and made the salute, and bowed deep to the throne, and said in a calm, steady voice, "As a groom of Lyonesse, I kneel to no one, but pay respect where it is due." Next to him, Morgan had curtsied deeply, so deeply, indeed, that Idris was afraid her knee would touch the ground. But she caught his eye, and he knew that her feeling in the matter was the same as his. The black eyes of Fisheagle rested on them. The face was without expression.

"We met at the New Deer, Prince," said Idris. "Your hunt, if you remember."

"Oh," said Murther, looking at him with his hot, bored eyes. "The hunt. The dragon or whatever it was escaped. We killed a sloth. Big one." He yawned. "His guts went everywhere. So *funny!* I don't remember you. The girl, yes, very tasty, ha."

The chamberlain was giving off waves of anxiety. Fisheagle's black eyes rested on Idris. The mind probed. But Idris's inner mind was full of the white smoke to come, and he had put only simple, basic thoughts outside a double muffle. Fisheagle's mind was horribly strong, sharp, and curious, though, and he could feel her levering at the corners of his mind. He looked at the floor. Something moved, darting. A mouse. Into the back of his memory came something Ambrose had said. *Study your enemy. Particularly his feet.* He put his mind into the mouse. He saw folds of cloth, then a kindly darkness as the little creature ran under the skirts of Murther's robe. This was better. He was not just standing there under Fisheagle's glare. He was studying his enemy, using the mouse's eyes.

Two pale columns rose before him: Kyd Murther's legs. There was something wrong with the heels. Something very wrong. . . .

"Away," hissed the chamberlain. The next courtiers were waiting on the stairs. Idris and Morgan slid away, were written on the skin, and let out of the tower.

"You didn't kneel," said Morgan.

"Nor did you." Idris was sweating. He had just seen a terrible thing.

Morgan met his eyes. She said, "There was no need," she said. She trusted him. He hoped she was right.

There was food, delicious food, red mullets, spits of snipe, a whole sturgeon that had been caught entering the Fal, strange thistle-like vegetables from Ar Mor, pies of fruits without name, honeys of heather and pine and sea-pink. Morgan dug in. Idris could not eat any of it. They stood and watched the parade of grave Knights and fat Captains and girls with pink feet and rings on their toes. Idris saluted the Knights, and Morgan chattered away charmingly, and the royal party came down from the Kyd Tower and mingled with its court. But Idris could not speak without thinking of what he had seen through the mouse's eyes.

"I'm glad my father's not here," said Morgan during a pause.

"Why?"

"It's not his kind of thing." A Captain waddled past, eyelids jeweled, wiggling his fingers at a pinkfoot. "Oh, look, here's Kay."

Kay was indeed threading through the crowd toward them, leading a man with hanging cheeks and the triple crown of Captaincy. Idris felt the blood drain out of his face. "Morgan!" cried Kay. "Idris! I beg to name Captain Ironhorse. Of the Westgate, you know! What a coincidence, isn't it? I expect you knew each other, all that time ago?" He grinned mischievously, hoping to cause embarrassment.

Idris looked into the Captain's stony little eyes, the eyes he had last seen through the spikes of Hell's Throat. He said, "I do not believe we did." Anger rose in him. "Ironbottom, you say?"

"Ironhorse," said Ironhorse, as if talking to someone very stupid. The fat brow creased below the tiara's rim. "But your face is familiar." Idris saw the stony eyes recognize him. "No," said Ironhorse. "I am wrong. I was thinking of someone else." He smiled, a smile totally false, and waddled away into the crowd. His robes looked shabby, and the gold of his tiara was certainly mixed with copper. He was a petty provincial Captain, but he was still poisonous enough to kill.

"I would have thought you'd have known him," said Kay, with a false innocence overlying a little grin of triumph. "I mean, Westgate's pretty small and mostly fallen down, so there can't be that many people worth knowing there."

"Kay, you are a pathetic snob," said Morgan. The grin turned to a sulky pout.

Idris felt suddenly weary. "One day you will be a useful Knight," he said and fixed the pale-haired boy with his eyes. He felt Kay lever at his mind, opening his mouth to snap back. *No*, thought Idris, *an argument with voices will not do. Well, since you want your way, have it.* He opened his mind and let Kay in.

Kay saw what the stagmen had seen. His face went suddenly white. Horror filled his eyes. *Idris*, he thought. *Sire. What have I done? What can I do?*

Use your voice. Undo the harm you have caused. Idris could feel the mind of Fisheagle suddenly burning. *And if it cannot be undone, be a loyal Knight of Lyonesse.*

Can you forgive me?

Nobody needs to be forgiven for being human. You have been my friend. Perhaps you will be my Knight. Kay was weeping. Idris would have liked to comfort him. But his eyes were following Ironhorse through the crowd. He was heading toward the royal party. To organize the arrest of an escaped monster? Without a doubt.

But before Ironhorse could reach the royals, a great bell boomed through the Mount: the warning bell for the Hour of Thanks and the ceremonies that followed. Marshals began to shoo the celebrants into their ranks. Ironhorse was far from the royals. Idris felt relief. The Captain would not be able to talk to anyone in authority till after the ceremonies and the procession, by which time the white smoke would have risen. Unless

266

Fisheagle had seen into his mind. In which case it was already too late.

"To the towertop!" bellowed the heralds, their horns blaring back and forth along the black stone walls

To the towertop they went, and looked north, to where the shadow of the tower lay on the slope of the Dark Tor, moving at a snail's glide toward the granite quoit on its summit.

"Part, Court!" cried the heralds. The crowd divided. Down the avenue they came, the Dolphin and the Regent — the Dolphin waddling, or perhaps hobbling, his burned-looking eyes flicking left and right, Fisheagle gliding, tall and slim. And Idris, looking at her, could not repress a sudden ghost of a thought. *This one killed the King and the Queen who bore me.*

The shining black figure hesitated for an eye-blink. Then it lifted an arm clad in shiny black and tipped with a long silver hand, black-nailed, and pointed and cried, "Rise to the Solstice Seat, Dolphin of the Realm!"

FIFTEEN

Kyd Murther glanced around him. Then he clambered up two steps onto an ancient seat of stone and slumped into a corner of it, glowering down at the court.

"The solstice comes!" cried Fisheagle. "A year ends, another begins! And the axle of time's turning is Kyd Murther, Dolphin of the Realm of Lyonesse, twelve years old this day!"

There was polite applause from the Captains. The Knights, Idris saw, merely pretended to be interested.

The shadow of Murther in the throne was a tiny crumb of darkness on the top of the shadow of the tower. "There is a black bull over there, and a burner, locked together in an iron cage. The bull is the old year, the burner the new," said Morgan. "Watch."

The shadow moved across the stone of the quoit, in the exact center of which was a little bull's-eye of white quartz. As the shadow touched the bull's-eye, harsh white light came into being, and the death bellow of the bull and the burner's mindscream roared out of the mountains. And while the light yet burned and before the first shocked howl of the scream had died, a great bell boomed in the tower.

"Praise the Well," said everyone. All the faces were solemn and removed. Idris did his best to fit in. But he was not thinking about the benefits of Wells.

He was thinking, in a rage as hot as the bull-destroying burner: This is a lie, and mixed with terror it holds the land in thrall. But I have seen the truth of Murther, and I know the nature of the lie, and within the hour it will be avenged.

He looked up and saw the dreadful face of Fisheagle. The eyes were looking straight into his.

"Blessed be the Well," she cried, in a harsh prey-bird's shriek. "And let no Cross be suffered to live."

Let it not, thought Idris, unmuffled, staring straight back.

For what he had seen through the eyes of the mouse during the robing of Murther was this. Murther, Dolphin of the Realm, sworn to abide by the Treaty that protected monsters from men, had fins that ran down the backs of his legs.

The Dolphin was Cross. And so must Fisheagle be.

"Blessed be the Well," murmured the crowd.

The bell boomed.

"Now we all go down to the Old Well," said Morgan.

Idris's mouth was dry as dust. He looked around. The eyes of some of the Knights rested on the Great Ambrose, as if idly. The moment for the white smoke was at hand. The stiltwalkers and tumblers and acrobats began their capers. The band's tarantara started a terrible baying and howling in the Mount kennels.

Was this the moment? Not all the Knights were looking at the Ambrose. Some were red with wine, or chatting to their neighbors. The tradition of the smoke was an ancient one. Was it just a curiosity?

Now was the moment he must decide. He risked putting his mind up to Kek. He saw the procession, a jeweled thread winding out of the Mount woods to the walled-in huddle of the Wellvale.

And something else.

In the back courts and yards of the Mount and in the stockades in the woods was a dark jostling, like black flies on a dead fish. He was looking down on the helmets of black Mountmen. Thousands of them. Tens of thousands.

His heart gave a mighty thump and seemed to stop.

The Knights in the procession had sharp swords, bright armor, and loyal minds. But there were no bows, and the armor was more ceremonial than useful. Every year for hundreds they had looked for white smoke and seen none. Certainly they were prepared for a fight but not for a battle. Fisheagle was ready for battle. Idris could make the smoke rise. But if he did, he would die in battle, and his Knights with him.

And in dying, he would have failed.

A terrible weariness spread through him. Cross or human, Fisheagle had prevailed.

There would be no white smoke.

The procession moved on. Serfs and prentices lined the road, scrabbling for coins flung by the Mountmen. The

Wellporches were decorated with bright hangings. Wellchoirs sang their enormous harmonies from each one, and from the chimneys high above brilliant colored smokes writhed against the lowering sky. The dwarf Cran was standing on the shoulders of a servitor outside the Ambrose porch. His little eyes were fixed on Idris. Idris returned his gaze. He shook his head firmly, once left, once right. The balance of history tipped. He had saved thousands of lives, but Ironhorse held his in the hollow of his hand. The dwarf sighed and slid down to the ground and scuttled off.

The procession moved on, the eyes of the Knights held away from the Ambrose now, a feeling of disappointment in the air mixed with relief. And at the back of it all, Idris thought he sensed a cold, scornful laughter.

Now he would be killed.

After half an hour the procession arrived in the square in front of the Old Well. Here, the Mountmen made a semi-circular wall to keep the people from the porch. Two servitors helped Murther from his litter, and Fisheagle glided onto a dais that had been raised before the porch's arch. Murther's sulky look had darkened.

Idris pushed to the front of the crowd, reckless of detection. He stood there and tried to believe that he had had a narrow escape. He did not believe it. Fisheagle had seen his thought. She wanted him to think he was beneath her notice, that was all.

A herald rose on the step of the dais. "The Kyd will go to the sword Cutwater," he boomed. "It is not to be expected that he will withdraw it from the stone, for he is as yet Dolphin, and not of man's estate."

"What rubbish," said Idris, too outraged to keep his voice down. A nearby Captain frowned, not believing his ears.

"Idris!" hissed Morgan, who had followed him through the crowd.

"Kyd . . . MURTHER!" boomed the herald.

Murther stumped across to the Wellporch and entered the shadows. Courtiers clustered around the entrance so that the interior was invisible to the crowd. There was a silence, then a patter of applause. A messenger came out and whispered in the herald's ear.

"A marvel!" cried the herald. "Kyd Murther, Dolphin of the Realm of Lyonesse, has moved the sword Cutwater!"

"Bilge," said Idris. People looked around at him.

"A thumb's breadth!" cried the herald. "Last year, a finger! This year, a thumb! Each year a little more! Our Dolphin approaches man's estate!"

Idris was looking at Fisheagle. She was gazing into the porch, her face bony and cruel. It was not the face of a mother whose son had proved his kingship. An angry glee rose in him. He knew what he must do. "The world should see!" he cried. "Let it see!"

Around him the crowd froze, unbelieving.

"There can only be one Rightful King in Lyonesse," he said, wide-eyed and innocent and inwardly raging. "Surely this is a marvel that all should see?"

Morgan kicked his ankle. She said, "She's looking at you!"

And indeed, Fisheagle's fin-crowned head had turned toward him, and the all-black eyes were on him, burning cold.

"It is not customary," said a herald.

Idris bowed coldly. He felt the scorch of Fisheagle's mind, deflected it. He had said what he must say, and the people had heard, and perhaps formed their suspicions. He turned and pushed his way back through the crowd. Certainly he had declared himself. But Fisheagle could do nothing in public. To make him acknowledge his claim was to risk him proving it. And if he proved it, Murther's claim would be shown to be false and Fisheagle's with it. No, she would not risk such a thing in public.

In private, it would be a different matter.

Morgan stood for a moment frozen in horror. She saw the people part in front of Idris. She thought: They heard him, and he is marked for death. Then she saw on many faces half-hidden looks of admiration. And she thought: They part out of respect, not fear. My Idris!

She found she was following him.

They pushed through the crowds, back to the Ambrose. As they mounted the stairs, Idris said, "I think I have cost you your life."

She could not make his words sound real. The Goldfinch Chambers were flooded with light. They were surrounded by beauty and luxury. Beyond the chambers was the close, happy world of the Wolf Rock. These were the boundaries of her existence.

She heard him say, "We must leave. Now." She found herself nodding, heard herself saying that she was ready to give up her life and start another, dark and terrifying, and meaning it.

She was happy.

Idris said, "Pack. Not much." He moved out to the balcony. The procession was passing below, heading back to the Mount. Nobody looked up. Nobody halted at the Ambrose porch. The new Kek was hovering on the updraft from a burner engine. The streets were emptying. The Mountmen armies had lit cooking fires at their mustering points. Surely he had not escaped Fisheagle's attention?

Morgan came back in and slung a pack on a divan. Digby was draped over her shoulder. "Idris," she said, "please explain."

"I'll show you," he said. "Bring the pack, and your bow, and plenty of arrows. We'll pick up horses from the stables." He was already out of the door.

She found herself trotting after him and was briefly surprised at herself. It was not just that he had turned hard and brown, with the sword in his belt and the ring on his thumb. It was that it was impossible not to believe in him.

Dusk was filling the deep street with shadows as they hurried the horses through the last of the parade leaving the Old Well Square.

The square itself was almost empty now. They tied the horses to a ring by a mounting block. "Hold my hand," said Idris.

She took his hand. "Where are we going?"

He led her toward the Old Well. For a moment a silence lay over the square, like, thought Idris, the silence of a giant wave that has traveled thousands of leagues, now risen, crest toppling, ready to break and smash and change lives forever. Morgan's hand was warm and encouraging in his.

They entered the porch. The carvings writhed black and sinister. "What are we doing here? It's dark."

"Light?" said the voice of Digby.

"Not too bright."

Digby hopped onto Morgan's head and began to emit a whitish glow. The pale beam wavered across the flagstones, and lit the sword Cutwater sunk deep through the door hasps and into the rock.

Idris said, "Pull it."

"Tch," said Morgan. She put her hand on the hilt and tugged. "No way. You know perfectly well."

"Watch," said Idris.

He leaned forward, put a finger under the crosspiece of the sword, and flicked it upward. Cutwater lifted in the air, turned once, and fell into his hand.

There was a silence.

"But . . ." said Morgan.

"You saw it," said Idris.

"But it's a story," said Morgan. "They told it to me when I was little."

"And it was true."

Morgan opened her mouth to argue. Then she closed it again, and shook her head, as if getting her thoughts straight. She took a deep breath. Her eyes filled with tears. Then she spoke. "Idris Wolf Rock House Ambrose House Draco, my brother by adoption," she said, "I beg you will accept my apology. Sometimes I have misbelieved, but I have always known you have a great destiny. I accept you now as Kyd Idris of the Vanished Children, Rightful King of Lyonesse."

"That's nice," said a deep, grating voice from the darkness outside. "But we don't." And into the pale-lit porch stepped two Mountmen.

·PART FOUR·

She tried to rest in the deep, but the darkgardens could not soothe her. She floated among the Helpers, but they were drawing close to their time, and there was no peace in them. She was weary of light, the cut of it in her mind, the wriggle and strut of the little people who hopped in it like live fish in a hot pan. She had thought that soon the world would all be dark and cool and drifting. . . .

But she could not hide it from herself. What had begun as a pinprick was now a gaping wound. A thing had been torn loose, an important thing, so that if something was not done, the wrigglers and strutters would gain courage and turn on her, and the plans long ages in the making would bleed away and become useless.

So back from the darkgardens she hurtled, through bitter black water and rock channel and stone Well chimney, to her body in the Kyd Tower. She entered the body with a sound like a roar. She picked up the creature in her chamber, a dog, a young one, and tore it with her teeth, and felt the rage shoot into every corner of her as its blood gurgled down the body's throat. And knew that the thing was no more than a small difficulty, which she could crush as she had all the others. The dear child would have to be strong and violent and without pity; but in this he was talented, thanks to her training.

Before, she had let her mind quietly into the kingdom. Now she would scrape it to the bone. And she would find the creature and his friends. Oh, it would be good, she thought, throwing away the dog, skin and bones now, sucked empty. Her men would go out, and the small Helpers, too, and they would hunt down this creature, this . . . Idris. And empty him. Would she throw him into a Well, or fill his emptiness with something else, and have him walk and talk and be hers? Her tongue ran around her mouth, licking up the last flecks of the dog's blood. She had not decided yet. The decision could wait.

She turned her face to the bronze shutters, eyes closed. The shutters wheezed open. Starlight crashed into the room; she could feel its nasty brilliance. She paused, letting her mind gather strength. She felt the power of it press against the inside of the lids.

Sea Eagle, Cross, False Regent of Lyonesse, opened her eyes.

SIXTEEN

The Mountmen were big, and they had swords at their waists and spears at the present. "You ought to learn to keep your voice down," said the bigger of the two. The spearpoints were leveled at neck height. "Now drop that sword, if you please."

Digby, out, thought Idris, over the thunder of his heart.

The light went out. Idris slashed Cutwater across the darkness in front of him. The sword moved smoothly and easily, as if it had eyes of its own. It went through something wooden, slammed into something meaty, and came back to the guard position. Beside him, Morgan made a sound between a sob and a gasp. One of the Mountmen started shouting. Cutwater's blade swept across again, low and wicked, and hissed through flesh. Someone screamed, or perhaps two someones. There was a crash of armor on stones. Then the world went quiet, except for a low moaning at ground level. Idris said, "Are you all right?"

Morgan made a small noise. Frightened, poor girl, thought Idris. Well, that makes two of us. His eyes were getting used to the darkness now. He hauled the Well doors open till they gaped wide. That would show people that there was a king on the loose. Then he stepped over the bodies on the ground and looked out of the porch entrance. The square lay empty. "Come," he said and pulled Morgan out by the hand. She was moving too slowly. The hunt would soon begin. Had already begun. Fisheagle had seen his mind and bided her time. She had been watching him, waiting for this moment. For how long?

It did not matter now.

There would be other Mountmen, many others. He put his mind out for Kek and saw darkness. The gull was asleep. Idris prodded it. Darkness, sea cliffs, white waves breaking. Too far away. No good. He looked across to the mounting block where they had tethered the horses.

The horses were gone.

Morgan was clutching his hand with both of hers. Her hands seemed suddenly surprisingly cold.

They were across the square now. He hesitated. Without the horses, he had no idea which way to go. Feet sounded in the road, nailed feet, running in step. A patrol. He pulled Morgan back into a doorway. "All right," barked a voice as the feet went by. "Into the square. Detailed search, fan out. Boy about twelve, armed. Girl similar, reddish hair. Dead or alive. Go."

Idris pushed violently back at the door. It gave. They were in an ill-lit room. The air was full of low voices and weed smoke and the fumes of apple madness, enough to sting the eyes. They were in the tavern on the corner of the Old Well Square.

Idris led Morgan to a table and sat her down. "Sunapple juice!" he cried, trying to sound like an innocent Wellminder out for an evening stroll. "Morgan, what for you?"

The room fell silent. "Leech, by the look of her," said the landlord.

For the first time, Idris saw Morgan in the lamplight.

The breath stuck in his throat.

The right-hand side of her dark red tunic was the wrong red. Blood-red. And wet.

She said, "Help." Her face was gray. Her lips were white. "Mountman. I think it was a spear."

Idris started around the table toward her. But the scabbard Holdwater somehow got between his feet, and he tripped and went facedown on the gritty flagstones.

"Clumsy," said Morgan in a tiny voice. The lids dropped over her eyes. There was a seep of bright-red blood at the corner of her mouth. She's dying, thought Idris, on his knees. And it was me that brought her to her death. Please. No. Not Morgan. He got up. The scabbard tripped him again. As if it had a mind of its own and was doing it on purpose.

It was doing it on purpose.

He pulled the baldric over his head. He laid the scabbard on the wound in Morgan's chest and looped the baldric over her gold-red hair. The silence in the taproom was deep as a well. From the Old Well Square came the sound of shouting and the crash of nailed boots kicking in doors. It meant their death. It was coming closer.

But Idris paid no attention. He was watching Morgan. And so was everyone else.

As the baldric went over her head she lay back in her chair, eyes dull, lids sinking, skin death-blue.

Then she smiled.

Everyone in the tavern drew in his breath at the same time.

An edge of pink was moving up her face. It vanished into her hair. Her eyes opened. The irises were green as ever, the whites clear and brilliant. She yawned, frowned, touched the bloody part of her tunic. "What's this? What a *mess*!"

Idris shook his head. He could not say anything. He found he was crying.

She touched the scabbard gently and looked at him and smiled again. The smile blurred with Idris's tears.

The voices in the square were louder now. The drinkers were staring. Two of them had dropped to their knees. One was staring harder than the rest — a thin man, with a ragged hood and breeches out at the knees. "Ambrosegroom!" he said.

"I know you," said Idris.

"Wayncull Hedger, what you saved," said the serf. "In the monsterstables of Ambrose, sir. Landlord's a friend of mine. Anything we can do, sir?"

"I remember," said Idris. Crash, went a boot from the square. "If your friend could lock the doors. And we must get away from here."

"Under me cloak?" said Hedger.

It was a small cloak, nearly see-through with wear. "No."

The landlord shot the last bolt. He said, "There's a way from the cellar to the barge-wharves. He'll show you." A battering came on the door. "Open!" cried a voice.

"Thank you, landlord," said Idris. Words bubbled up in him, and he turned to the drinkers. "Good people, you are the first in Lyonesse to know that I am your King. In token of this, you will see that the doors of the Old Well stand open, for I have taken my sword Cutwater from the stone. I shall return. Until that day, live peaceably, and tell the world quietly what you have seen, and spread word of the proof. On that day, we will march together to save this land of ours."

Mouths, hanging open. An awestruck silence.

"Open!" roared the voice again. This time the kick was accompanied by the sound of splintering wood. Idris gripped Morgan by the hand and ran after Hedger.

SEVENTEEN

The landlord hauled up a trapdoor, shooed them down a flight of steps, and said, "Go!"

The trapdoor closed. There was no light. "Go where?" said Idris.

"Digby!" cried Morgan.

A green glow lit barrels, bottles, and dirt. Hedger rolled aside a barrel. Behind it was a black hole in the wall. "In here, my liege and lady!" he cried, shooing them into the tunnel. There were clonking sounds as he blocked the entrance. "Get 'ee on!" he cried. "Get 'ee on!"

"Spiders!" squeaked Morgan.

"Aren't any," said Idris, brushing webs off his face. The tunnel sloped downhill. After a hundred paces it became wet underfoot. It joined another tunnel, bigger, stone-floored, one of the routes by which monsters were brought from the Wells to the wharves. The tunnel must have something to do with smuggling. Idris made a mental note that, when he returned, the landlord would pay no taxes, ever.

The tunnel was sloping gently upward now, the entrance a gray disc of night. Then they were in the open air, in a muddy yard of wagons behind the lakeshore, crawling between wheels and axletrees.

"Where now?" said Morgan.

Idris had no idea. These were the wharves where the monsters were loaded for the sheds by the dam. He could already hear shouts in the tangle of sheds and warehouses behind them. And he could feel something worse than that — a scorch in the ether, like a great freezing lamp beam: the mind of Fisheagle, searching.

At the same time, Hedger's mind showed him a woman and three little children. Hedger's family. Hedger was terrified, too, for his family, not himself. But so strong was his faith in his rightful king that he would risk even them.

Idris felt proud and humble and strong. He knew his duty.

"Leave us here," he said.

"One good turn deserves another," said Hedger. He bowed, radiating relief, and sidled into the dark.

The sounds of the pursuit were still faint. Between the waggon wheels Idris saw the dark shift of the lake, and against it, tied up at the quay, the shapes of the barges that took cut monsters down the lake to the work sheds by the dam.

"This way," said Idris, with a confidence he definitely did not feel. They crept out of the shelter of the waggons, onto a quayside of sooty stone. "We'll get onto the road," he said.

"Down the north side of the lake and over to Castle Ambrose." Without horses or food. Some hope.

They began to walk back toward the Great Road, keeping in the cover of the carts. A noise came from ahead: the squinch of boot nails on stone. A voice said, "Line abreast. Keep up, blast you." Idris saw the long, wavering gleam of starlight on spearheads. A line of men was walking through the carts toward them. They were checking carts and buildings, slowly and thoroughly. They had no need to hurry. There was nowhere for a fugitive to go except the lake.

Morgan had seen it, too. "So?" she said, in a small, high voice.

There was only the lake.

A dim light came on in a corner of Idris's mind. He said, "This way." He made himself sound calm. He led her swiftly back and across the quay to where the barges were moored. They lay in line alongside the quay, shifting like tethered beasts. The water sloshed dank and poisonous against their side. "Into the boat."

"Me? On one of *them*?" said Digby. "No *way*!"

"What makes you think anyone is giving you even the teeniest thought?" hissed Morgan.

"The carts will come down from the Wells when Darksolstice ends at midnight," said Idris. "They'll load up the monsters for the sheds by the dam. We'll go with them."

"In the *monstertanks*?"

Idris said, "Yes." He felt a strange silence fall on the world. He said, "Muffle. Double muffle. For your life."

Then it was on them: a roaring beam of mind playing among the buildings, prying open every cranny, and behind it a feeling of claws and nails and a tearing beak.

It passed.

It would be back.

They scuttled up the gangplank and onto the barge.

Idris felt the warning silence again. He lowered Morgan into a tank, hid her bow under a sack, and climbed after her. It was wet, and it smelled of monsterslime and lake water and rotting iron. But when the mind of Fisheagle came back it roared over the top of them, unable to penetrate the metal.

Boots tramped on the quay. Torchlight reddened the barge's rigging. He and Morgan sat close, Cutwater in Holdwater across them. He could feel her shivering. "How long?" she said.

"Soon."

They waited.

It was not soon. The feet marched away. The hours passed. From time to time the mind of Fisheagle scorched over them. Morgan's head slumped on Idris's shoulder. After a while, Digby said, "Call me stupid, but what will you do when they put a monster in here and fill up the tank?"

"Breathe through the bars."

"But it'll eat you."

"It will have been cut."

"Oh," said Digby in a small voice.

It was cold and Idris was hungry, but he must have dozed off. The next thing he knew was a gush of cold, acrid water and the squeal of a crane-sheave and something big and heavy plummeting into the tank. The grille slammed down, and he and Morgan were standing on tiptoe and breathing with just their faces above the harsh, smelly water. Something screamed in his mind. For a moment he felt a wild urge to leap on deck and run. Then he realized that this was only a monster, probing at his muffle. *Monster,* he thought at it, *be silent.*

Soon I am forever *silent,* said the monster in an indistinct voice. *For they have cut my limbs, and my teeth, and never again will I swim in my darkgarden with the red fish swimming.*

Monster, said Idris, *what is your name?*

My name is Driftflower.

Driftflower, it is true that you will not see your darkgarden. But I will tell your fellows your name, and when I have stopped this cruel commerce between our worlds you will be remembered.

Feet came on deck. Boots walked toward them. Someone was checking the tanks.

"Breathe," whispered Idris. "Go under."

"But —"

"Go!"

The feet were by the next tank. Idris grabbed Morgan's sleeve and pulled her below the surface. He felt her struggle, then go limp. The boots sounded through the tank. They stopped.

Help, said the monster. *There are people hiding in here. Let me go, I have told you.*

Morgan's arm had gone rigid under Idris's hand. He tensed against the hooks that would come down and drag them out and take them back to Fisheagle.

A voice said, "Yeah, right, hundreds of 'em." An iron hook jabbed spitefully. The monster squealed. The boots walked away. Idris put up his face and breathed, heard Morgan do the same. There were more boots, shouts, ropes in blocks, the flap of a sail. The deck moved underfoot. The tankwater tilted, as if the boat was heeling to the breeze. That meant that the tank was flooded at one side, so the monster could stay there, and clear a few hands' breadths at the other, so there was room for Idris's and Morgan's breathing. They felt the boat move away from the quay. Morgan squeezed Idris's hand. We are free, thought Idris. Though we are in a cage, and it is very cold.

He put a hand between the bars and felt for the lock. A fumble, a soft click. The grille came free. Idris raised his head carefully.

The barge was sailing through darkness. The crew were in some sort of shelter at the back end. Smoke rose from a stovepipe. "Keep low," he said. He crawled out, dripping, closed the cage grille, and helped Morgan after him.

They crept forward between the tanks, soaked and shivering. When Idris put his head up, the lakewater reflected a cold stripe of moonrise. Against it stood the Welltowers, already reassuringly small with distance, and behind them the cruel fang of the Mount. He could not feel Fisheagle's mind.

The front end of the barge was empty. They huddled in some old sacks under the foredeck. "Where are we going?" said Morgan, trusting him completely now.

"To the Sundeeps," said Idris.

"Why not the Wolf Rock?"

"We are dangerous." Fisheagle was horribly swift. Morgan's family might already be captive or dead. "Safer to go to Ambrose."

Morgan was silent. She was thinking about the people of her tower. Today had started as a party. Now, life could never be the same again.

Idris sat and shivered with more than cold. The world was broken. Then the sword came into his mind, and he felt the strength of the land in him. He took Morgan's hand and felt her anxiety ease. Almost immediately they both fell asleep.

He was woken by a finger digging into his ribs. "Something is happening," hissed Morgan. "Keep still."

There were boots on deck. A monster screamed. Machinery clanked and groaned. Pulling aside a corner of the sacking, Idris saw that it was daylight. An iron tank was rising into the air on a crane hook. Beyond the crane was the stone wall of a shed. Serfs were hauling ropes attached to the tank. "They're unloading," he said. "We'll have to wait."

"Don't just sit there, *do* something," said Digby.

"Shut up or we'll let them cut your foot off," said Morgan.

The barge rocked as the weight came off it. Voices, feet, machines. "Back on duty a glass after sunset," said someone. The crew's boots went from wood to stone. The voices faded. Cautiously Idris raised his head.

The barge was alongside a quay. Behind the quay was a group of sheds. Idris put his mind out. He felt no people.

"All clear," he said. "We'll make clothes out of these sacks. They'll think we're serfs. We'll get off the boat and find somewhere to hide. There must be stables here. We'll wait for night, take some horses, and start across the Poison Ground. We will stay with the Hospitallers. Then we'll go on to Castle Ambrose."

"Or to my parents," said Morgan.

Idris had been considering that. Tower Draco was in the greatest danger. "Too dangerous," he said. "Fisheagle will expect us to go to them."

"So they're hostages," said Morgan, her voice rising.

"Nothing will happen to them as long as we're alive," said Idris. What Morgan had said was true. "We go to Ambrose."

Using Cutwater, they hacked crude smocks from the sacking and slit other sacks for hoods. They were prickly, and they smelled terrible. But when Idris looked at Morgan he saw not a monstergroom of Knightly descent but a small, bent serf.

"Let's go," he said. "Don't stride. Shuffle."

293

"Teach your gran to churn butter," said Morgan, hiding her worry behind a thick serf accent.

Idris hung the sword down his back, covered it with the cloak and hood, and looked around. All clear. "Wait," he said. He shuffled down the hold of the barge to its back end. In the shelter was a box that held half a loaf of bread and a heel of cheese. Stuffing them into his hood, he shuffled back to Morgan, who was hiding her bow under her cloak. "Walk."

Kek had woken. He was high above, resting on the wind. Down he swept toward the huddle of sheds by the Great Road, with the boxy barges alongside and the two little serf figures shuffling across the open quayside and into the long storage shed with the stable at its end. "Kek," said Kek, and settled on the rooftree.

And waited.

It was dusk when Idris awoke, the early dusk of the year's first day. The taste of the barge sacks was still in his mouth. Morgan was asleep on the hay beside him.

Sounds were coming from the quay. Tanks were swinging back onto the barge, full of something from a series of carts. Metal ores, perhaps. Through the hay on which they were lying came the sound of hooves on stone.

Idris touched the sword and felt its strength in him. Then he woke Morgan and pulled her into a far corner of the hayloft. They pushed up a rampart of hay. Feet clumped on the stairs.

A man with a pitchfork started throwing hay down a hatch. "That'll do," said a voice from below. "Pub?"

"Captain said watch the horses," said the man with the fork. "Rebels around."

"Good luck to 'em," said the voice downstairs. "We can watch out of the pub window."

The man with the fork pitched a final bundle and disappeared. Hooves shifted on cobbles, and a horse snorted. The stable door slammed.

"Ten minutes," said Idris. "We can't go across the dam. We'll have to ride by the Poison Ground."

They had saved the last of the bread. They ate it now.

"Shall we not stay by the lovely lake?" said Digby, sounding nervous. "Idris?"

But Idris had already gone. Digby jumped onto Morgan's shoulder from the beam where he had been sitting. They followed.

The stable was full of horse breath and dung smell. Digby's greenish glow shone on the flanks of a dozen broad-chested horses. Morgan chose two, pleased to find something only she could do. There was only draft harness in the tack room, so she put on halters and hoped for the best.

Idris was striking his steel with a flint. The tinder glowed and popped into flame. "What are you doing?" said Morgan.

"Covering our retreat." He picked up a handful of hay and

lit it from the tinder. "Shoo the horses out as soon as I open the door. Ready?" he said, hand on the bolt.

"Ready," said Morgan.

Idris drew the bolt and pulled the door open. The night was black. He threw his burning wisps of hay into the manger. The flames caught and ran. Smoke rose and spread over the ceiling. Morgan ran outside with the horses, followed by the others, whinnying and jostling. Idris followed, heaving himself onto his horse's back by its mane. Flames were licking from doors and windows, casting a red glare over the lake and the dam. Hooves thundered in the shadows. Up the road, a door burst open and men spilled out, shouting. "Come," said Idris, lying low to the horse's neck and pulling its head around.

The night air whipped past. The two great horses galloped away from the flames and into the thick darkness over the Poison Ground. Idris and Morgan were hungry, and sore from the caustic Wellwaters, and they had nothing to put over their faces against the vapors of the Ground. But they had escaped the Valley of Apples and Fisheagle, and that for the moment was something to make the blood warm, and take the sting out of the fear of a whole army pursuing them and the worry about what lay ahead.

It did not last.

After ten minutes, Idris felt his horse's stride become uneven. The animal slowed from a canter to a trot, from a trot to a lurching walk. "She's gone lame," said Morgan, after an inspection by Digbylight. "You'd better come up behind me."

So they turned the lame horse loose and Idris climbed up behind Morgan. On they plodded, much slower now, into the black stink of the Ground. The horse had been working all day. It wanted its stable, there was no doubt about that. Finally it stopped. Morgan kicked it with her heels. No result. "Do something," said Idris.

"If I had a saddlecloth, a bridle, and some oats, I might be able to," said Morgan. "As it is he wants to go home, and I don't blame him."

"All right," said Idris. "We'll walk." They dismounted and took off the halter. When the horse arrived back it would be thought that it had run from the fire. They stood and listened to hoofbeats fade into the night silence of the dead land. Then they started walking.

It was a cloudy night, without stars. Digby cast his greenish glow, which showed the road and a disc of marsh. "I can hear monsters," said Morgan. So could Idris, loud and insistent. They were not trying to charm him. They were wild and rejoicing, totally alien.

"This is the Colony," said Digby. "What you call the Poison Ground."

"You could go and join your friends."

"No, thank you," said Digby. "I have always felt out of place in my world. I prefer humans of destiny like you two."

"Walk," said Idris.

It was a long, weary way, one foot in front of the other, hour after hour through the stones and mud, up river levees, across plank bridges, down the other sides, on again. Idris tried unmuffling for a moment. Monster voices roared into his mind. Hastily, he put the muffles up again, but not before he heard that bigger mind, more powerful, beak and claws and fury, searching: Fisheagle.

Idris touched his sword. He and the land of his fathers were at war not only with the Mount but with a whole dark, bitter, watery world.

Very well, he thought, grasping Morgan's hand. It is in the open now. We shall prevail.

On they trudged, on and on, until the ground started to rise and a breeze tore the fog aside for long enough to show the loom of a hill. There were trees up there, scorched and leafless above the fog, and a ring of stones like teeth.

By the stones there stood a figure, dark and still.

Idris's hand went to the hilt of Cutwater. The blade seemed to catch in the scabbard. When he finally drew it forth, it felt heavy as stone in his hand.

He moved stealthily forward. Against the sky he saw the figure lift its head. "At last," it said. "What kept you?"

The voice was the voice of Ambrose.

Idris and Morgan ran up the mount. "How did you find us?" said Idris.

"You found me," said Ambrose. "There are stones here. Fisheagle has wrecked it with her poison. But the stones hold enough power to sweeten the place."

Beside the stones stood a tent, pitched in clear air. Below the hill, the vapors of the Ground spread corpse pale under the moon. They crawled into the tent and found blankets. They slept.

EIGHTEEN

Next thing Idris knew, a light shone on the cloth walls. There was Morgan sleeping yet, and the fierce angles and hollows of the face of Ambrose.

"Up," he said. "The kingdom is being turned upside down and shaken. We will go to the Sundeeps, and I will put you on the road to raise your armies and take your revenge. We will eat as we ride."

"I don't suppose you brought anything raw?" said Digby.

"No doubt you will catch some unfortunate rat later. Greetings, Morgan. You and I will walk together." They rose, and moved ahead, misty silhouettes against the first paling of the dawn. Idris saw Ambrose speak, then Morgan shake her head violently and put her hands to her face. His mind understood what Ambrose was saying. It was terrible news.

Mountmen had come to the Wolf Rock six hours after Darksolstice. Five retainers were dead. It was not known what had happened to Uther and Nena. No trace of them had been found. The tower had been burned. Perhaps they were in the ruins. Or perhaps — probably, even, Ambrose thought, but there was no way of being sure — they had escaped, been smuggled away, and were hiding with friends before they could be spirited to Ar Mor or Iber. Idris felt for Morgan, deeply. She had comforted Idris and taken him in to her family, and because of him this terrible thing had happened. He must comfort her as best he could, as a friend and a brother.

And as her King, said a small voice in his mind

As the light grew, he saw that Morgan was holding Ambrose's hand like a little girl, and her face wore a dazed expression. Idris guessed that Ambrose had used his arts to protect her mind from the full horror of what he had told her.

"Now we ride," said Ambrose.

The ponies were of the Sundeeps breed, wiry and agile. On Morgan's saddle were slung her bow and a quiver of arrows. Soon they left the road and traveled across what looked like trackless swamp. They were heading north, riding parallel to the western margins of the Poison Ground. A sharp breeze was blowing out of the west.

Idris sent his mind to Kek. The black margins of the Ground passed under him, league on league. There was the oakwood, and farther west, far down the Old Road, the Wolf Rock and its tower.

Idris's hand went to the hilt of his sword.

It was bad to hear about it. It was much worse to see it.

The roofs and floors were gone. So would be the furniture, the hangings, the small, worn treasures the family had gathered over seven hundred years. All that remained was a shell of blackened stone.

He turned to Ambrose. The mage's head moved side to side. *Say nothing.* Morgan was staring straight ahead, so she would not have to look in the direction of the ruins of her home, many leagues distant though they were.

The ruins, which by the kindness of Uther and Nena had been Idris's home by adoption.

Anger burned in Idris's heart. He was riding through blasted swamp that had been green fields, hunted by traitors and usurpers across a monster-haunted wilderness where peace and plenty had once prevailed. He would fulfill his destiny and put this great wrong right, no matter how long it would take and what it might cost. It was for this that Ambrose had taken the trouble to save him from the Westgate all that time ago. Well, Ambrose would be repaid.

He loosened Cutwater in Holdwater and settled himself in the saddle. And Idris Limpet of the Westgate, now Kyd Idris House Draco, rode hard with his comrades for the Stone Downs, starting his journey to raise the armies with which he would right the wrongs of Lyonesse.

As the sun was sinking, the ground began to rise. Soon they were riding through scrubby oakwoods, discreetly skirting neat farms in the clearings. The woods became sparse and gave way to rolling grasslands dotted with shepherds' huts behind windbreaks of yew. It was a beautiful land, and Idris found pride in every blade of grass. As evening approached, a green tumulus cast a long shadow over the turf. Beside it waited a little group of ponies. "Change," said Ambrose.

"Can't we rest?" said Morgan.

"Not till the castle. Look, there's food."

"Good," said Morgan listlessly. Idris was worried about her. She had had a mortal wound, and news nearly as mortal. Whatever arts Ambrose had used on her were fading. She was pale and haggard. They ate, honeycomb on hard, delicious biscuits. Then Ambrose poured liquid from a silver flask into a small cup and handed it to Morgan. "Drink," he said. "A tonic."

Idris took the cup after Morgan. The liquid tasted mild and sour. But something spread through his limbs and into his mind so that he forgot about flight and pursuit and destruction by fire and was filled with joy and pride and energy. Morgan's color had returned, and her eye had brightened.

Three minutes later they were in the saddle, cantering for the high ground to the northwest. The air was fresh and clean. The hooves drummed and the blood pounded. Morgan dropped back so she was riding knee to knee with Idris. "Look!" she cried, pointing upward, red hair flying.

A lark hung hovering on the edge of vision, the merest mote of a creature, pouring forth its endless, unrepeating song. Idris reined in. The notes tumbled from the heavens like a blessing. "In winter!" said Morgan, brilliant-eyed. "An omen!"

They sat a moment on their fidgeting ponies, listening to the music flowing over the long slope of the down. Then Idris frowned. Into the corner of his hearing, underlying the larksong, had come another sound, distant and ferocious. The wind of a huntsman's horn.

Ambrose had heard it, too. "Ride," he said. *"Ride!"*

There were no larks anymore. There was only the setting sun spreading blood up the sky and the yowl of hounds on a breast-high scent.

Worse than hounds, much worse. They had heard this evil yelling before, at the New Deer and from the kennels of the Mount. This was the music of halfhounds.

"Faster!" roared Ambrose.

The sun sank below the horizon. The sky turned from blood to hot iron, and still they rode, the foam blowing back into their faces from the ponies' muzzles. Suddenly on the crest of the next down, a ragged circle of stone stood against the red sky.

"The Dog's Quoit!" cried Ambrose. "Into the circle!"

As they spurred up the hill, Idris's pony must have caught a whiff of the halfhounds, because it squealed and bolted forward and leaped the heel stone, so he arrived inside the circle clutching its neck. His hands slipped. Idris hit the turf with a thump and lay winded, still hanging on to the reins, looking up at the cold blue, in which the stars rode bright and steady.

"Keep clear of the stones!" cried Ambrose. "Blindfold the ponies!"

As Idris looked past the stones and down the hill, the hounds burst from scent to view and the inside of his mouth turned to sand.

There were a score of them, dark shapes lolloping up the hill, eyes fiery red, tongues swinging through teeth that glowed yellow and green. Idris's head was ringing, but he was not frightened. Ambrose's cordial? No. The righteous anger of a King. Cutwater flew from Holdwater and was in his hand. The strength of the kingdom entered him. He said, "Morgan, behind me."

"No," said Morgan through her teeth. Her bow was in her hand.

"Help!" said Digby, who had leaped to the top of a menhir.

"Stay there," said Morgan, nocking an arrow. She drew and loosed. A hound rolled over. Its companions turned on it and tore it. Its spilled bowels glowed phosphorescent in the dark. In the shadows behind the hounds, a shadowy horseman shouted, "Tear them and eat them!"

Ambrose raised his hand. A ring on his forefinger caught the reflection of a blue-white star brilliant at the zenith. He began chanting in an unknown language.

Two hounds were ahead of the pack. The first hurdled a stone. From the safety of his menhir Digby spat in its eye. It screamed. While it was screaming, Idris cut off its head. He ran through the next and heaved Cutwater's blade out of the stinking carcass. The main body of the pack would be at the circle any second now. There were too many for swords. Ambrose's chanting grew louder and deeper. Suddenly a slim blue beam of light lanced from the star and into the ring on his finger. "Shut your eyes!" he shouted. A blast of . . . something . . . roared out of his hands. Even through his closed lids, Idris saw the stones blaze incandescent. The air filled with the stench of burning dog. "Open!" cried Ambrose. "Idris!"

The stones were as before. But the hounds were ashes, except for one, in midair, leaping at Idris's throat. The sword Cutwater moved in his hands, or his hand moved the sword, which he could not tell. The dog's body went one way, its head another. Its blood smelled of decaying fish.

Silence settled over the Dog's Quoit. Somewhere a curlew called. Beyond the curlew drummed the hooves of the huntsman's horse, fleeing. "He will return, and bring others with him," said Ambrose. "Now ride."

Many weary leagues later, they rode down the avenue of mica stones and under the arch of Castle Ambrose. People brought them food. Ambrose spoke. Idris and Morgan were too tired to do anything but listen.

"We rest, then leave for the Sundeeps," he said. "Fisheagle knows you are the Wielder of the Sword, and since the Dog's Quoit that you are with me. We have destroyed their hounds, but they have worse in their stables. The Armies of the Mount are already on the march." He drank from his emerald-green beaker. The flesh of his face looked eaten away with tiredness. "Idris, I thought you were a fool. I was wrong. You have done the best that you could have done. If the Knights had risen, you would have died. If you had stayed in the Valley of Apples, you would even now be drowned in a Well. Whatever fate it was that directed you here, it was a good one."

"I suppose it was Wayncull Hedger," said Idris, giving credit where credit was due.

"The instrument of destiny may as easily be a monster-mazed serf as a king." Ambrose raised his glass to Idris and drank. "Idris and Morgan. We must make sure that you get a good start on the road to Ar Mor. I only wish I could come with you."

"What do you mean?"

The eyes disappeared into the deep cavities beneath the brows. "I am afraid that we must part. You must go to find the armies that will save Lyonesse. The only way I can help you do this is by . . . departing."

"What do you mean?" said Idris.

"To raise the forces that will save you I must put myself beyond help," said Ambrose. "Perhaps I shall find a way to return. Perhaps not."

"You saved me," said Idris. "I forbid it."

"Either I go alone into silence, or we go all three," said Ambrose. "And if we all three go, Lyonesse becomes a Poison

Ground, and its people are left to filthy water and the teeth of monsters. The land demands that you go. It is out of your hands."

There was a silence. Then Ambrose smiled, haggard but warm. "Perhaps I shall be able to whisper to you from the place where I shall be. Now. You will take ship with Captain Penmarch. I have sent word to him. His ship the *Swallow* will be cruising off the Westgate for a week after the full moon. He will fly a red pennant from his masthead. He will take you to Ar Mor and King Mark in his palace at Ys, who as I told you before is my friend since I built him the stonefields at Carnac. Speak to him well, and he will help you raise your armies. But go carefully until you leave Lyonesse, for the land is roused against you."

"Come with us," said Idris. "You have been seen. You are in danger."

Ambrose passed his hand over his face. "Impossible. Now. I have some instructions for you and I must give them while there is yet time. Morgan, I have had news that the people of the Wolf Rock live but are in hiding, and you will see them again one day, but it must not be yet."

Morgan said, "I rejoice that they live." A tear ran down each side of her nose. Idris put an arm around her. He could feel her weeping with grief and anger. So brave, he thought. My friend.

"We will go to the Sundeeps. And there we will contrive our deaths."

"Deaths?"

"The grave is an excellent hiding place," said Ambrose. "Particularly if you are not in it. Now go to bed."

Idris's old cell was as cold as ever, the straw mattress as hard, the blankets as thin. He was pulling off his boots when there was a knock on the door.

"Enter."

And in came Orbach. "Sire," he said and went down on one knee.

"Rise," said Idris, too tired to be embarrassed.

"I wondered . . . might I look at the sword?" said Orbach. Idris showed him Cutwater, and Orbach nodded. "Nice balance," he said. "Nice work. Oh, very choice." He seemed to want to say something else. Idris waited.

"It is like this," said Orbach in a reverent mumble quite unlike his usual voice. "You was a useful student, sir. Dead useful with a weapon and with a tasty attitude, know what I mean? So I hereby offer you my service."

Idris felt a warm glow of encouragement. "I accept and with gratitude," he said. "But I must go out of Lyonesse with Morgan. Swear on Cutwater you will spread the word that I will return and do what I can to save Lyonesse from the Wells and the sea."

"I do so swear," said Orbach.

"And I," said Idris.

Orbach bowed, and backed out of the door.

"Good night, sire," called Morgan bravely through the wall.

"Good night, subject," he said, yawning.

He heard her blow a raspberry and was glad she had at least recovered her rudeness.

Then he went to sleep.

When he awoke, a heavy wind was blowing and rain was coming in at his glassless window. They breakfasted while it was yet dark, wrapped themselves in cloaks, and plugged steadily westward. All day they heard nothing but the beat of hooves and the buffet of the gale in their ears. Through the eyes of Kek, the view was of hills that came and went among scudding drifts of vapor, and of three figures on ponies, one big, two smaller, toiling across the rust-colored moors. Backward Kek would not look. Idris could feel the pressure of many minds to the east. And all that lay ahead was the sea, gray and cold and drowning.

Night was falling as they toiled over the pass into the Sundeeps. Ambrose lit a pale fire on his helm and cantered down the path at dizzy speed. The forest closed in. Then they were on the lakeshore, passing the hearth of the stagmen, cold between its menhirs. "Stay close," said Ambrose and led them over the icy water to the tower without lights. Morgan gasped with delight at the tower. "What is this?" she said.

"My house," said Ambrose. He yawned. "And my tomb, at least for a while." He saw both children looking at him, horror-struck. "Don't worry. Not yours. Tomorrow we face the Armies of the Mount."

Morgan had been looking around her at the simple stone room. "How will this place resist a siege?" she said.

"Oh, we'll probably manage," said Ambrose. "Zupper?"

Idris woke in the night. He could hear voices in his mind. There was Ambrose. And two others, enormous voices, speaking a language he did not speak but that he could understand. They seemed to be making a plan. *The children will leave,* said Ambrose. *I will remain.*

It is good, said two voices, and Idris caught a glimpse of two minds huge and wild as cave systems, winding back chamber on chamber to when the world was young and hot and ferny. They were huge enough to make even the King of Lyonesse feel extremely small. Too small to worry about anything, really.

He went back to sleep.

It was still dark when he woke. As he descended the stairs Morgan was three steps ahead of him. Ambrose was at the table in the main room. "Come," he said. He took them down a curling staircase. At its bottom was a huge chamber with a stone bed, a wall of books, and many benches covered with devices of whose use Idris had no inkling. "This is where I must spend my eternity."

"What on earth are you talking about?" said Morgan.

Ambrose smiled kindly. "So straightforward, you Knights," he said. "There is a red dragon and a white dragon that live in the Sundeeps. Idris has seen them swimming in the lake. They disapprove of monsters, being from an older world. They have agreed to destroy the Armies of the Mount and guard me thereafter from the malice of Fisheagle. In return, I have agreed to try to find a way for them to reproduce themselves. They are immortal. But they are the last of their race, and they wish it were otherwise, so they would like some children." He smiled. "I do not hold out much hope. But they will certainly keep me here till I succeed."

"No!" said Idris.

Ambrose put one hand on Idris's head and the other on Morgan's. The hands felt warm but very heavy. "Be comforted, both of you. Know that when I sought the Vanished Children, I did not know what kind of brats I would find. But now I have discovered them and known them, I can go to my eternity happy."

Idris found that there was something in his throat, and his eyes were pricking with tears. Then another thought broke through. "Children?" he said. "More than one child?"

"I told you. When Angharad's maid stole the newborn boy from beside his dead mother she knew that the fury of Fisheagle would come upon all the children of Angharad. So she took the girl, too, and left her with a Knight whose own daughter had died. Uther, in fact, of the Wolf Rock."

Idris looked at Morgan. Morgan looked at Idris. They were in a chamber where their most trusted friend was to spend eternity trying to breed dragons. Nothing was surprising anymore. "So you are my older sister," said Idris and felt a deep, true joy.

Morgan smiled at Idris. She took his hand and said affectionately, "Happily there is very little family resemblance."

"You have a lifetime to talk," said Ambrose. "But in an hour it will be dawn, at which point there is an army to be destroyed. So might I now have your attention?"

NINETEEN

Twenty minutes later, Idris and Morgan pushed Ambrose's shallop out of the watergate and launched forth upon the pool. Unlike the punt this was a sea-going boat, with a mast and a sail struck down in its bottom. The night was dark, the air still, and a sheet of mist covered the water, whether naturally or by Ambrose's art they could not tell. Idris drove the boat into the lake with long strokes of the paddle, keeping low, so as not to break the mist's skin. He could feel thousands of eyes in the mountains around the lake. They made him tense and nervous.

"Look out, dragons about," said a voice somewhat muffled by the mist. Idris jumped.

"Digby!" said Morgan, delighted. "I thought you'd gone!"

"While you're here, row," said Idris. "And be quiet."

Digby extended an oarlike fin and started making vigorous yet silent swirls in the water. By the far shore, the river current caught the hull. The bank began to slide by, a thicker darkness in the dark. Idris heard Morgan draw in her breath sharply.

He followed the direction of her gaze. He saw why.

Against the eastern sky, the horizon bristled with horses and men and engines. A rumor of voices and a clatter of arms came from up there, and even through his muffle he could hear the scream of burners consumed in war machines. He shivered. All this was for him. "Faster," hissed Morgan. "Get us out to sea."

"No," said Idris. "We watch." A stillness had come on his mind. A terrible thing was about to happen, and it would not be right to avoid seeing it.

Yesterday's wind had abated. The boat slid down the river and into the little estuary. The light was growing. Halfway along was a dark patch that Idris remembered as a reedbed and behind it a grove of trees standing black against the sky. "Here," he said, and drove the boat's nose into the reeds. The tall grasses closed behind them.

They crawled up the bank. A shoulder of ground hid the lake. "I'm going up a tree," said Morgan.

Idris climbed one of his own. In the upper branches he stopped.

The lake lay flat and gray in the dawn calm, the forest furring its banks, the tower pale and lovely on its island. The mist had cleared. Somewhere among the crags a horn sounded, long and thin and brassy. On the peaks and ridges around the lake, smoke rose from machines and light crawled on moving armor.

All to kill a boy in a tree.

It was lonely, being a King.

Farewell, said the small, clear voice of Ambrose in Idris's mind.

"Farewell," said Idris.

"What?" said Morgan in the next tree.

"Nothing," said Idris. It was a lot less lonely to be a King with a sister than a King without one.

Something was happening on the lake.

A figure had appeared on the towertop. It held up its arms. Two more figures, smaller, stood one on either side. *ARMIES OF THE MOUNT,* said a huge voice in his mind and the minds of the watchers. *KNOW THAT I AM THE MAGE AMBROSE, CALLED GREAT, AND THAT THESE ARE THE CHILDREN IDRIS AND MORGAN, CALLED "VANISHED." OUR TIME IS NOT NOW. WE GO DOWN INTO SILENCE. FAREWELL.*

"What's he doing?" hissed Idris.

"He's made dummies," said Morgan. "The one who is you is even wearing a crown. He's so *funny!*" But she was crying as she said it.

A dull rumble shook the trees.

"The lake," said Morgan.

The surface was writhing as if huge fish were moving underneath. A fin the size of a boat's sail broke the surface and circled. It was white as milk and heavily spiked, like the fin of a great bass. Another fin broke the surface, a fin like the first, except that this one was a deep blood-red. The fins carved huge whorls in the water at the far end of the lake. They paused a couple of heartbeats. Then they turned and began to move in line abreast.

They moved swiftly, ever more swiftly down the lake. They swept past the island. Ahead of each fin other things were breaking the water, making foaming white wakes. Two crests, four eyes, four nostrils, two heads the size of houses. Then necks, great gleaming shoulders, wings, opening, beating once, twice, wings the size of hay meadows. And two huge dragons, one milk-white, the other blood-red, were flying, dripping, gaining height, the wind of their wings bowing the treetops to which Idris and Morgan clung.

"They say that the Old Magic is gone," said Idris. "They are wrong."

The dragons swept out over the sea, banked, and turned, still climbing. Up they went, up, high enough for the as yet unrisen sun to glitter milk-white and blood-red on their scales.

Then down. Down they swept to where Ambrose and the little figures stood on top of the tower. Down to where the Armies of the Mount were marching rank after rank over the hillside and through the forest to the lakeside. Down, down, like thunderbolts.

From the snouts of the dragons leaped hammers of blue fire.

The tower went first, melted like wax. A roaring cloud of steam shot into the air from the lake. The dragons swept low over the hillsides, methodical as reapers, cutting down the Armies of the Mount, men and machines, quick, merciless.

Idris heard a shriek of terror from thousands of minds, then silence.

The steam of the lake rose and filled the Sundeeps.

Slowly Idris and Morgan descended their trees and crawled through the reedbed and into their boat, and the tide carried them onto the broad bosom of the sea.

When he could think a little bit, Idris put his mind up to Kek. The gull was very high. The lake and the hillsides leading down to it were hidden beneath a quilt of steam. In all the land east of the Sundeeps only one thing moved: a horseman, ear to his horse's neck, galloping as fast as hooves could carry him away from the crags and toward the Mount, bearing the news that its armies were destroyed, but that so were the Great Ambrose and Idris and Morgan, the Vanished Children of Lyonesse.

Fisheagle and Kyd Murther might sleep easy in their soft black beds, if sleep they did.

But not for very long.

There were two huge, sliding splashes from the lake. The Red Dragon and the White had returned to their home, where they would start their task of guarding Ambrose through the long ages of eternity.

Idris caught Morgan's eye. There were tears on her cheeks. He smiled through his own. Then he bent his back to the oars and pulled out to sea. The sea was a comfortable place for a Limpet of the Westgate. Idris was in need of comfort just now.

Three hours later the peaks of the Sundeeps were low on the horizon. The breeze was light, the swell a gentle heave. Morgan was sitting in the middle of the boat, holding on to both sides. Her knuckles were white. Idris put up the mast and hoisted the little lugsail. The wake began to chuckle down the boat's side.

"It's tipping *over!*" said Morgan.

"Heeling," said Idris. "It's meant to."

The peaks fell astern. The Wall followed them south. The North Sundeeps buoy went past, green with copper-rust. There were bread and cheese in a box and water in a barrel.

"When do we get to the Westgate?" said Morgan.

"Two days, depending on the weather. We can spend the night on the Great Bank, if we can find it."

Actually it was Kek that found it: a green-topped comma of white sand running along the line of the ebb tide, with a red-and-white-striped beacon on it, and the ruins of a fisherman's hut. The little boat's nose grounded on its beach as the sun was going down. Idris and Morgan collected a pile of driftwood and lit it in the lee of the hut. They sat wrapped in rugs. They thought of Ambrose, but happily; he had used his art to be sure of that. Digby was off somewhere, hunting something raw. Idris felt easy back in the salt smell and the sea rustle. Morgan felt out of her element.

"What happens if Penmarch isn't at the Southgate?"

"He will be."

She leaned against him, chewing a bit of marram grass. "What do you think of having a sister?"

"All right."

"Only all right?"

"If I were a poet from a distant land, I would say that it is a very wonderful thing. And that my life has been empty until now. And that while it is good to be a King, it is very good to be a King with a sister. But I am from Lyonesse, where we do not speak of our feelings if we can help it. So I will say none of this."

Morgan was eyeing him with deep suspicion. "So you mean it is all right?"

"Absolutely lovely, your Royal Highness. Is that what you wanted to hear?"

Morgan then chased him over the dunes with a bit of driftwood until he cried for mercy.

The moon rose huge and silver, one day off the full. Idris sat on the beach and looked in the general direction of the Westgate. Harpoon and Ector would be so proud of him, if they knew he was alive.

If they were alive themselves.

TWENTY

The next morning but one, the boat was threading a maze of low yellowish banks of sand, through which the tide poured like a river. The Wall ran a league to the left. Far ahead the tops of towers caught the light. Idris's heart leaped. The Westgate!

He turned the boat's nose for the Wall, sliding across the tide. There was a watchtower two leagues north of the Westgate, a little fort, always empty, with its own little harbor. The boat slid briskly down the waves, rounded the end of the little breakwater, and came alongside the small stone quay. Idris tied it up and slung a couple of rope fenders overboard to cushion its side as it rose and fell with the breathing of the sea.

"Come," he said. "We'll walk down the Wall and I'll show you the Westgate."

"Not safe," said Digby. "Don't like it. Ononono. Let's get out of here."

"He's right," said Morgan. "We're supposed to be at sea, not ashore."

But Idris was within reach of the Limpets, and he would not have listened to the Old King himself. He pulled a cloak around his shoulders and ran up the steps onto the Wall. At the top, he looked down at Morgan sitting on the quay.

"Come *on!*" he shouted, so close to home, impatient to show her.

"And who zackly are you shouting at?" said a voice at his shoulder. Idris turned, his hand going to his sword. A man in dark-blue gateguard uniform had come out of the turret. Idris vaguely remembered him as Davis Stree, one of the greediest of the gateguards, a smuggler's bribetaker, no friend of Ector's. Davis frowned. "Do I know 'ee?"

Davis was a nasty piece of work, but Idris was too excited to be suspicious. "No," he remembered to say.

Davis's brow creased. "I swear I knows you."

"I used to stay with Ector Limpet," said Idris, casual as he could manage, though he felt as if he might explode. "How is he these days?"

"Oh very well," said Davis. Idris felt his face split in half by a great grin of delight. Then he turned cold, for he saw that Davis's eyes were suddenly narrow and cunning. "He's on duty at the harbor till midnight. You'll catch him if you go down there in your liddle boat."

"Oh, don't worry," said Idris. Something was wrong. Gently he leaned his mind on Davis's. *This is him*, it was saying. *He'll come in and we'll collar him and I'll have the reward. I'll have so much beer.*

"Fine," said Idris, dry-mouthed, already backing down the

steps, his heart hammering. They were waiting for him. There would be no Ector, no Harpoon, no brothers and sisters. He was full of fury and despair.

"Who is that horrible-looking man?" said Morgan.

"A horrible man," said Idris, fingers already fumbling at the mooring lines.

"What about your family?"

"Gone." Idris tried to keep his voice steady. He was already paddling out of the little harbor. Outside, he pulled up the sail. He pointed the boat as close to the wind as it would go. The best he could do was crab along parallel to the shore, a long bowshot out to sea.

"Oh," said Morgan. "I'm sorry." He had been so happy. Now he was hard and grim and closed.

"They've gone somewhere. Like yours."

"Yes."

Silence. Both of them hoped it was true. Neither of them believed it.

The wind was rising, and the swell was tipped with little white fringes of foam. Their present course would take them close past the entrance to the Westgate. Any boat could come out and snap them up.

Idris knew he had behaved like an idiot, not a King. A whole army had perished, and Ambrose had gone down into silence, and Idris had wasted it all with his selfish impatience.

Ahead, the towers of the Westgate grew.

Idris said, "That man's gone to warn the town."

"What are we going to do? Can't you sail farther out to sea?"

"No. The wind's wrong."

Up a wave, down a wave. They were running along the town Wall now. Idris glanced up and saw the Fort where this had begun. How the world had changed since then —

"*Idris!*" shrieked Morgan as the boat slewed away from the wind and scooped up water. "Will you just stop thinking about your family? Because us getting killed will not do them any good."

The gate towers were coming abeam. His heart lifted. If there had been a boat ready it would surely have been out by now, waiting to catch them. Idris found himself looking right into the harbor.

There was a boat coming.

He looked out to sea. There was a boat there, too. No. Not a boat, a ship. His heart beat hard. A good-sized ship, half a league a way, roaring down the wind under a white tower of sail. And from the top of the mainmast there flew a long, long pennant of brilliant scarlet.

"They're catching us," said Morgan, still looking at the boat racing out of the harbor.

It was true. The boat was one of the six-oared gigs, for use by Captains only. A fast boat. Ironhorse manned his with the hardest fishermen and Mountmen he could find, and raced it against other gigs, who took care always to let him win.

"They're faster than us," said Idris. "They'll catch us." He tried to still the storm in his head so that he could feel the mind of the gig's coxswain and grab it. He got a glimpse of something fat and pompous. Then he felt Fisheagle's mind, still searching for his. He closed up again.

Morgan was stringing her bow. "The fat one," said Idris.

"HALT IN THE NAME OF THE MOUNT," roared a voice from the gig. "IDRIS LIMPET, YOU ARE FIRST CROSS AND NOW TRAITOR. THE LAND IS RAISED AGAINST YOU. THERE IS NO ESCAPE."

"Nasty pompous person," said Morgan, stretching an arrow back to her cool green eye. She loosed.

"STOP, OR WE — AIEEE!" cried the voice. Shouts rose from the gig. The oars tangled. It slewed sideways and fell behind.

"Who did I just shoot?" said Morgan.

Suddenly Idris's grief was gone, replaced by a fierce joy. "Ironhorse," he said.

They shook hands. A buoy slid by. Idris sent his mind up to Kek.

Captain Ironhorse was lying on his face, yowling with agony. An arrow was sticking out of his bottom.

"Good shot," said Idris.

"I was aiming for his head."

"Well, you got him in the brains."

Morgan giggled. Then the smile fell off her face. She said, "What's that?"

Another boat was sliding out of the harbor. As Idris watched, a huge white triangle of canvas rose up the mast and a white mustache appeared under its bow. His heart sank. She was the *Pride of Westgate*, a corsair chaser, old but still dangerous.

But the *Pride* was a sailing boat, and like all sailing boats, she could not sail straight into the wind. And the ship on the horizon was no longer on the horizon, but a long bowshot away, great plumes of white water roaring from her stem, men up in the bow, waving. And above it all, snapping in the breeze, that great glorious red pennant. The *Swallow*.

Then the *Swallow* was upon them, and there was a roar of flapping canvas, and a rope snaked down from the deck. "Make that fast!" cried a round red face at the rail. "Off we go!" Idris made a round turn and two half hitches, and the ship's canvas stopped flapping and started to draw, and the wake roared down her side. Two long, heavily tattooed arms reached down and gripped Morgan and Idris by their wrists and swung them upward. And away tore the *Swallow* down the channel toward the open sea, while the *Pride of Westgate* wallowed in the harbor mouth, gave up, and returned to her mooring, but not before Idris had seen two men on her foredeck wave to him and bow deeply. He felt a warmth spread in him. There were two more of his subjects who looked forward to his return.

"Good morning," said a voice. It belonged to a small man with wild sea-blue eyes and a peaked woolen cap of the kind worn by sailors. "I am Captain Penmarch, at your service."

Idris named himself and Morgan as House Ambrose mon-stergrooms, in the Manner. Captain Penmarch bowed at the mention of Ambrose's name.

"And I must thank you," said Idris, "for saving our lives."

"Sir," said Penmarch, and though he smiled his face was pale and tight, "it is your sister you should thank, for shooting that fat Captain. And I must tell you that our lives are not yet saved. Rather the reverse, indeed. For there will be dirty weather, stinking filthy awful dirty weather, between here and Ar Mor, not to mention a lot more Aegypt corsairs than usual, a-cruising for fair-hair slaves. And our foremast is not as I would wish it, being broke halfway through and splinted, as you would say. It may be that you will find yourself looking back on this after-noon's work as a charming amusement."

"I doubt it," said Idris.

"Look there," said Penmarch, pointing to the west.

A dark shadow was tearing over the water toward them.

Then the wind hit like a battering ram, and there was no more speech.

All the time the *Swallow* had been bearing down on the shallop, the cloud had grown lower and darker. Now it was dragging its dirty belly along the sea, and the wind was scream-ing. Idris caught a glimpse of the towers of the Westgate sinking behind the spray of the waves bursting on the Wall. Then the towertops had gone, and so had the Wall, and all that remained was rain and wind. Such wind! Wind that howled out of the west so that the *Swallow* flew south down the channel over a sea knocked white and smoking, one tiny rag of sail drum-tight on her foremast.

Idris noticed that Captain Penmarch was eyeing the foremast. It was bending nastily in the gusts, the bend worst in a place where it was splinted with beams and lashings. If the foremast went, the mainmast would go, too.

But there was nothing to be gained from worrying. Idris went to where Morgan was curled up in her coil of rope. She was green, except for her lips, which were blue. "Cheer up," he said and put an arm around her to warm her up.

"I think I'm dying," she said.

"Just seasick," he said and gave her a hug. She managed a sort of smile.

So there they lay huddled, while night fell and the wind shrieked and the wounded foremast groaned and the land of Lyonesse tore away down the churning white wake, mile after stormy mile. Morgan slept, her head on Idris's arm. Idris stayed still, not wishing to disturb her. Eventually he fell asleep, too.

When he woke he was teeth-chatteringly cold, and the world was gray in the dawn, and things were different. The wind was still shrieking, but the waves had grown, towering over the ship's side. And there was another thing.

In place of the little handkerchief of sail of the night before, the *Swallow* was carrying a dangerously big foresail. The wind was behind them now. Every time the ship came to the top of a wave, it thumped into the sail, and the shrouds groaned, and the splinted place on the foremast moved and squealed. Captain Penmarch was at the steering oar. The sea astern was horrible. The waves were the size of hills on the land, curling over and spilling drifts of white water down their steep gray fronts. But that was not what froze Idris's blood.

A bowshot astern was another sail, gray in the grim dawnlight, bearing the mark of a trident. Below the sail was a beaked ram painted scarlet, a fierce ship-ripper tipped with a bronze skull, parting two enormous white wings of spray. Behind the ram was a sleek hull. The ship ran down the front of a wave and vanished in a trough, leaving only the top of a mast visible, then came up again as the next wave ran under, much closer.

Idris scuttled aft, clinging to the bulwark. "What's that?" he said.

"That," said Captain Penmarch, "is a pretty fine specimen of your Aegypt corsair. But don't worry, we're holding him with the big foresail."

Idris did worry. Westgate people knew all about corsairs. Corsairs came from Afryk, to the south of Iber. Their ships were fast and seaworthy. When they captured a Lyonesse ship, they murdered unsellable members of the crew and took possession of the remainder and the cargo. People and goods they shipped up the great rivers to Aegypt, where they sold them in dusty markets: the strong to work their mines, the clever to add their numbers, the beautiful for work too horrible to think of. . . .

"We may make Ys," said Penmarch, leaning against the

tiller. "It's hard to reckon in this breeze, but we can't be farther than ten —"

He might have been about to say "leagues." But at that moment a cross-sea surged over the swell, and the *Swallow* slewed across the wind, and the foresail flapped once, then cracked full again.

And the foremast came down.

It came down with a groan, and the vanishing of its rigging left the mainmast unsupported, so that came down, too. One moment the *Swallow* had been flying away from the slaver across moving mountains of water. The next she was wallowing in a trough, lying to her masts and rigging, without power or direction.

"All *haaaands!*" roared Penmarch. Then, to Idris, "If you can use that sword, now is your moment." Then he was away, shouting orders.

Men spilled on deck. All carried knives or swords or clubs, but most of them looked as if they would rather be somewhere else. Cutwater was in Idris's hand. Morgan was by his side, her bow in her hand, her hair whipping in the gale.

"Hide," he said. This could not be happening, not after all they had gone through.

"No."

Then there was a roar of sails, and the corsair ship crashed alongside, and with a yodeling shriek the corsairs swarmed aboard.

Idris heard Morgan's bowstring twang. He heard her curse and say, "Wet," and glimpsed her drawing her dagger. Then two men with black beards and green brass helmets were upon him, and Cutwater took the legs from under the first and the throat out of the second, and then there were three, no, five more, too many, and somehow his back was to the ship's side and a black-bearded giant was coming at him with a club. He raised Cutwater to strike. As the sword went back it seemed to give a sort of wriggle and slid somehow from his hand, and he felt the wrist-loop go over his fingers and away, and heard a despairing cry from Morgan, and felt an awful sense of double loss. Then the club was swinging toward him, and he jerked his head back to avoid it, but not far enough. Red light bloomed in his eyes, and horrible pain, and he fell backward over the ship's side and into the raging sea.

TWENTY-ONE

Pain. Horrible pain in the front of the head. Eyes like red-hot iron balloons. Salt in the mouth.

Idris moved his arms and legs. He felt wet stone under him, and a slimy tangle of seaweed. He managed to get on to his hands and knees. He was sick. He lay down again. He was cold. Very cold. He went to sleep, shuddering.

There were dreams. There was a black place, smooth and warm, with little red sparks and blue fish that swam. There were Harpoon and Ector and the Precious Stones and the Boys all waving, but he knew he would never see them again. And there was Morgan.

His eyes slammed open.

He was lying on a beach of stones, tangled in ropes that seemed to have lashed him to a stump of mast. There was weed on the beach, brown and dreary, and other drift-wood, and huddled things that he knew were bodies. The sea beat against the beach, cold and gray. Strangely, there was no Wall.

His heart lurched. Where was Morgan?

He struggled out of the ropes and clambered to his feet. He walked along the high-water mark. The bodies were dead. Some had drowned. Some had died of wounds. None of them was Morgan. He heard a sound behind him. His hand went to his sword —

Or where his sword should have been. His fingers found an empty scabbard. Memory returned.

"Kek," said the sound. It was Kek.

Idris sat on a rock and put his face in his hands.

He had been driven from his kingdom. He had found his sister and now lost her forever. And the sword Cutwater was at the bottom of the sea. The scabbard Holdwater was at his belt. But a scabbard without a sword was a mockery.

A mockery that saved your life, said a small voice in his mind. *How do you think you survived?*

The voice sounded like Ambrose, tiny and far away. Another one gone forever. All gone, thought Idris in his misery. And I am alone. The tears were hot on his face.

"Kek," said Kek.

Idris looked up. The gull was sitting three feet away, watching him with a beady yellow eye. It put its head on one side. It seemed to be saying: Yes, it is hard to imagine things being worse than they are now. But you have got a loyal gull. Not everybody has one of those.

"All right," said Idris sulkily. He blew his nose on a handful of seaweed, which was worse than not blowing it at all. "All *right*."

The gull spread his wings and staggered into the air. He caught the breeze and soared. Idris put his mind up to the gull. Behind the beach he saw a green slope studded with rows of standing stones.

He climbed painfully to his feet and began to walk.

A path led along the seaward edge of the stonefields. After a couple of bays, he saw a man walking toward him. The man was elderly, wearing grubby white woolen robes. Idris wondered if he should hide. But the old man had a mild look, and besides, what else did he have to lose? "What place is this?" said Idris, when he came up to him.

"Hard by the city of Ys," said the man, speaking with an odd accent. "Who are you?"

"Idris," said Idris. "I have been shipwrecked. My sister has gone."

"Bless my soul!" said the elderly man. "My poor dear fellow! Come, come, come, come!" He hustled Idris around a headland to a low thatched inn. Idris said that he had no money, but the old man pushed him in at the door and handed him like a parcel to a stout, motherly woman who hustled him into a tub of hot water and made him dry himself with a rough towel and sat him down and fed him crab soup with wild garlics. The crab soup reminded him of Harpoon, and his sadness increased.

"I have unhappy news," said the old man, when Idris saw him again an hour later. "Coastwatchers have reported back.

You are the only one alive, I fear. Of those who came ashore, I mean. There is no body of a girl, though."

Idris nodded dully. Beyond the open door a cart laden with useful wreck washed up from the *Swallow* was rumbling toward the town. Morgan was lost.

"What was it that happened?" asked the old man.

Idris explained, low and dreary, out of good manners, not a desire to talk. He did not care if he never talked again.

Morgan was gone.

"Corsairs? A blood-red sail? It is Bizound. He is the worst of the Aegypts. You are lucky not to be in his slave hold," said the old man, undoubtedly trying to cheer him up.

Idris shrugged. "My friends are there," he said. "I should be with them."

The old man was saying something.

"What?"

"You have arrived in our land from who knows where," said the old man. "It is the Manner that you should come to our King and tell him who you are. He is a good man, and will welcome you. This I know, for I am the Stonekeeper, trusted guardian of his stonefields."

Mention of the Manner brought Idris to his feet. Out of habit, his hand went to his sword hilt. It found vacancy. Lyonesse was gone from him. "Permit me to name myself," he said. His titles processed through his mind. Standing here with an empty scabbard in this place without a Wall, they seemed pompous

335

and foolish. "I am Idris Limpet of the Westgate, and I thank you for your kindness," he said.

"Really?" said the Stonekeeper. "Come. I will take you to the palace."

Idris allowed himself to be led through the muddy streets of Ys. Inland of the town they came to a hillside, in which were bronze gates framed with great sarsens of granite. There were passages inside filled with woodsmoke, many people, and the music of harps, wafts of excellent cooking. Idris paid no attention to it all, trudging after the Stonekeeper in his new, empty world. After a while they came to a great hall columned with oak trunks. Light was falling from a shaft on to a man who sat in a chair of crude granite on a dais. "So enter the presence of Mark, most excellent King of Ar Mor, Duke of Ys," boomed a voice. There were more titles. Idris did not hear them. The King looked too small for all his names. He was like a Sundeeps pony, small and energetic in the stone chair, with fierce black eyes and curly black hair into which were twisted bits of gold wire.

"Good morning," said little King Mark, as the echoes of the herald's pomposities died in the vaults. "You have been shipwrecked, I think."

Idris said, "We were attacked by Aegypt corsairs, and I was cast up on your majesty's shores. Allow me to name myself. I am Idris Limpet of the Westgate in Lyonesse."

The little King sat forward in his chair. The dark eyes drilled into Idris's. He said, in a voice surprisingly gentle, "It is a terrible thing to be shipwrecked, and to lose your friends to death and the Aegypts. You are welcome in my lands. There are many here from Lyonesse."

Idris bowed.

"Your Manner is nobler than your name," said King Mark. His eyes strayed to the empty scabbard at Idris's side. The brows drew together a fraction. "Limpet, you say. Have you cousins in Ar Mor?"

"I do not think so."

"Stonekeeper, hither," said King Mark. The Stonekeeper approached. The King murmured in his ear. Then he looked at Idris, a strange look, somewhere between doubt and respect, the hot black eyes again burning into his. "My country is yours," he said. "Go, but come again when you are ready. There may be things of which we should speak."

The Stonekeeper led Idris out of the palace, down the granite-paved road into the low streets of Ys, and halted in front of a broad wooden door. "Here, I think," he said and knocked. The door opened.

And a point of light bloomed in Idris's mind, a point that brightened and spread until it was like the sun in splendor.

For the woman standing in the doorway was smooth-faced and fair, and from the corners of her eyes there ran the tattooed cat whiskers of the Fishers. It was the face of Harpoon. And there was Idris, hugging her and being hugged back, and a thunder of feet in the house, and the rest of the family crowding around. And Idris separating himself from the mob, and being shooed inside, and Ector Gateguard standing with his hat in both hands, bowing, saying, "Welcome home, er, sire."

"Please don't," said Idris.

"But it's true," said Ector.

"All right. I command you not to. I'm just Idris. I'm home."

"Well, then," said Ector, and the grin split his face, and Idris was helping Harpoon put the shells on the table and admiring the dolls the Precious Stones had made out of driftwood and boxing with the Boys, and the darkness went away until it was no more than a cloud on a distant horizon.

"So here we are," said Ector to the family after zupper, "where there are no Captains and no monsters and the King is fair and the people are good."

"And so is the wrestling," said the Boys.

"And we may swim and not be killed," said the Stones, together. "Have you tried it? It's lovely!"

"Now," said Harpoon, when the shell plates were cleared away and a fire of wreck was spitting green in the hearth. "Idris, you can tell us what you've been doing all this time."

Idris looked around at the faces of his family. Ector and Harpoon would have an idea of what had happened to him; they might even have told the Stones and the Boys. After all, they had been chased away from the Westgate one step ahead of the Mountmen. Of course he should tell them everything. They would be so proud.

But they would be proud of their Idris, not the person he had become: a King without a kingdom, who had lost his sword, and his sister, and his destiny, and become a lump of driftwood on a foreign shore. So he would be their Idris: Idris Limpet, back with his family. He had had some strange adventures and learned a lot. But all that was behind him now.

Ector was smiling at him, nodding encouragingly. Harpoon's eyes were deeper and more understanding. She knew what must have happened, and what it must have meant to him. He came to a decision.

"Doing?" he said. "Oh, I went to a new school and learned some new things." He paused, basking in the joy of reunion, the simple happiness of being Idris Limpet. "But it is very, very good to be home."

Darkness, all was darkness. The darkgardens were beautiful again. There was no need to endure the torment of the light. For the things that had been torn away had been made good, and the Realm was secure, and the gathering of the Helpers around the Wells continued, steady, untroubled, heading remorseless as death for the day when they would break forth and conquer.

The bronze shutters of the Kyd Tower were closed. On the black stone bed the human form of the Regent lay without motion, the breath a mere zephyr, keeping the sluggish blood moving enough to ward off decay, no more. The hawk face was still. Nothing could disturb it: not the reports of the Mountmen who watched, not the shakings of the ground as the Wells shuddered to the tides, not the screams of children tormented by Kyd Murther in his blood-red apartments in the next tower.

And Idris, whose departure had brought this peace, lay fast asleep in a small bedroom in a small house in Ys of Ar Mor. He did not dream, not of Morgan, nor of the sword Cutwater, nor of the creatures of the Sundeeps or the creatures of the Wells. He did not dream because he had put his dreams away.

As the sun of Ar Mor rose, it touched the swirling patterns chased in the gold of the scabbard Holdwater, hung by its baldric from a nail on the wall. The scabbard was empty. Perhaps it wanted to be filled. Or perhaps in hanging by Idris's bed it was performing a work of healing.

The light reflected from Holdwater shone into Idris's eyes. He squinted and groaned. Outside, Ys was stirring itself for the new day. Idris pulled up the covers, and turned on his side, and slept on.

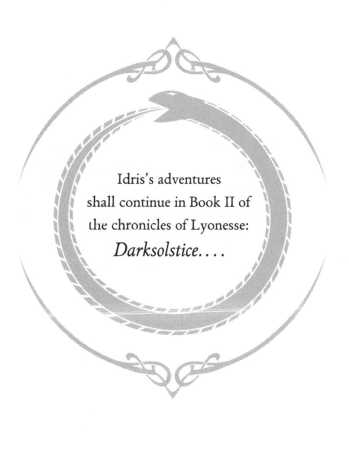

Idris's adventures
shall continue in Book II of
the chronicles of Lyonesse:
Darksolstice....

AUTHOR'S NOTE

To the reader of Lyonesse:

I was born into the watery world of the Isles of Scilly — a few paradisiacal crumbs of granite scattered over the turquoise sea thirty miles west of Land's End, Britain's most southwestern point. The islands are dotted with prehistoric tombs and, at low water, the remnants of cyclopean walls can be seen snaking from island to island along the bottom of the sea. My mother's family has lived there for six generations. My childhood was full of tales about a sinking of the land that transformed Scilly from a range of mountains into an archipelago.

In the tales, it was not only Scilly that had sunk. In the mid-eighteenth century, fishermen in the Atlantic trawled up window frames that they assumed came from a drowned village. A petrified forest lurks deep under the sands of Mount's Bay. Just as it was common knowledge on Scilly that Lyonesse had sunk, it was also common knowledge that Lyonesse had been the home of the proto-legends of Arthur, or Idris as he was called. We believed in dragons, monsters, star and stone, and that all actions had consequences. I was born in a room overlooking the body of water from which the sword Excalibur came, and into which it was flung. I grew up with the certainty that Arthur and Tristan and Morgan and the rest of them originated here and in the related French Atlantis of Ys. While Lyonesse has featured as a springboard for the wilder type of fantasy, it has had no real chronicler. I decided that this was something I needed to put right.

In a properly constituted legendary universe, Lyonesse cannot sink as a matter of mere geology. It is human hubris that must cause the inundation, and human virtue that must strive to keep it above water. Idris, I was assured since earliest years, was a good person because he saw that his actions had consequences for others; Murther/Mordred and his monstrous gang were evil because they were interested in the hoggish pursuit of power for its own sake, whatever the consequences for other people and the world. Certainly, some readers may find in the story of Lyonesse parallels with the world we live in now.

The battle between the dark and the light lives strongly in my heart. So do the stones and islands of Scilly that are all that remain of the mountains of Lyonesse, and the sun that still shines over Lyonesse, and the gales that still blow there. I visit them often. I am glad that I now have a chance to take you with me.

A note on language and sources: Two notable research sites have, of course, been Scilly and the library of Trelowarren, home of the greatest of the antediluvian manuscripts.

Unhappily the Old Tongue, in which most of these stories were originally told, is now extinct. For certain words I have had to use modern equivalents, which are not always precise. For instance the ancient *hvaachn* has become *monster,* losing in the process its original sub-meanings of death-beast, enemy, firewood, and helper; and *puttaiyur* has become *corsair*, which is as close as a modern mind can come to this particular form of seagoing slaver and plunderer originating in what is now North Africa.

Sam Llewellyn
The Tower
Tresco
New Deer Moon, 2008

Lyonesse

Castle Ambrose

The Moors

The Sundeeps

The Dog's Quoit

The Stone Downs

The Banks

The Old Road

The Westgate

The Wolf Rock

The Broken Wall

Scorrin

The Marsh

N